tHE SINNERS OF St BENEDICtS BOOK 2

PRINCES & WOLVES

ALSO BY E.J. KNOX
Little Nymph
Prince of Thorns

the Sinners of Saint Benedicts
Gods & Angels
Princes & Wolves
Men & Monsters

Rivermont Royals
Reign
Rival
Ransom
Resist
Redeem
Rage
Rebel
Ruin

Rivermont Royals Reveals
Obsess
Infatuate

AS ELIZABETH STEVENS
the Trouble with Hate is…
Accidentally Perfect
Being Not Good
Popped
the Art of Breaking Up
the Roommate Mistake

Heaven & Hell Chronicles
Damned if I do
Damned if I don't
Damned if I know

THE SINNERS OF ST BENEDICTS BOOK 2

PRINCES & WOLVES

ELIZABETH STEVENS WRITING AS

E.J. KNOX

Kinky Siren
an imprint of Sleeping Dragon Books

Princes & Wolves
by E.J. Knox

Paperback ISBN: **978-1925928389**
Digital ISBN: 978-1925928372
Hardcover ISBN: 978-1925928396

Cover art by: Izzie Duffield

To letting go and moving on,
Neither of which I'll be doing with these characters just yet.

Contents

Author's Note

This is a dark, angsty, contemporary high school enemies-to-lovers romance with enough steam to melt your screen. Do not engage in public consumption unless your poker face is impenetrable.

Do not read if you don't like broken alpha males claiming what's theirs, a feisty heroine determined to break the bonds of an unwanted future, or complicated love triangles full of passion and dirty words.

This story features the heroine in sexual situations with both love interests. While not considered cheating by the characters, you may have different feelings (and that's okay). Proceed with caution.

This book is written using Australian English. This will affect the spelling, grammar and syntax you may be used to. It might come across as typos, awkward sentences, poor grammar, or missed/wrong words. In the majority of cases (I won't claim it's infallible, despite all best efforts), this is intentional and just an Aussie way of speaking (it took my US beta readers a bit to get used to). I can't say 'the' Aussie way, since we seem to differ even within the same state. Just think of us as a weird mix of British and US vernacular and colloquialisms, but with our own randomness thrown in. I still hope you enjoy it, though!

CHAPTER ONE

Apollo took my hand and kissed the back of it. "I feel like I don't have to finish my salad," he said as we sat at our table in the dining hall that night.

"I feel like you should eat your salad," I countered with a laugh.

Apollo gave me puppy dog eyes as he brushed his fingers along my cheek. "But I ate my chips. Chips are a vegetable."

I tried not to smile and further encourage him. "*A* vegetable. Singular. Salad is multiple vegetables."

"Not if it's lolly salad," Marco said with a cheeky grin around whatever he was shovelling into his mouth.

I wasn't really sure what to say to that. I was smiling at Marco and trying to think of a reply when movement to my left pulled my focus.

Valen was standing up, his vape pen hanging from his mouth as he pulled his hoody up over his head. His eyes glanced around at everyone, and he paused when he saw we were all looking at him.

"What?" he snapped.

"You heading out...or...?" Apollo asked, slight hesitation in his voice.

I didn't know if there was really a change in Valen over the last week, or if I was seeing one because he and I had changed.

Had it really only been last Sunday when I'd snuck out of his room in nothing but a jacket and heels? Had it really only been Monday when we'd both been practically adults and realised this could work, that we could do this moving on thing? That had been six days ago.

And since then, life had gone back to the way it had been months ago.

Well, almost.

"Can a man not go for a piss without the fucking inquisition?" Valen asked Apollo as he blew out a torrent of smoke around his head.

"You're mighty defensive for a guy just going to take a slash," Marco observed.

"You just concentrate on whatever the fuck a lolly salad is."

Valen's eyes darted over me as he walked out, and I realised I was fiddling absently with his cross at my neck. And fully visibly, too, as I was wearing an open collared top. His hand lifted, then jerked up to tug at his hood like he'd been subconsciously reaching for something he shouldn't be.

Suddenly nervous, I cleared my throat and turned back to Marco, who was regaling us all with his perfect lolly salad recipe.

A body dropped on my other side with a tray of dinner, and I actually jumped. Apollo's arm tightened around me.

"You right, babe?" he laughed as he nodded to Florence, as the body who'd just appeared beside me. "Flo."

She kicked her chin to him in perfect imitation of Marco and didn't even correct him. "Yeah, hi."

"Where have you been?" I asked her.

She shrugged as she tucked into her dinner. "Art room. Big project. Not going well."

"I'd offer to help, but..."

She smiled at me. "But you suck at Art. I know. I've just got so much to do before the retreat. And if that all goes well, then..."

As Florence talked, mainly just nervous chatter that I knew was her way of working through her worries, Apollo's hand was busy roaming my body under the cover of the table. For all intents and purposes, he was chatting with Marco and Gage across the table from me, and I was listening to Florence. But in reality, our attention was on each other.

Apollo's body encased my own as he ran his hand slowly up the inside of my leg. His thumb brushed over my clit and pleasure shot through me that I wouldn't feel bad about. I wouldn't apologise for letting Apollo touch me like that. I wouldn't let myself doubt wanting him to do so much more.

Valen was out of my system, and I was going to see where this new spark with Apollo went. There were worse people to be physically attracted to than the man you were contractually obliged to marry.

I slowly lay my hand on his leg and squeezed gently. He dropped his lips casually to the spot under my ear and kissed me. I felt his smile as he kept teasing me and tried not to smile in return and raise Florence's suspicions. There was letting Apollo touch me at the dining table, and there was other people knowing about it, even my best friend who would have been all for sexy shenanigans right under the nuns' noses.

"...and if that goes well, I might get to go to Paris," Florence finished, and I forced myself to look like I'd been paying attention.

"That sounds like a lot," I said.

She sighed. "It feels like a lot but, if it's what I need to do, then it's what I need to do. Miss D'Arras thinks I've got a real shot but fuck it's a load of work. I shouldn't have left it all to the last minute."

"You shouldn't have, but you wouldn't be you if you didn't," I reminded her, and she smiled.

"If you're in need of stress relief," Marco said with a sinfully sexy grin all for her, "ye know where I am."

"Do you want to get out of here?" Apollo whispered in my ear as his thumb rubbed my clit more firmly. I was pretty sure I knew what he had in mind.

I turned to look at him and our noses brushed. He pressed a kiss to my lips and nudged my nose with his. His eyes were bright with humour.

Being with him like this, my heart fluttered, and I couldn't stop smiling. I felt like the walls of my prison had stopped closing in, like my planned life wasn't going to just be utter shit being married to a man I'd lost all connection with. We still had a long way to go, but the possibility was there.

It just needed fostering and exploring and, just then, I was more than happy to foster and explore it.

So, I bit my lip, ran my hand further up his leg and leant my forehead to his. "What did you have in mind?"

He grinned with all the sexy charm that Apollo Callahan possessed. "My room is awfully lonely…"

"Oh, you talk to inanimate objects now, do you?" I laughed.

"Babe, I'm fucking God. I know everything."

He couldn't even get through the first sentence without laughing and I joined him. He brushed some hair from my face and looked me over, full of warmth and… And love.

"What do you say?" he asked. "Interested?"

I pretended to think about it, like it was a hardship. "Okay, but I get to pick the movie."

Apollo leant his lips to my ear. "I wasn't planning on watching a movie," he said, then nipped my earlobe playfully.

My nipples responded and so did my clit.

I leant into Apollo, my hand sliding up his leg and stopping just shy of his crotch. I saw the heat in those deep sapphire eyes. Heat for me. I could see how much he wanted me. I could see he was thinking about all the things he wanted to do to me. With me.

I wanted that, too. I wanted to explore this. Us.

"I like the sound of that," I told him.

Relief flooded his eyes, like part of him had thought I'd shut him down. That there was my Apollo, Frenella's boy. The one who I knew, without a doubt, loved me.

I kissed him, took his hand, and stood up.

"You leaving?" Gage asked as he looked between me and Apollo.

Apollo wrapped his arm around my shoulders. "We are. We'll be in my room. I don't want to be interrupted."

Gage looked us over with a slightly less amused eye than Marco. "What do you want us to do about the race?" Gage asked.

Apollo shrugged. "You know what to do if anything goes wrong. There is no circumstance in which you come to me tonight, understood?"

Gage saluted and Marco nodded. Beside them, Fender both saluted and nodded.

"God's word is law," Fender said with a wry smirk.

Apollo nodded. "You know it. We'll see you lot tomorrow."

"Tomorrow?" Florence said to me with a wry smirk of her own.

I gave her a wink, took Apollo's hand, and started leading him out of the dining hall. He made a great show of following me out, informing anyone who'd listen that he'd 'follow this woman to the ends of the world'. People were clearly paying attention. They were supposed to pay attention. Apollo wanted them all to know he was taking his girlfriend to his bedroom. Or, rather, that his girlfriend was taking him to his bedroom.

It wasn't until then that, after all the subtle changes I'd gone through the last few months, I realised people *were* looking at me differently. Not better or worse, just different. I felt like I was under more scrutiny, like the whole school was watching where this new behaviour between God and his intended was going.

I felt like I'd finally earned it. I felt like it was about damned time people saw more of the real me, not just the meek little princess going gormlessly to her fate. Valen brought it out in me. Apollo saw it and he wanted it. Florence had always said I was meant to be the goddess of Saint Benedicts, and I was finally starting to feel like it.

I didn't leave Apollo's room until after midnight. The hallways were dark, only the low lighting of after hours to light the way of those students who were out of bed past lights out.

And I felt good. Not just in the physically satisfied after blissful orgasms kind of good, but good and free and light. I was very aware that the freedom I now felt with Apollo was a very different freedom to the one Valen gave me, but it was no less because of it. I felt optimistic about my future for the first time in five years. I felt like I might not lose all that made Apollo good and mine. Life was looking good.

As I skipped down the cheeky service stairs, I ran into a body I recognised well. He wasn't going to stop, clearly.

"Hi," I said as he made to pass me.

He paused, a frown crossing his face as he looked me over in the near dark. "Uh, hi."

My fingers played with his cross at my neck as we just stood there and looked at each other in silence.

The way my heart beat in my chest, I knew he'd never really be out of my system. How could he be? Valen Kincaid was over six foot of brooding tall, dark, delicious and dangerous. Danger that was made all the more appealing by the knowledge that he would never be a danger to me. Not the way he was to others. Had I not put a stop to whatever was happening between us, he certainly would have been a danger to my heart, but never to my life.

"Do we talk now?" he asked, his eyebrow rising.

I licked my lip uncertainly. "Do we not?"

He shrugged. "We didn't before."

"So, we're just going to spend the rest of our lives in forced proximity, hating each other like always?"

"What do you suggest, princess?" he asked, but the moniker had lost most of its contempt.

"I thought we could be civil. For Apollo at least."

He scoffed as he looked away from me, sucked on his teeth, then looked back to me. He took a step toward me, the nearness of his body causing mine to hum. I could feel how close he was, how very nearly he was touching me, but just...not.

"You want civility, princess?" he asked. "How civil does this feel?" His voice was a purr that made my nipples tighten and my clit tingle.

"Perfectly civil," I answered. Lies. But I could do this. "We fucked each other out of our systems, remember?"

His lip rose in a snarl, then he breathed out deeply and kicked his head to the stairs behind me. "I suppose God's finally laid claim to what's his."

I knew what kind of claim he was insinuating.

I swallowed hard. "No, actually. He hasn't."

The boy was happy to stick his face between my legs until I was moaning his name in pleasure, but I couldn't touch him.

Valen looked surprised for just a moment. "Well, don't let me get in your way."

"I won't. I'm not."

"When he finally does want to claim you, you should let him."

"I will."

"Good. Because we've fucked each other out of our systems and everything's fine."

"Exactly. He can do whatever he wants to me."

"Good." Valen was doing a very good impression of Grumpy Cat.

I nodded. "Good." So was I.

We stood there in awkward silence. I knew I needed to go back to bed, but I couldn't bring myself to walk away. I noticed he didn't either. Neither had he moved away from me. Our clothes brushed against each other in the semi-dark.

"You never came back to dinner," I finally said.

He shrugged. "No. I had...shit to do in Bieityn."

I couldn't help the jealousy sneaking into my voice when I asked, "Shit?"

For a split second he hardened. Then he softened. Then he settled on neutral. "My brother needed...backup."

"Kane," leaked out of my mouth and I'd never heard myself sound so pathetic or scared.

Valen looked me over. His hand rose like he wanted to comfort me, then fisted and he pushed it into his pocket. "Neo," he answered, but there was so much in that one word.

There was an understanding that Kane terrified me, an acknowledgement that that fear was justified, and a promise that he'd never let Kane hurt me. I didn't know how he'd conveyed so much in just one word.

It still wouldn't set my heart steadying anytime soon. Kane Kincaid was a man who set my response to heavy fight or flight mode. And my ability to fight was entirely non-existent.

Valen seemed to be able to sense my panic.

I felt his fingers almost imperceptibly rub mine where they hung by my leg, and my eyes flew to his face. It was almost unreadable, and it wasn't the light – or lack thereof – to blame.

"You're safe, love," he whispered as his fingers barely touched mine again, like he had to stop himself touching more of me.

I nodded. "No. I know. I..." I searched his eyes. "I know, Valen..."

He looked into my eyes for the space of a few more heartbeats, then cleared his throat. "Best get yourself to bed, princess. Don't want to be caught out and about at this hour."

He started back up the stairs and I forced myself not to turn and watch him go.

"Night, Valen," I murmured into the dark, telling myself I didn't wish it was his bed I was going to.

Chapter Two

Things continued to go from good to better with Apollo.

A large part of me knew that I was throwing myself all in as a way to tell myself I was over Valen, but it wasn't all one-sided; Apollo met me halfway. He didn't just meet me halfway, most of the time he came to me.

Months ago, Florence and I had talked about how Gods didn't go to princesses, and I'd wondered if maybe princes did. Apollo certainly seemed to be doing his best prince charming impression.

He knocked on our dorm door so often that Florence had imposed a 'text first' policy on him. Not that he heeded her. Because if my best friend and my future husband could go out of their way to antagonise each other, then they would.

I loved them both.

But having them in the same vicinity for too long was never a good idea.

"You know the maid of honour has to deal with the groom for at least the duration of the wedding," Apollo said to her the next Tuesday. "That's like a whole day. Minimum."

Florence shot me a look and I knew what she was thinking. Apollo hadn't once brought up the wedding. He'd talked about the future and how Florence would have to put up with him for the rest of her life. But he'd never mentioned the wedding before. Almost as though, before, the wedding was just a formality we all had to get through – because obviously Florence would be my maid of honour. Now, though. Now he talked about it like it was something to be excited about.

"If you say destination wedding, I might kill you," Florence told him.

He smirked at her, layering on all his arrogant amusement and entitlement. "That, Flo, is a wonderful idea. What do you say to Hawaii, sweetheart?" he asked me.

"Trite and clichéd," Florence responded. "And my name is Florence."

"And what would you suggest, then?" he asked her, not even bothering to give her shit about answering to 'sweetheart'.

She looked him over like she found him utterly lacking. Probably because she did. "Something intimate," she told him, her voice softening. "The little church in Bieityn your parents use to make you go to every Sunday of the holidays until they gave up telling you what to do. Reception at the Callahan Estate, of course. But not in that hideously ostentatious ballroom. Out in the gardens. In Spring, just as the weather's turning. Flowers everywhere. The bride barefoot, running through the topiary with her skirts in her hand."

"Not that you've thought about it at all," I commented.

We'd talked about my wedding. Not often and not in huge detail, but it had come up. Bits and pieces.

"I'm an artist, what do you expect?" Florence answered. "I've pretty much planned the decor of little Apollo Junior's delivery room. It's what I do. I visualise."

I spluttered at the mention of my previously unnamed child. "On that note, we're leaving."

"Good riddance," Florence said, looking at Apollo. "Although, he's quiet for once."

And he was indeed quiet for once. There was a thoughtfulness about him, but I couldn't tell exactly what he was thinking about.

"I'll see you later," I told her.

Florence nodded, watching Apollo with a strange expression on her face. Almost as strange as the one on his.

Deciding it didn't need dwelling on, I took Apollo's hand and steered him out of our room.

"What are you thinking?" I asked him as we headed for his room.

He shook his head like he was clearing it of something. "What do you think?"

I smiled. "About what?"

"Florence's suggestion."

"I don't know that it was really a suggestion. More like a…vision board." I'd heard her use the word; I was hoping I'd used it correctly.

"Still. What do you think?"

"About being married at the church, then running barefoot through your mum's immaculately manicured shrubbery?"

He nodded, his hand squeezing mine for a moment. "Yeah."

I didn't suddenly start to worry that he was thinking of doing it next week. Rather, I chose to think of it as a maturation of our relationship. It was inevitable, this marriage, so why not talk about it in a healthy and productive way?

"I don't hate it," I told him honestly.

He smiled softly. "Is that Harlow-speak for you actually do hate it?"

I laughed and leant against him. He wrapped his arm around my shoulder as we walked.

"No," I said. "I guess I haven't really given it much thought. It's not something I wouldn't want to do, though."

"Would you prefer Bora Bora?"

"Uh, no. Definitely not."

"Good."

"Do you want the little church and a barefoot bride?" I asked him.

"The bride gets to pick her own footwear – or lack of – but I like the sound of the church. I– We've spent a lot of time there. Fetes and services."

"Plus, it's just really sweet."

He chuckled as he held the door to the boys' dorm open for me. "Plus, it's really sweet," he agreed.

"Your mum would probably faint from excitement," I said as we started up the stairs.

He nodded. "Oh, I've no doubt."

"Where were they married? Your parents?"

He scratched his head. "Amalfi Coast. Yours?"

"The Isle of Bute," I answered with a grin.

"Scotland?"

I nodded. "Oh, yes. Family tradition."

"Your mum's side then?"

"Yep."

"Her family has a place there, don't they?"

"If by place, you mean castle, then yes."

He smiled warmly as he opened his door for me. "So, are we expected to be wed in the family castle on the Isle of Bute?"

In a perfect world, we would. I'd spent years fantasising about my wedding being so similar to my parents' but modernised of course. And yet, I'd given up the dream five years' earlier.

"Mum would no doubt love it," I said. "But let's not pretend that Archer Callahan would allow it for his only son."

Apollo sighed. "No, I guess not."

I shrugged as I dropped onto his couch. "It's okay. If we really wanted, we could just go to the closest registry office and really piss him off."

Apollo laughed and sat beside me. "I like you like this," he said, his arm sliding behind me.

"Like what? Cynical and sassy?" I teased.

He nodded as he leant towards me. "Like this." He searched my eyes. "It's like you're being honest again, for the first time in a long time."

"Are you suggesting I've been lying?"

He shook his head and his nose bumped mine. "No. Not lying. Not really. And it's not hiding either. When we were little, you had this...fire about you." He ran his fingers down my cheek. "It went away for so long. I didn't notice until it was back. And, baby, is it back," he chuckled.

"And that's good?" I asked, fighting a smile.

His nose bumped mine on purpose this time. "It's fucking amazing."

He pressed a kiss to my lips and things heated quickly. Apollo's hand slid up my side to cup my breast, as the other went to the back of my neck.

Suddenly, he was leaning his forehead to mine.

"Are you a virgin?" Apollo asked me.

I hesitated.

Did I lie? Did I tell him the truth? What if he asked more questions?

"I...don't need – want – details," he clarified. "I just need to know."

I opened and closed my mouth a couple of times, then shook my head. "Uh, no."

I wasn't sure how apologetic to be. After all, I was supposed to be the pure one. We'd never talked openly about it, but it was obvious that I was expected to stay faithful. Whether because he thought it was my duty or because of who he'd thought I was, I didn't actually want to know. Apollo had never said directly, never said anything, like he just assumed. But his Angels had said plenty. They'd been the ones threatening a beating to any boy who talked to me when I was new to Saint Benedicts and my ownership had yet to be established.

But years of worrying, and I needn't have bothered. He didn't blink. Didn't bat an eye. He just took in my words and nodded.

"Okay. Good."

I was the one blinking. "Good?"

"Yeah, good." He nodded and breathed out with a shaky laugh. "You're... Fuck, how do I put this?"

"The princess," I suggested with a wry smirk.

He grinned. "The princess. *My* princess. I had to keep you... You were supposed to be..."

"This is fast becoming the opposite of good, Apollo," I warned him.

He chuckled. "Yeah. Right. Sorry. No, it's just... It takes a lot of pressure off."

"Pressure?" I asked, still not sure how this was a good thing.

He nodded, adamant.

Suddenly, gone was the boy I'd known most of my life and, in his place, was a man. A God. This Apollo wasn't Archer 2.0, he was completely his own man. Here was the Apollo I heard whispered about in the halls of Saint Benedicts. He was the man you knew could do unspeakably pleasurable things to your body, and thrill ran through me as I realised that he was looking at me like he wanted to do *all* of them. To *my* body.

Apollo leant towards me. He lay his hand splayed over my upper thigh and my hip, his thumb dipping precariously close to my centre. His eyes bore into mine with determination and desire.

"I don't have to feel bad about what I want to do to you anymore," he said, his voice low and seductive.

There was a part of me that fluttered and warmed and got nervous about this change between us. Then there was the part of me who'd known Apollo most of our lives and knew there was never a reason to be nervous with him.

"What do you want to do to me?" I asked him, teasingly, almost like I was daring him to do them right then.

His smirk was unbelievably sexy. "Oh, you have–"

A muffled, "Apollo," accompanied a knock on his door.

He rolled his eyes at me. "What?" he yelled towards the door.

"We need you," came Valen's voice through the door.

For all the flutters I had with Apollo, my body went crazy at the sound of Valen's voice.

Apollo rolled his eyes again and headed for the door. "Do you need me?" he asked as he pulled the door open. "Or do you–?"

Valen stalked in, took one supposedly uninterested glance at me, and turned to Apollo. "Machette's dead."

"What?"

"Machette is dead. I'm really not sure how else I can put that," Valen snapped.

Apollo frowned. "Fuck. What happened?"

Valen's eye slid to me quizzically.

Apollo waved away whatever the question was. "Yeah, Harlow's here. Who cares? What happened?"

Who cares?

What happened to men's business, and the women looking the other way when they saw too much? Was this seeing too much? It had to be. Someone was freaking dead. Did I just pretend to be heavily invested in that spot on the carpet? Did I sidle out of the room almost comically obviously?

Who cares?

I cared. Very much.

This seemed like a serious breaking of protocols, and I didn't much care for that. No one had actually said there were consequences to the women finding out about the men's business, but I understood they were implied. Just because I didn't know what they were, didn't mean I couldn't be afraid of them.

Valen sighed as he scrubbed a hand over the stubble on his jaw. "The Rossanos paid him off and he turned. Battista put him down before he could do much damage, and took a bullet for his troubles."

"I knew taking Machette in was a fucking bad idea. Dad wouldn't fucking listen," Apollo muttered.

"Vinnie's threatening worse than a couple of bullets if you don't show your face."

"It's a fucking Tuesday," Apollo huffed. "I do have class tomorrow."

Valen shrugged. "No one cares if I miss class. I'd be more than happy to go show Vinnie just how inconvenient his timing is."

"You can't kill Vinnie Rossano."

Valen's eyebrow rose. "Can't I?"

Apollo smirked at him. "You could. Easily. But I'm not giving that order." He pinched the bridge of his nose and stretched his neck as he thought. Finally, he sighed, "Vinnie's got a niece, yeah?"

Valen nodded. "She's enrolled here."

Apollo's nod was terse. "Get the boys to pay her a visit. Give her some time in the boot of one of the cars until Vinnie starts to see sense–"

"You're going to kidnap her?" burst out of me and they both turned to me like they'd forgotten I was there.

Apollo shrugged. "It's just kidnapping."

"Just kidnapping?" I repeated and he nodded. "Just kidnapping someone we go to school with?"

"You say that like it's the first time." Valen scoffed.

He was glad I was here. Glad I was seeing this side of them. A side he knew would shock me. If he thought that it would make me want him less…then he was right because I was totally over him.

Apollo shrugged. "We need her for leverage. Vinnie Rossano's a piece of work and, if he's turning Dad's men, then I need to do something."

"Turning? Like you're playing at war?" I said.

"Our peace is tenuous, babe," Apollo said, like that was supposed to appease me.

"Oh, and kidnapping his niece isn't going to make him retaliate?"

Apollo pointed at Valen like he'd thought of something. "Get Fender to keep an eye on Harlow and tell the boys to watch their backs. Tell them why if you want. Sooner Vinnie knows we've got his niece, the quicker this will go."

I frowned and crossed my arms. "I don't need a babysitter. No one's bothered me before."

"No one's got past one of us before," Valen said snidely, and I didn't want to think about what he was implying.

I ignored him, the blazing beacon that he was, and kept my gaze on Apollo. "Why don't you just put me in the boot with Vinnie Rossano's niece?" I suggested.

Apollo huffed. "Fuck's sake!"

I glared at him. "Is this why the women aren't allowed to know the men's business? Because there'd be no kidnapping or torture or any of the 'fun' stuff?"

"Because they're too soft to do what needs doing!" Apollo snapped in perfect imitation of his father, then looked instantly apologetic. "Just... Leave the stuff you don't understand, babe. Please." He sighed and looked at Valen. "At least put the niece in the backseat," he said resignedly, as though that would make me forgive him for his outburst.

"I'll leave you to your night of petty crime," I told them and made to walk out.

Apollo reached for me, but I kept my arm out of his grasp.

"Leave the stuff you don't understand," I repeated back to him as I headed out the door.

"Fuck!" I heard Apollo yell.

Before I reached the top of the cheeky service stairs, Valen was beside me.

"Does he think promoting you to babysitting duty is going to make me feel better about this?" I asked him.

"You're fine with me killing people," Valen said as we headed down the stairs, "but Apollo talking about kidnapping someone is appalling? You expect that little from the big, bad wolf but not your prince charming?"

I stopped and looked at him. "It's the *way* he discussed it. Like it didn't even matter. Like–"

"How do you think the Kincaids plan their assassinations, princess?" he asked quietly. "You think we sit around with our blankies and hot chocolate, crying about who gets to do it?"

"I..." didn't know what to say. "No...?"

"Then, what?"

I blinked a few times. "I don't know."

"This is our lives, princess. We live this every day. People die. Kids are used as leverage. We run fights. We take bets on car races. We handle weapons, putting in thousands of hours of training to make sure we don't kill the wrong people. This is our world. Your world. And no amount of wishing otherwise will make it so. I suggest you do as your forebears have done and look the other way."

I glared at him. "So, you think I'm soft, too."

He took a step towards me. Then another. On his third, I took a step back and hit the wall behind me.

"I think you can handle anything Apollo can, and more. But you don't have to, so I'd rather you didn't have to worry about it."

"It was okay when I was worrying about what I *thought* you got up to. But now I know, it's not okay?"

"That's not what I'm saying."

"Well then, what are you saying?"

He hit the wall beside my head with his open palm and beared down on me. "If I could change this world, I would," he snarled.

The unsaid words lingered in the air between us. *If I could change this world for you...*

Then his voice lowered, but it was no less vehement. "But no amount of wishing it otherwise will make it so."

His nose almost imperceptibly brushed mine, then my cheek, before his head hung over my shoulder.

"No amount of wishing, love."

When it felt like my heart would crack, he pushed himself away.

"Come," he commanded as he continued. "Vinnie'll be out for blood when he hears what stunt God's pulled now."

I put my hand on his arm and he jerked away.

"Whose blood, Valen?"

"Whoever's he can get."

Chapter Three

Apollo hadn't left my side all night. I knew he was making up for the other night when I'd walked out in him. Our interactions had been stilted since then. This might be our world and there might be little I could do about the killing and the kidnapping, but I wasn't going to let him treat me like a… Well, a woman.

My interactions with Valen had been fairly non-existent since he'd posted up outside our door and I'd left him there to bitch to Florence about stupid boys. By the time Florence stuck her head out the next morning, he was gone, and there was no way of telling how long he'd been there or what he'd heard us talk about.

I found I didn't much care if he'd heard it all. My annoyance. My sexual frustration. My wishing life was easier so Valen could keep rocking my world. My wishing life were easier so Apollo would just do it instead. My missing Valen and feeling conflicted about Apollo, but excited about Apollo and thankful Valen and I were over.

In fact, he probably had heard it all, decided I was completely insane and good fucking riddance, and that was why he wasn't coming anywhere near me as he drained that bottle of whiskey across the bonfire that Friday night.

But, with Apollo's hand constantly on me, his attention directed squarely at me, I hadn't had much time to feel Valen's eyes not leaving me. Even Florence was impressed with Apollo, although she was currently off somewhere with Marco.

Apollo had won significant points in Florence's scoreboard when he'd not just ignored but refused three separate Magdalens' attempts to get their hands on his cock. And one of them had even started unzipping his trousers, even with his arm around my shoulder. She'd given me a look that I'm surprised didn't kill but, by God's side, I felt invincible and decided that worrying about Magdalens' wrath would be a problem for future Harlow.

At some point in the night, a wild howling and hooting came from the woods. The opposite direction to the school. It wasn't the drunken, playful howling of Marco looking for Valen. It was the kind that made goosebumps prickle on your skin and had fear shooting down your spine.

As my hand tightened on Apollo's arm, I looked around for Valen. I couldn't help it. Fear pierced me and Apollo was by my side; I needed to know where Valen was. I wasn't sure if I was worried about his safety or knew he'd do anything to secure mine. I hoped the latter, because my eyes didn't search for Florence until I'd seen Valen was on high alert and ready for whatever was coming.

Florence was safe with Marco, but he was locked in a silent exchange across the bonfire with Apollo, Valen, Fender and Gage.

The rest of the party was paused like they were trying to decide if this was a joke that the Saints had organised, of if it was serious.

Another set of howls and hoots, closer this time.

A very definite voice echoed towards us; "I'm coming for blood, Callahan!" and the sound of a gunshot.

My hand tightened even more on Apollo's arm as his grip on me did likewise. Valen was running to us before the echo had finished ringing out through the trees.

There was a second of confusion, like people were still wondering if it was a joke, before suddenly the whole party broke into movement. Kids were running in all directions. Some were all for themselves. Some were looking for friends or lovers before they took off. But all of them were running back to the safety of the dorms.

Someone hit us and I was pulled out of Apollo's grasp. I saw him reaching for me, then strong arms were around me and Valen's body was positioned between me and the direction the noise was coming from.

"Happy now?" Valen growled at Apollo from over my head, and there was no sign of how much he'd been drinking.

Apollo's smirk was carefree, but his eyes were hard. "I'm fucking God, Valk. I just need to remind these fuckers."

Valen snarled at him like the wolf Apollo treated him. "Great, how are you going to do that?" he asked as Marco dragged Florence over to us.

She caught my eye, and we exchanged a silent panic. Her hand found mine and Valen finally let me go as I gravitated to Florence's arms. We hugged each other tightly as Fender and Gage arrived, and the Saints discussed their battle plan. With every howl or hoot or gunshot from the woods – each closer than the last – Florence and I both jumped.

"I can manage with Marco and the boys," Apollo was telling Valen.

Valen's eyebrow rose in the flickering bonfire light. "I'm the best fighter you have."

Apollo nodded. "Exactly. So, I need you with the girls. We need as many of us here as possible, and you're the only one who can protect the girls alone."

"I'm not going to take offence to that," Marco said, pouting and Florence whacked him.

"Any one of us can look after the girls if any of them get through," Gage said. "Let me take them. You'll miss me less here."

Apollo almost looked swayed, but he shook his head. "No. I'm not risking Harlow's safety–"

"Gee, thanks," Florence said, unable to stop herself from sassing Apollo, regardless of what was happening around us.

Apollo grinned at her, his eyes still cold and calculating. "Stay with Harlow, where you belong, and you'll benefit."

The noise was getting too close for comfort.

All the guys looked in that direction.

"Have you got your gun?" Apollo asked Valen.

He nodded once. Apollo returned a single nod.

"Good. Go. Be safe."

The two men clasped hands and I didn't know what passed between them, but I'd never seen them so serious. But then Valen was grabbing my arm and dragging us towards the dorms. I gripped Florence's hand tighter so we wouldn't be separated.

"Slow down," I told him. "Your legs are like twice as long as our entire bodies!"

Valen whirled and pulled my body into his as he bared down on me, heedless that Florence was standing right there. Danger, protection, and annoyance swirled around him and wrapped around me as he fixed those grey eyes to mine.

"You will do as you are told and you will do it without question," he said, his voice dangerously low and it sent a tingle through me. "There are times I will indulge your rebellious streak, but this is not one of them. Come."

He went back to dragging us, and it was all Florence and I could do to keep up while we shared a look at his words. He'd never given any indication that there was anything going on between him and me in front of anyone. I didn't know if Florence and I thought he was doing so now because we knew something had happened, or if the situation was making him not care what Florence did or didn't know. The thought was enough for me to know that he was worried. And if he was worried then there was something to worry about.

Valen didn't slow until we got back out of the woods and the lights of the school grounds were falling on us. I could see there were a few kids still running for the dorms. There had been the occasional gunshot during our mad dash through the trees, but otherwise relative silence.

After the woods, there was a swath of grass and then the path that would take us to the dorms. On the path, there was a collection of nuns, peering at the woods and, no doubt, us as well. They weren't chasing after the fleeing students, or even calling out after them. Uncharacteristically, Valen swerved towards them.

"What is going on, Mr Kincaid?" Sister Agnes asked.

"Infiltration. We're sorting it."

"We abide a lot from 'God' and his 'Angels', Mr Kincaid," she said slowly. "Since Saint Benedict's conception, we have allowed a lot to slide. But you would do well to remind the Nameless that business is not to be conducted on school grounds."

"You think I have any control over any of them?" Valen asked her sarcastically.

Sister Agnes just blinked slowly like she couldn't care less. "It is conveying a message, Mr Kincaid. Is that not your job?"

"I will convey your message, sister," he replied, his tone icy and heavy with warning.

Sister Agnes held her own. The woman didn't flinch under the wrath of Cillian Kincaid's son, God's tame wolf, or any of Valen's other roles he was forced to play.

She just nodded, looked us over and swept away with the other nuns. Her final unspoken parting instruction to go to bed and stay there was felt by all three of us.

"Come," Valen huffed at me.

"What is going on?" Florence asked him. "Who were those people, and whose blood are they after?"

"Is this anything to do with Vinnie Rossano?" I asked.

Valen stretched his neck like he was trying to stop himself from answering or turning.

"Vinnie Rossano?" Florence cried. She pulled to a stop, which forced me to stop, which forced Valen to stop.

Valen was not pleased. "We need to get inside. The sisters will put the whole fucking place on lockdown in..." He seemed to be counting, "seven minutes. If you're not in your dorm by then, I can't guarantee your safety."

But Florence was more stubborn than all the Angels put together. She shook her head. "No," she laughed humorously. "What the fuck is going on? What did that idiot God do to piss off Vinnie Rossano?"

Valen huffed. "We haven't got enough time to cover all of Apollo's idiocy. But that's not Vinnie Rossano."

"Okay, so who is it?" Florence asked.

Valen growled, letting go of me and flailing his arms.

"I'm not moving until you give us some answers, wolf-boy," Florence pressed.

Valen stepped up to her, but she was about as cowed as Sister Agnes had been.

"I'm about to run out of patience with the two of you," he snarled at her.

"Tough fucking luck," Florence answered.

Valen was still up against her, chest-to-chest, and he pointed at me. "I expect this sort of disobedience from her, but I will not tolerate it from you. I don't care what she's told you, my restraint goes no further than her. Do you understand me?"

Something sizzled between them. An understanding. Florence knew Valen knew. Valen knew Florence knew. There was an unspoken agreement that it didn't need to be explained, and the expectation it wouldn't be discussed seemed given.

"Throw your weight around all you like, Valk," Florence said. "But you wouldn't dare touch me knowing what it would do to Harlow."

Oh, brilliant.

Not only did they both know that they both knew there was something – had been something – between Valen and me, now Florence was antagonising him, too. It wasn't enough that she rile up God, she wanted to test the decency of a man well-known to have none. And drag me into it, to boot.

"Don't use me in your disagreements," I told them. "This is

between you."

Valen growled and it was fucking sexy. "I will answer any question about tonight that you have. Once you're in your dorm room," he promised her.

She seemed to be in bullshit detecting mode. Finally, she nodded. "Okay."

Valen nodded, then led the way to the girls' dorm. He didn't bat an eyelid at the girls who squeaked and hurried out of his way as he charged up the stairs and straight to our room. He opened the door, ushered us in, stepped in, then closed the door behind him.

"Ask your questions," he demanded as he went to check our windows like he actually thought someone might try climbing in them.

"What is going on?" Florence asked.

"Someone's come looking for vengeance."

"That's hardly an answer."

"I said I'd answer your questions, not give you a fucking lecture in response," he said, turning to her as he crossed his arms. "Next question."

Florence rolled her eyes. "Why has someone come looking for vengeance?"

"Because God is drunk with power and he's crossing boundaries he's never even pushed before."

Both Florence and Valen looked at me and I was going to pretend I didn't read the implication on their face; God was drunk with power because of me.

"Okay." Florence seemed to be thinking.

A great klaxon sounded through the building. It was the signal for lockdown.

"Any more questions?" Valen asked.

"Who did God piss off?"

"No one you need to worry about."

"That's not a good enough answer, Valk."

"God fixed a car race. Marco made sure Fender won it. The losers are coming for payback."

Florence rolled her eyes again in her typical exasperated with Apollo style. "Fucking idiots. The pair of them."

"Fucking idiots," Valen agreed. "Is that it?"

Florence looked him over like she was considering. "Would you give me any more answers if I kept pushing?"

"I said I'd answer all your questions."

"I wasn't sure if I should believe you."

"Valen's many things," I said quietly. "But he doesn't lie."

"If I can help it," he added, as though that was a very important point.

"Is Apollo going to be okay?" I asked.

Valen gave a single nod. "He's got the other Angels. Those coming for him will barely put a scratch in him."

"Barely? That's hardly a comfort."

"It's comfort enough for me," Florence commented dryly as she dropped onto her bed.

"If that's it, I'll be in the hallway. Lock the door and do not open it for anyone but me," Valen commanded. "Understood?"

A thrill ran through me just at the word and the memory of the way he usually used it. There was a look in his eye that made me think he was playing on that now. But then I blinked, and he was back to just his usual, stony self.

"Understood," Florence said when it seemed obvious that I wasn't going to reply.

He left and we busied ourselves to take our minds off what might be happening in the woods. After I was changed and in my pyjamas, I opened the door a crack and found Valen sitting on the floor with his back against the wall like he was a very tired sentry, his vape pen in his hands. Tired, or bored.

"Are you planning to be here all night?" I asked him.

He leant his head against the wall. "Someone has to be."

"You don't need to help Apollo?"

He rolled his head to look up at me. "Yes."

"Then why don't you go? Or does even God's tame wolf not have a way through the nuns' lockdown?"

The ghost of a smirk lit his gorgeous lips as he looked down the hallway away from me. "I could get out of here blindfolded and bound–"

"That's certainly an image," I said suggestively.

His eyebrow rose as he looked at me from the corner of his eyes. "That mouth on you," he whispered, almost reverently.

I shrugged. "Am I supposed to be the little princess again?"

He shook his head slowly. "Fuck, no. Not with me." He shifted and cleared his throat. "It doesn't matter to me."

"Of course not," I said, a note of teasing in my voice. "What does it matter to you the dark and sinful, erotic things that go through my mind?"

I didn't know what made me push him – almost test him – like that. Maybe it was the fact we were both a little drunk, but I couldn't help myself.

He gave a humourless chuckle. "Nothing. It doesn't matter to me at all."

I leant on the door frame. "Can I get you anything?" His head twitched like we both knew what I really wanted to offer but wouldn't. "Bottle of water? If you're hungry, I'm pretty sure all we have are biscuits."

"Water would be great."

I nodded. "Back in a second."

"What are you doing?" Florence hissed as I closed the door. "I have no where to go, so you two can't fuck in here."

I smirked at her as I went to the mini fridge. "I'm not doing anything."

She nodded. "Sure. I'm just melting over here from imagined burning hot chemistry between the two of you."

"If you bring up waterboarding again…" I warned her, getting a bottle of water.

She shook her head. "I honestly don't know what the point is. I could put my headphones and my eye mask on?" she offered.

"There's really no need. We've fucked each other out of our systems."

Florence rolled her eyes. "I mean, clearly not, but…"

I pulled the door open again and leant down to pass Valen the water. His eyes darted down my top. I assumed he was copping a look at the goods on display…until his eyes narrowed. His hand shot out and grabbed my wrist to stop me standing back up.

"What is wrong with you?" I asked.

"Where the fuck is my cross?" he snarled, and it sent a pleasant tingle of anticipation shooting right through me.

My free hand went to my neck, and I suddenly remembered the whole deal before the party.

"I forgot to put in on again after my shower," I told him. "I was late, and Florence needed the bathroom."

His eyes narrowed further. "You forgot?"

I nodded. "Yes, Valen. I forgot. I forget a lot of things."

He let my arm go and I stepped back. He stood up swiftly and boxed me against the wall. Oh, how I wished we weren't in the middle of the girls' dorm hallway. At least no one else was around.

"Do ye now?"

I swallowed hard but nodded.

"And did you *forget* we'd fucked each other out of our systems, or do ye need another reminder?"

Um, yes, please. I would love another reminder. But I couldn't tell him that.

"I'm fine." I wasn't.

He raised one of my hands above my head with the arm he wore his cuff. He left it in line with my eyes, and I saw the flash of silver chain hiding under it that belonged to my cross. His other hand went to my hip, and it seared my skin through the fabric of my pyjamas. I wanted him closer. I needed him closer. And I couldn't fucking have it.

"Then ye won't forget to wear my cross again, will ye?" he asked, his voice low as he dipped his lips to my ear.

I wanted very badly to argue with him, remind him that I wasn't an object he could just order around, but I also wanted him to order me around. I wanted him to want me to wear his cross. It was the closest we could ever come to meaning anything and I didn't want that to change.

"No, Valen," I told him. "I won't."

And I wouldn't. I wouldn't even take it off to shower if that was going to risk me forgetting to wear it.

"Good. No go inside and put it on. Now."

"What will you do if I don't?" I sassed.

"Be very thankful," he said slowly, "that Florence is in there."

"Why?" I asked, my clit tingling and my nipples tightening. "Because otherwise you'd punish me?"

He pressed his very hard erection into my heated pelvis. "Yes."

I arched my back to press against him. "Even though we're over?"

"You will always be mine," he said so quietly I was sure he hadn't meant to.

He finally pulled away from me and looked deep into my eyes. My heart hitched in my chest and my stomach tightened and fluttered in a totally different way. I didn't know what to say. I didn't know how I felt. Here we were, supposed to be over and done and out of each other's systems, but it definitely didn't feel like it. And it felt like we both felt the same.

I cleared my throat and slid towards my door with a nod. "Good night, Valen."

He inclined his head. "Good night…Harlow."

As I turned the door handle, I realised I still had the water, so I held it out to him. He took it, his fingers lingering against mine.

"Thanks," he said.

I tucked my hair behind my ear. "Thank you." He seemed to know what I was thanking him for, but I clarified anyway. "For protecting me."

He took a breath. "Forever."

I gave him a small smile that I saw returned in his eyes if no where else on his face. I gave an awkward nod, and slunk into my room, collapsing on the door to close it behind me.

"So?" Florence asked.

"I'll always be his," I said quietly.

Florence shared a grin with me. "That's good?"

I nodded. "I think so. It shouldn't be, but it is."

She shrugged. "Don't let anyone tell you how you should feel, Harlow," she reminded me.

I made a mental note to follow her advice.

Not that it helped my conundrum.

I wanted to make things work with Apollo.

But I still wanted Valen, too.

Chapter Four

No one bothered to explain what had happened at the bonfire party. Apollo seemed fine except for a couple of scrapes. Marco had a slightly bigger wound in a split eyebrow. Gage seemed fine. And Fender had got himself grazed across the abdomen with a bullet, so he was a little sore but healing well.

The next morning, Florence had left for an Art retreat, leaving me and Apollo free to do nothing but each other all weekend. And Saturday was looking like it might finally be the day it all happened.

I was in Apollo's room, and we still had a couple of hours before dinner.

His hand ran up my leg as I straddled his lap on the couch. Our bodies rubbed together as we kissed. I'd already unbuttoned his shirt to run my hands along his body, and my top was on the floor. My hands were in his hair, and his other hand was up my skirt.

He deftly circled my clit, sliding over me easily with nothing but my own juices. Pleasure tightened in me. My body tensed. His lips dropped to my neck, and I sighed as the tingles shot straight to my nipples.

"Fuck, Apollo," I breathed as he worked me closer and closer to orgasm.

"You going to cum for me, sweetheart?" he asked.

I nodded. "Yes. Make me cum. Please."

His fingers worked me faster as I balanced on that precipice. Then my whole body clamped around his as it finally crashed over me, and

I felt the smile on his lips against my neck.

Without any warning, he stood up, with me in his arms, and threw me on his bed. Before I had time to utter a single question, he was lying over me. His lips found mine and his finger slid thrust inside me to pump me steadily.

It did have to be said that he'd learned the best ways to bring me to multiple orgasms and he wasn't afraid to get creative. But then, I guessed that's what happened when he was relying on his fingers or his mouth and refused to put his cock in me.

But we were on his bed and clothes had started to come off…so maybe it was going to be today?

As a much more gentle but no less amazing orgasm washed over me, my hands reached for his belt. He didn't stop me, so I undid it and his pants. Still, he didn't stop me, so I slid my hand inside them. I stroked his shaft and felt the rumble of an appreciative groan vibrate through his chest. He was rock hard for me.

His lips trailed down my cheek, my jaw, my neck. His hips began to rock with my rhythm as he fucked my hand slowly, his fingers thrusting in and out of me in time. We were so close to finally having sex.

"Wait. Harlow, stop," he said, pulling my hand out of his trousers.

I looked him over. "What?"

He looked down at me and I thought I saw a war waging in his eyes.

"Apollo?" I asked.

"I…" He grunted in frustration, pushed away from me and stalked out of the room, tucking himself back in his trousers but not even bothering with his door on his way out.

He'd just left me there, totally hanging, watching his door like I expected him to come rushing back through it with a thousand apologies on his lips. When it became apparent that wasn't going to happen, I stood up, straightened my clothes, found my top, and decided I wasn't waiting for him to come back.

I paused in his doorway wondering if I *should* wait for him, then shook my head before slamming the door behind me. Apollo was nowhere to be seen. He clearly wasn't going to turn around and come after me. I wanted to say that it was a sign of how well he knew me, but there was a part of me who knew he was just taking the easier road. Then there was an even smaller part of me who felt that he didn't come back because he didn't care enough — that he'd never care enough.

"Stop it," I snapped at myself, heading off the thought that Valen would have come after me. "He wouldn't have either."

Neither of them would, and I told myself not to blame them.

Valen and I were done and, even when we weren't, it was never going to be anything; he had no reason to come back.

Apollo and I were new; we were still working out what a real relationship looked like. He was trying to give me space. Even if he used that space to lose himself in a Magdalen, he thought giving me space was what I needed.

I wanted to not fault him for that. And most of me didn't.

But there was also a part of me that just wanted to be angry and annoyed and confused and spend a whole lot of my father's money on useless shit in Bieityn. So that's what I was going to do.

As I barrelled out of the boys' dorm building, Marco saw me.

"Oi, oi, missus. Where's the fire?" he asked, throwing all his lazy charm behind his words and his eyes.

I rolled mine. "Not in the mood, Marco."

"Haven't seen the delectable Florence around this weekend."

"She's at an art retreat," I snapped.

"Are ye okay, missus?" he asked, his tone soft and gentle.

I huffed. "No."

"Can I help?"

I sighed as I thought through the logistics of my plan. "Up for some light chauffeur and escort duty, Marco?"

"And just how much would ye be paying me?" he teased.

I frowned. "With my pleasant company," I sassed.

He grinned. "Perfect. I'd love to. I've got no plans."

I nodded. "Then take me to your vehicle of choice."

"Oh, you wouldn't want that, missus," he said as he led the way to the boys' garage. "Saturday evening ride down the hill on me bike would be my choice."

"Fair. Thanks for the warning. Your second choice of vehicle, then."

"I just so happen to have the keys to Valk's Viper," he said with a mischievous smirk, swinging said keys around his finger.

"Oh, good. So, I'll be risking death while in the car, then risking death when we get back to Valk waiting on whomsoever nicked his precious baby?"

Marco looked at me askance over the hood of said Viper. "Ah, he won't kill *you*, missus," he assured me. "And he'd sooner kill me for driving you in anything else."

"You say that like he cares about my safety," I said flippantly as I got into the front passenger seat.

Marco dropped into the driver's seat beside me. "Now, that. He'd rather die than let you know that."

I looked at Marco for a second, but there was no sign of anything on his face. His tone had implied far more than he should know – or guess – or probably that I should know in return. And yet, it implied it heavily. His manner, though, suggested I was imagining things.

"Okay, so where are we off to?" he asked as he turned on the car.

"Anywhere with an exorbitant price tag."

"You shopping away your problems, missus?" he asked, and the sympathy was buried very deep in his tone.

"You lot drink or fight or fuck, or whatever else it is you Saints do," I told him. "I swipe a piece of plastic."

"Us *Sinners*," he corrected me, "could show you a thing or two."

I gave him a snarky side-eye. "Come now, Marco. You know Valk would never let that stand."

He snorted. "Aye. Ain't that the truth."

Marco drove me down the hill to Bieityn, making small talk. Or rather, doing all the talking like we were having a pleasant conversation about things ranging from the weather to God's heir assumptive to the latest English assignment.

"Ye'll want to start at *Marta's*, I presume?" he said as he found a park.

I sighed. "Unless you're aware of them adding rainbow to the menu at *La Freeze*?"

"Alas, they have not. The closest stock I know of is Saint Bens or the Estate."

Well, I wasn't going to either of those places. "*Marta's* it is, then."

"Are you looking for anything particular?" the Marta in question asked as I perused her rack of overpriced designer labels.

"Not really," I told her, and she knew that meant 'leave me alone'.

"Of course, Miss Vanguard. Let me know if you need anything."

I nodded and she wandered away.

Marta had survived years in Bieityn purely by knowing who was a student at Saint Benedicts, who lived in Bieityn, and who was a tourist. The first two, she left to their own devices because they'd either spend their money or they wouldn't. It was only the last one she pestered and wrung a sale out of.

"What do ye need from me, missus?" Marco asked.

I kicked my head to indicate the lounge chairs outside the fitting rooms. "Take a seat and I'll pretend I'm asking for your opinion."

He gave me a deep, wide grin. "Can do."

I took a bunch of random things that caught my eye into a fitting room and started getting changed. The first outfit I tried was a long white culotte with a bright orange blouse and green scarf.

"Is the next faculty dinner Wonka themed?" Marco asked, not bothering to hide his shit-eating grin.

"Shut up," I told him, but I felt a smile threatening and my mood lightening already.

I lost track of the outfits I tried on and showed him. A lot of them were intended to be ridiculous and get a smile out of both of us, but he seemed over-eager to find fault with all of them regardless.

By the time he wasn't very impressed with a magenta number either, claiming it washed me out, we were both grinning from ear to ear and I'd almost forgotten why I'd essentially stormed down to Bieityn to waste a bunch of Dad's money.

"Do you even know what that means?" I asked him.

He shrugged. "Does it mean the colour will stain your skin when you sweat in it?" he asked, and I couldn't tell if he was serious or taking the piss.

I shook my head. "Fine. Next."

The big black floor-length dress got a firm head shake.

"No. Hard pass," he said.

"What? Why?"

"You look like you're going to a funeral."

"Yeah, yours if you keep this up," I muttered as I hiked up my skirts and headed back into the fitting room.

"If you wanted someone to fawn all over you, you should have God sitting in this chair."

Suddenly, I remembered why I was in Bieityn with a view to spend a lot of money.

"If I don't see your God for the rest of the weekend, that would be fine by me," I snapped through the door.

"Did ye want to talk about it?" he asked slowly as I came out in an emerald green sequin dress, and his jaw dropped.

It had spaghetti straps, hugged my figure tightly, and had a massive split up one leg. It was a little more spangly and sparkly than I'd usually go for even when the aim had been to seduce Valen.

"Fuck me," Marco breathed as he leaned forward and rested his elbows on his knees. It echoed the sentiment I'd thought upon seeing myself in the mirror.

"What?" I teased, checking myself out in the larger mirror. "No comment that I look like a radioactive asparagus, or look like an extra from a seventies movie?"

He shook his head. "Nah, missus. Not this time. You look proper lovely. Got a do in mind?" he asked as he leaned back again.

I shook my head. "Probably too garish for Christmas. Although, I'm sure Archer would approve based solely on the price tag."

Marco grinned. "Aye, but Mr Callahan also thinks that big fancy bar in his ballroom is the height of sophistication."

I snorted. "Are you questioning Archer Callahan's taste?" I joked

Marco held up his hands in defence. "I wouldn't dare question a sitting council member of the Nameless, missus. But I would question the basis of God's so-called taste."

"Your tastes are more simple, are they?" I asked, honestly wanting to know more about him.

He shrugged. "Us Angels come from different stock. Those like the Kincaids have money to spare, but we all live differently. Our idea of decadence is different. We don't want our women draped in pearls and diamonds."

"What would you prefer them in? Leather and tattoos?"

His smile was wide, and both teasing and companionable. "Whatever she wants."

"I get the feeling this is an O'Malley thing. The Kincaids sure don't seem to appreciate women. Theirs or not."

"Aye. They're a different breed again. Most of us at least appreciate our own, even if we don't much care for anyone else's."

I gave him a rueful smirk. "And what about your God's woman?"

His smile widened further, and he huffed a rough laugh. "Aye, missus. Most of us appreciate our God's woman, too. We're contractually obliged after all."

"Oh, well. If you're contractually obliged," I teased, and we shared a friendly smile.

"You're different, missis," he said gently.

I looked down at my hands. "Am I?"

"Don't misunderstand me, please. I mean it in a good way. You've got more balls on you. More you're own person."

"You mean I'm not the quiet, demure little princess anymore."

He shook his head. "Nah, missus. Ye'll always be that, but you're not afraid to show your claws anymore. When you need to. It'll serve you well."

I fiddled with the stupid giant crown on my finger that I hadn't had time to take off before leaving school. "A woman isn't supposed to see the men's business, Marco..."

"They're not..." he agreed, waiting to see if I'd continue.

"And yet I've seen more in the last two weeks than in all my years before."

He nodded slowly. "God's...a right cocky bastard, that's for sure." He scratched his ear. "Way I see it, missus. There comes a point where the women in our world become kind of invisible. It's ironic really, as to become invisible, ye first have to become special." He shook his head. "I'm not making any sense."

Weirdly, he was making a kind of sense. It was a theory I thought I could at least follow the points through to their conclusion.

"Like, the more we're a part of our man's life, the more we see?" I clarified. "Except we have to pretend we haven't, everyone else pretends we haven't, and we're not supposed to talk about it?

Marco nodded. "Exactly."

I sighed. "I don't think I'll ever really understand this world, Marco."

His nod this time was more solemn. "Aye, me mam says much the same."

I huffed. "And she's an O'Malley. I've got no fucking hope."

"Would swiping some plastic make you feel better?" Marco asked kindly, indicating the dress.

I looked down at myself and smiled. "Yes. I'll change, buy this, then how about we grab some dinner?"

"I could eat."

We dropped my totally unnecessary purchase off at the car, then decided on where to eat. We didn't go to *Bieito*, though I didn't doubt they'd find a table for me. Instead, Marco showed me a little burger place where all the boring, normal locals frequented. Everyone there seemed to know him and greeted him with warm smiles, open arms, and free beer.

It was honestly the most normal I'd felt in…forever. This felt like the way life was supposed to be. It's what all the movies and TV shows said normal life was. Just laughs and greasy food and no one worried about your bank account or what you could do for them or how many carats sat on your finger or strands at your neck.

It was late by the time Marco and I were heading back to the car.

"You still should have let me pay," I insisted.

"Nonsense," he replied. "You said you'd pay me with your company. And you did."

"I'll not have *you* treating me like a kept woman as well."

He laughed. "I wouldn't fucking dare. Besides, I can claim it as a business expense."

I froze. He kept walking.

"You claim stuff as a busi–?" My words were cut off with a scream as foreign arms grabbed me from behind.

Fight or flight kicked in and my legs flailed like champions, they just failed to hit anything useful.

Marco was in fight mode within seconds. I saw him turn and size up whoever had me. I saw recognition cross his features.

"You don't want to be here," he told them.

"Don't we?" the guy at my back asked as two more stepped out of the shadows around us.

"You want me to put another of your boys in the hospital? It'll be my pleasure."

"There's three of us, O'Malley, and only one of you. Or are you counting your woman?"

"I'm not *his* woman," I grunted, trying to get free of the guy who held me.

I finally got a hit into his crotch. It wasn't much, but it was enough for him to loosen his hold on me. I thrashed until I fell to the ground then scrambled over to Marco as fast as I could. I felt the skin of my knee rip on the pavement, but that was the least of my worries.

One of the other guys lunged at me, but Marco was there, putting himself between me and danger. He already had a knife in his hand.

"You're not gonna want to watch this, missus," he said to me as he and the other guys looked like they were waiting for someone to make the first move.

"You out with Callahan's girl, O'Malley?" the first guy sneered.

"That's not Harlow Vanguard," another jeered. "I heard she was so fucking ugly Callahan wouldn't touch her even for the Vanguard fortune."

The three of them laughed and I felt anger surge through me. I got to my feet, frowning at them as impressively as a particularly cheesed off Sunday school teacher.

"Well, you heard fucking wrong," I snapped, and I heard Marco sigh audibly.

If he was annoyed with me, he didn't show it. "We gonna chat, or we gonna do this?" he asked.

Then it went off and I totally lost track of what was happening. Glints of silver flashed where knives caught light, but Marco kept them all away from where I was pressed against the wall and trying to stay out of the way.

One of Marco's opponents went down and didn't get up. I didn't much care at that point if he never did again. The second one ran as the first one dropped, and the third – the guy who'd grabbed me – was lying on the ground with Marco's knife at his throat.

"This is done, now," Marco snarled at him. "Do we have an understanding?"

The guy nodded as furiously as Marco's blade allowed. "It's done, but if Callahan crosses another line, we take blood. Starting with his girl." His eyes flashed to me, then he pushed Marco away, got up and ran off after his fellow.

Marco dropped to his knee and breathed heavily. I rushed to his side and fell down next to him.

"Are you okay? What can I do?" I put a hand to his side, then pulled it away to find it slick with blood. "Oh, fuck."

"Oh, fuck," he seemed to agree.

"What can I do?"

"Car," he said.

I awkwardly got under his arm and pushed us to standing.

"I feel like you're not really helping me here," I said, trying to break the tension it seemed only I was feeling. I wasn't sure if I wanted to remember that this was their life.

"Probably because I'm not."

"You better run, O'Malley!" someone called from behind us, but I didn't have the stability to turn around.

"Oh, my God!" I wheezed as I struggled under the weight of Marco's arm. "What do you want me to do?"

He fired off a shot behind us from a gun I hadn't even seen yet. Based on how wayward it seemed – from the person with zero knowledge of such things – I assumed it was intended as a warning shot.

"To the car, missus," he answered, far more wheezy than me. "You're going to have to drive."

Panic welled in me. More than having random hands grab me in the dark. More than seeing Marco fight to what I suspected was someone's death on my behalf. I couldn't drive the fucking Viper!

"Me? Drive Valen's prize possession?"

"He'll be too busy bitching about all the blood I leave in it to worry about you behind the wheel."

"You are bleeding a lot."

"I am bleeding a lot," he agreed.

We got him into the backseat of the car with one more shot fired behind us in answer to one that sailed past my head alarmingly close. As I climbed through to the driver's seat, my desire to not be outside the car longer than necessary was fully justified as a bullet hit the back of the car.

"Go!" Marco shouted.

I scrambled to get the seat in some semblance of usable to me and peeled out of the park with squealing rubber.

"Valen's going to kill me," I muttered. "He's going to actually kill me."

"We're coming in hot," Marco said.

I flicked my eyes to the rear-view mirror and saw the glow of a phone. I didn't know who he was talking to.

"Come alone. Just you, Valk." A pause. "Blood loss. Barely conscious. Gonna need a fuck tonne of stitches. The Viper's got a bullet hole in it. But the missus did get a nice new dress."

I careened up the hill, taking the twists and turns far too quickly, but thankful at each one that my father had insisted not only that I learn to drive auto and manual cars, but also that I take that defensive driving course. It had been more like a stunt driving course in disguise, but it was serving me well just then.

Marco had been silent too long.

"You still with me?" I asked.

"Yeah. Just. Valk's gonna meet us... Garage..."

"Shit sticks," I muttered as I slammed my foot to the accelerator.

The car leaped through the Saint Benedicts front gates and fought for traction on the gravel drive. I almost lost control but managed to spin the car to a stop just outside the boys' garage. I saw a figure run towards us as I climbed out. I recognised Valen's figure instantly. Part of me wanted to run to him and throw myself in his arms and make him tell me everything was going to be okay, but I had to get Marco some serious help.

Valen paused when he saw me, then was running faster. As I went to open the back door to get Marco out, Valen's hand closed on my arm and whirled me to face him.

"Where are you hurt? Where's Marco?"

I batted him away, but he clung to me. "I just scraped my knee. Marco's the one who needs stitches."

"This isn't your blood?" His hands roved over me professionally, like he was looking for wounds.

I shook my head. "No."

"Fuck," he breathed, and it sounded all relief.

For a moment, I thought he was going to pull me to him and kiss me. For a moment, I think he thought he was going to as well. But he didn't.

"Marco's in the back," I told him.

Valen wrenched the back door open and exclaimed at the sight that greeted him. "Fucking hell!"

Marco gave him a bloody grin. "Just you wait til you see the bullet hole."

"What the fuck happened?" Valen demanded.

"The spineless fucking Black Bloods came sniffing around for more retribution. Thought picking a fight with one of God's Angels would be funny."

"I thought we dealt with them?" Valen said.

Marco's already glassy gaze flickered to me.

"What?" Valen asked.

"They'll have put a target on Miss Vanguard's back."

"How? They wouldn't recognise her."

"It's my fault," Marco said.

"No," I told them both. "I'm the one who outed me."

"They said if God fucks them again, then they're coming for her first."

"Fuck!" Valen grunted, slamming his hand on the car door. "I leave you alone for five fucking seconds and you go and get a target on your back! And the fucking Black Bloods? I might never let you out of my sight again!"

He finished his tirade inches from me, his chest rising and falling rapidly. Mine was skipping and tripping and not at all sure how to take his words.

"Be more careful," he ordered.

"Or what, Valen?" I asked.

"Or I will never leave your side."

How did he make that sound so delicious but so threatening at the same time? His tone suggested I wouldn't enjoy it, history suggested I very much would.

"As impressive as your protective streak is," I said sarcastically, "Marco need serious medical attention."

Valen took a deep, steadying breath. "You mention this to no one. Not even Florence. Especially not Apollo."

"Why especially not Apollo?"

"Because the ijit would use it as an excuse to provoke the Black Bloods," Marco wheezed.

"Instead of heeding the warning," Valen finished for him.

"What am I supposed to do now?" I asked.

"Go back to your room and go to bed."

I looked at Valen. "Seriously?"

"And you do not leave school grounds without me or Marco." Valen looked to Marco. "You're gonna have to earn that double time now."

"I know. Now can we fucking get on before all me wounds clot and close by themselves?"

As Valen went to help Marco out of the car, I lay a hand on his arm. He looked at me quizzically.

"Floss is away. I don't... I don't think I should be alone tonight..."

Valen either refused under the circumstances to or just didn't see anything sexual in that. He nodded.

"I'll get Marco to the doctor, give you time to clean up, then come and check on you."

I nodded. "Thanks."

I hurried to my room, thankfully seeing no one to comment on my blood-soaked appearance. The back of my neck prickled like I was being watched or followed, but I forced myself to believe it was just my heightened nerves.

I was just climbing into bed, clean and changed, when there was a knock on the door. My heart tried leaping out of my mouth, but the familiar if stern face of Valen appeared around it and my heart settled in place once more.

"You decent?" he asked, coming into the room and closing and locking the door behind him.

"More decent than the last time we were locked in a room together. If that's what you're asking?"

He dropped to the floor by my bed and rested his head against the wall before closing his eyes. "I wasn't, but good to know."

"I take it you're staying?"

"You said you shouldn't be alone tonight."

"I didn't expect you to care."

"It's my job to care," he growled.

"Except it's not," I reminded him. "It's your job to care about Apollo. I highly doubt your contract states you're responsible for the mental wellbeing of his intended bride."

"What do you want me to say, princess?" he sighed. "Do you want me to say I'm here because I care about you?"

"I thought you didn't lie if you could help it?"

He opened his eyes and looked at me. "I don't. I'm here so you don't do anything stupid like run to Apollo and risk him doing something stupider like running after the Black Bloods like he's fucking untouchable. I'm here because my contract states I'm responsible for keeping Apollo alive. I can't do that if he decides to actually play God."

I looked him over, wishing that wasn't the only reason he was staying in my room overnight. He didn't give me anything. His gaze was hard, his jaw was set, and his mouth was tight. Then he closed his eyes again like he was just going to sleep where he was.

"You can at least sleep in Florence's bed," I offered.

"Florence would kill me," was his answer.

"No, she wouldn't."

"She would have no qualms doing anything to me, and I wouldn't lift a finger to her in return."

"Why not?"

"Because I know what that would do to you."

I sat there in stunned silence for a moment.

"Go to sleep, Harlow. And let this be the last time I have to sleep on the floor for you. At least for a week."

I felt a smile rise unbidden and snuggled down in the bed as though that could hide it.

Despite the fear of the events of that night, I felt safe with Valen. It wasn't long before I was asleep. When I woke up, the only sign he'd been there was the lingering scent of his favourite vape juice.

Chapter Five

The next day when I saw Apollo, we said nothing of the day before. Nothing about him storming off. Nothing about me going to Bieityn. Nothing about Marco's fight. Nothing that might have made it obvious that either of us knew how Marco got that wound.

It was business as usual, and it felt like we were both going to pains to keep it that way. I knew my reasons, and I tried hard not think about what Apollo's might have been.

As we walked through the school ground, Apollo slid his hand into mine. "I've got to do something tonight. Do you think you could come?"

"What kind of something?" I asked.

He smiled. "Just a…thing."

"Is this a pearls kind of thing or a jeans kind of thing or–"

"Jeans definitely."

I smiled at his certainty. "Okay."

But I wasn't smiling quite so widely after dinner when Marco pulled up to what looked like a dodgy arse warehouse in the closest industrial town to Bieityn.

"Where are we?" I asked Marco.

He looked at me like he did not want that job. "I'm going to let the ijit explain that one." He winced a little as he swung out of the car too quickly.

He joined me on the passenger side, and I looked him over.

"Are you sure you're okay?" I asked.

He nodded. "Healing like a fucking charm."

"I'm sorry," I said to him, again.

He shook his head. "I will not tell ye again," he warned.

He'd told me plenty of times it wasn't my fault. It still felt like it was. Maybe If I hadn't given myself away, he might not have had to fight so hard. Maybe if I hadn't run to Bieityn in a fit of annoyance at Apollo, he wouldn't need to be healing at all.

I opened my mouth, and he made a noise that told me exactly where to stuff my next thought. I snapped my mouth shut and nodded.

"It is my privilege to keep an eye on ye, missus," he said carefully, like he was really telling me something. "Don't diminish it just because it's new to ye. We Angels have taken and will take worse again for our God."

I took a breath and nodded. That made sense. "Okay. I won't. Thank you."

"For what?"

"For taking the time to explain things to me like I'm not an idiot."

"Ignorance put on you by our world doesn't make you an idiot, missus," he said as he led me to the door. "I sometimes wonder if ignorance really is bliss."

Marco held out a hand for me to stop before banging on the door. A clichéd little eye slot opened up and two bloodshot eyes stared out at us. They were close set and narrowed as though who dared to try and enter such a secretive and exclusive establishment.

"Marco, ye're late," the booming voice said.

"God has me on chauffeur duty," Marco answered.

The eyes swivelled to me. "He wanted her here?"

His incredulity and Marco's reticence wasn't filling me with confidence, neither about what type of place this was nor what was going to happen in it.

"God's word is law," was all Marco would say.

The eyes seemed to shrug. "All right, then. Welcome to the Club, Miss Vanguard."

He pulled away, slid the slot closed and wrenched the door open. And all my worst fears were confirmed. Beyond the door was clearly an underground fight club. Even to the person who knew nothing about the realities of such things. I knew enough about popular culture to recognise one when I walked into one.

There were disgruntled, dirty men everywhere, with booze and/or a smoke in hand, and not just tobacco by the smell of it. Now and then, I saw the slightly more put together styling of a Saint, or one of their older male family members. I was sure I saw Gage and a couple of other Saints in the corner sniffing something harder off a woman's naked body. And in the middle of the warehouse was a cage the likes of which I'd seen in relation to MMA fights, however I'd managed to ingest anything about that. But it was so much less clean. The two fighters in there just adding to the blood splatter as the gathered men cheered or booed them on.

The lighting was poor, and my eyes watered against the smoke as much as the smell, as Marco ushered me to the bar. He stayed behind me, one hand on my elbow, and I assumed he had the best vantage from behind me in case anyone came out of the shadows.

"Drink, missus?" he asked, and I nodded, still not bold enough to actually say anything.

Why in the hell had Apollo wanted me here?

Marco held two fingers up to the woman behind the bar and she brought us two glasses of amber liquid. I didn't care the glasses were a little dirty, I just threw it back and nodded for another.

"In need of some courage, missus?" Marco teased, but there was a hard glint to his eyes.

"Why am I here, Marco?"

"I would say it was because God was worried about his top Angel getting in that cage later tonight."

I felt like my heart had stopped. My whole body went cold. "What?" I asked.

My eyes swivelled to the cage, and I saw the victor's arm being lifted to the crowd. The other guy lay at his feet and didn't look like he was standing on his own feet any time soon.

Marco nodded as he threw back his drink and we picked up our seconds. "But then that would be questioning my God."

"Valen's going in there?" I asked.

Marco nodded as we both tipped our drinks back and motioned for a third. "Valk's going in there tonight."

A new contender was led into the cage and a great roar drowned out the rest of the noise in the place. He was huge. I was sure he was twice the size of the guy they'd dragged out from the previous fight.

"And there's his competition," Marco muttered, throwing back drink three.

"Valen's fighting *him*?"

Surely even Valen couldn't hold his own against a guy that size? Pure physics had to be against him.

"And he's a nasty fucker," Marco whistled, leaning on the bar.

"You know him?" I asked.

Marco nodded. "Bratva boy. A Volkov. One of Valk's kin on his mam's side. Sure won't treat him like it, though."

"Bratva? Valen's family?" There was a lot to unpack in that sentence. And the name Volkov sounded familiar for some reason.

Marco nodded as a concerned frown marred his features and he rubbed his thumb over his nose. "Even for Valk, this is a fucking stupid idea."

My heart thudded in my chest. "What? Why?"

He scoffed, but it was humourless. "Peskov's gonna wipe the fucking floor with him," he said, more to himself than me. "He's a fucking dead man."

I grabbed Marco's arm and made him face me. "A dead man?"

I shouldn't have reacted that way. After all, I couldn't stand Valen, and the feeling was mutual. Right? Why would I care if he was alive or dead? Not that Marco called me out on it. The closest he came was a glint in his eyes that really could have been anything else to do with the conversation.

And all he said was, "If Peskov doesn't do it, Callahan'll be first in line."

"Cillian wouldn't let him!" I cried.

Marco scoffed. "Valk's old man'll hold him down for Callahan to land the first hit."

Now I frowned. "Why?"

Marco gestured around. "This?" he asked, and I nodded. "This is one step too far. Us Sinners can run this fuckery, but if God's right hand takes part and gets himself injured and unable to do his duty? There's a fuck tonne of contracts being broken then, missus."

More contracts. Seemed our world was built on them.

"How much danger is Valen in, Marco?" I asked carefully.

Marco sucked his teeth as he looked back to the cage. "Valk's on a path of destruction of his own making, missus. Pushing God just that little bit further. They're both out of control. How much danger?" He took a deep breath. "I don't think he'll stop until he's got himself killed and all."

So much for Valen thinking Apollo's peacocking was idiocy. It seemed he was now joining in on it. And why? Because of what happened in Bieityn the day before? Or something else? Valen seemed to think Apollo egging on the opposition would be stupid. Was Valen doing it purely so Apollo wouldn't?

My heart pounded uncomfortably in my chest, and it was suddenly very difficult to breath. I looked around but couldn't see Apollo anywhere. The room was full of shouting and jeering. Alcohol and smoke invaded my nose. I felt my hand start shaking and fisted it.

"You all right, missus?" Marco asked, putting a hand on my arm.

I forced a smile and nodded. "Of course. Fine. Why?"

His eyes were kind. "Because I can imagine this is a lot. Are ye worried about last night?"

I shook my head with all the bravado I could muster. "No. No. I'm fine." I wasn't.

There wasn't just kindness but concern in his eyes. "They didn't know who you were, missus. Now they do, I can't say it'll get any better."

I nodded as though I actually had any idea how our world really worked and told myself my heart wasn't trying to climb out my mouth. "I know I'm in good hands with you, Marco."

It was a testament to the gravity of the situation that he didn't make a joke out of that. I think I would have preferred if he had.

"The Angels won't let any harm come to you, Harlow," he said, and I think it was the first time I'd ever heard him use my name. "Even the idiots who'd rather get themselves killed."

Idiots like Valen.

I took a deep breath and looked around again, aiming for a calm and collected changing of the subject. "And would you tell me to avoid the toilets here, Marco?"

Humour lit his concern. "Depends how desperate you are, missus."

To get a second to myself before I fell apart in front every hardened arsehole in this seedy underground club? "Uh, let's say quite."

One corner of his lips tipped up. "If ye make your way that way, you'll find yourself in the back. Amenities are much nicer back there."

I took a breath. "You don't need to come with me?" I teased. It was more a plea, really.

"Any fucker stupid enough to touch you tonight deserves what's coming to him."

I felt my eyebrow rise. "And that stops me getting touched how?"

He smirked. "If anyone touches you without permission, I will resign from my post."

"You're very confident."

He nodded. Once. "I am."

Then I would be, too. "Okay. Back soon."

These fuckers might not be stupid enough to actually touch me, but that didn't stop them practically rubbing their eyes all over my body. Faces leered at me through the shadows and poor lighting. I wasn't quite sure that it was enough to get me over any imminent meltdown, but it felt like turning back to Marco now would be admitting some kind of defeat. I could do this. If I was going to survive this world, I would have to do this.

I held my head a little higher, pulled my shoulders back, and affected an air of superior disinterest that I modelled after Archer. It didn't stop the looks. It didn't stop me reading on almost every face what they'd do to me given half a chance; I'd find no pleasure in it, and they'd get more because of that. It did stop the instinct of flight from taking over. Once again, the mantra of 'fake it until I make it' served me well.

Once I hit the corridor to the back, I felt slightly safer. The lights were out in this section, but it's not like the rest of the place had been brilliantly lit. Then hands grabbed me roughly and pushed me against a wall. The manic beating of my heart slowed when I smelled him.

My heart started pounding for a very different reason. My stomach fluttered. My clit tingled. And a deep well of desire opened up in me that I feared I'd never manage to close again. We hadn't been this close since I walked out of his bedroom two weeks earlier.

Had it really only been two weeks?

"What in the ever-loving fuck are you doing here?" he snarled. He was beyond angry, but my nipples still tightened.

"Lovely as always, Valk," I replied smoothly.

He dropped his nose to my neck. "I won't ask a second time, princess."

"Apollo wanted me here for your fight." Apparently.

"Why?" I could hear the surprise in his voice.

The darkness made me bolder. "I don't know. Maybe he wanted me to talk some sense into you."

"You say that like this wasn't his idea," he answered, his voice humoured now.

It sent a chill through me, and goose bumps broke out along my arms. Being this close to him, in the dark, was a very bad idea. I was suddenly less worried about his life and more worried I'd give into the sizzling attraction that still blazed white-hot between us.

"This was Apollo's idea?"

I felt him shrug. "He *thinks* it was his idea."

"You're manipulating him now?" I asked, thinking that didn't sound like Valen. "Do you think, if the two of you do stupider and stupider things together, he'll never find out you betrayed him?"

His body was so close to mine. Every fibre of me was hyperaware of him, despite being unable to see much of him. He pressed against me closer, and I could feel the anger rolling off him. It must have taken a lot of effort for him to not press his hand against my throat, but I felt it twitch beside mine.

"What we did takes two, love," he said slowly and pointedly.

My fingers brushed his. "But I don't owe him anything, Valk," I said sweetly. "I never promised him anything."

I could feel the anger emanating from him.

My fingers slid up his hand, over his wrist, and I met no resistance. "You're not wearing my cross," I said. He wasn't even wearing his cuff.

I felt him twitch but I didn't know if he was trying not to come closer or walk away. "I couldn't risk losing it in the cage," he said softly. He still sounded angry, but like he was trying very hard not to lose his shit with me. "Come. I'll take you to Apollo."

He pushed away from me with what seemed like some effort, and I followed him further down the corridor. He finally pushed his way into a back room that was clearly used as a changeroom. Apollo was in there, sitting at a couch and talking to another guy like they were the managers working out the cut of the fight. If that was how it even worked.

"Apollo," Valen said harshly, and Apollo turned.

When he saw me, he smiled. "Babe!" he said, and I wondered if it was just an alcohol buzz or something harder that he vibrated with.

I went over to him, and he wrapped me in a warm hug and kissed me deeply. He didn't feel overly high, he wasn't sloppy or anything. But he felt…reckless.

When he finally pulled away, he took my hand and brought me over to the couch. "You can take thirty percent off the top if Valk wins," he said as he sat and, given his hand in mine, forced me to sit with him. He relaxed back and put his arm around me.

"Thirty? Cocky little bastard," the other guy said, ignoring me entirely.

Apollo shrugged. "It's Valen fucking Kincaid. You gonna bet against him, Cundy?"

"He's fighting Peskov," the other guy, Cundy, pointed out.

Valen scoffed as he went to a locker and started pulling off his shirt. "I've fought Peskov," he said.

"Aye," Cundy said. "And he put you in the hospital for a month."

It felt like every single organ tried lurching out of my body at once. "What?" escaped me as barely a whisper.

"I'll be fine," Valen said.

Cundy threw his hands in the air. "Fine. All right. I'll take it. Thirty if Valk wins."

Apollo nodded. "Pleasure doing business with you."

They shook hands and Cundy walked out. Apollo looked to Valen, and I followed suit. Valen was wrapping his hands in what looked like bandages. It was enough to take my eyes off even the gorgeous body he had on display in just a pair of light shorts. Valen's eyes flickered over me, and I dropped mine. I felt Apollo shift.

"Where the fuck's your cross?" Apollo asked Valen. His tone was a mix of concern and accusation.

My eyes flew up but, if Valen was feeling anything remotely close to guilt, he didn't show it. He just looked resignedly bored.

He just shrugged. "It's fine, man."

"No fucking way," Apollo said. "You never take that off. What happened to it?"

Valen gave nothing away. "Chain must have broken."

"You lost it?" Apollo was indignant, but it seemed more like indignant on Valen's behalf.

"Must have."

"But… But your cross?"

I looked between them. There was obviously some nuance here that I was missing. Something they knew that they didn't seem to think I needed to know. A few weeks ago, I wouldn't have needed to know. Now, with that very cross burning against my skin, I needed to know.

"It's fine," Valen said. "I can get another."

"No, you can't. I know what it meant to you. There's no fucking way anything's replacing that."

My heart jumped in my chest.

I'd assumed that, like any student at Saint Benedicts, Valen wore a cross because it was the done thing. We got them and never took them off. Were buried with them. But sentimentality only came after years of wearing it every day and it becoming special over a very long time.

Him giving me his hadn't meant anything more than that it was one-upping Apollo's ring. The ring I couldn't wear during class, but the cross I could.

Hadn't it?

"Just leave it, Apollo," Valen said, his tone a warning.

"I won't leave it. Where'd you last have it?"

"It doesn't matter," Valen snapped.

"Since when? You just suddenly stop caring that your mum's gone and it's your dad's fault?"

Valen's eyes did slide to me now. There was nothing else about him to suggest it, but that action alone told me Apollo's words were information I was definitely not supposed to have.

"Leave it," Valen snarled, his tone a final warning.

"Dude, we can–"

"I said leave it!" Valen roared. "Fucking…" He mumbled as he stalked out of the room.

"Huh," Apollo muttered, his fingers playing unconsciously with a curl of my hair.

"What?" I asked, trying desperately not to sound too interested.

Apollo shook his head and kissed the side of mine absently. "Nothing. He… He loved that cross. It was the last thing he had of his mum."

"The last thing?" I gulped.

Apollo nodded. "Yeah. When he was born, she'd done her job. Finally birthed another heir for the Kincaid line after the disappointment of his sister, then the Kincaids were done with her. She took Valya back to the Volkovs and left Valk with the Kincaids. He hasn't seen or spoken to either of them since. His mum left the cross with his grandmother to give him on his confirmation. That was it."

It confirmed my theory that the Kincaids cared as much for women as they did for people who didn't pay them on time.

Apollo breathed in, then stood up. "Ah well, let's go see how much damage Valk can do."

I shook my head. "I might just wait in here."

He looked me over, seemingly only just realising that the first time he'd actually brought me into this part of our world he'd chosen probably one of the most violent things he could have. He nodded slowly.

"Ah, yep. Probably a good idea. I'll… I should…"

I nodded. "No. You go. I'll be fine." I hoped.

He seemed torn, but then nodded and hurried out.

The jeering and cheering was muffled, but I still heard every rise in volume that no doubt heralded a particularly impressive hit. I just didn't know who was, in fact, doing the most damage. I closed my eyes and forced my breathing into a slow and steady rhythm. My leg didn't get with the program and jiggled the whole way through.

Finally, Valen stumbled in alone. He was bandaged, and cuts and bruises were already blossoming across his body.

He looked at me like he was surprised to see me. "Princess?"

I stood up quickly. "I was…waiting for Apollo."

"You didnae come and watch?" he seemed to be teasing, his accent thick.

I shook my head. "Forgive me for not wanting to see you being a total idiot."

He scoffed. "Would a total idiot win?" he asked as he went to his locker.

"Yes." I unclasped his cross.

I walked over to him and put my hand on his arm. He turned to face me, a question on his swelling face. Even for all his stupidity and the swelling, he was still achingly gorgeous.

I held my hand out to him with his cross on my palm. "You should take this back," I said softly, knowing it was the right thing to do but not wanting to lose the one part of him I could keep.

Valen's eyes searched mine. I couldn't tell what was going through his mind. I'd expected him to be angry or at least affronted, but he wasn't. He seemed resigned. To what, I didn't know.

"I cannae do that," he said simply.

"Why not?" I asked.

"Because it was a gift."

"Valen, it was your m–"

He wrapped his hands around mine, his cross tight in the very centre. "It's yours now, love. My mother is a shadow hanging over my life. You are a light. If it is to be a reminder of anything, it should be a reminder of us."

I realised something. "You're high, aren't you?"

He inclined his head. "Aye. Nikolai can be a little heavy-handed with the morphine."

"Are you in a lot of pain?"

He scoffed and gave a tiny smile. "Not right now."

I fought my own smile as I nodded. "Then maybe now isn't the best time to be talking about this."

"It's the best time," he said casually.

"Why?"

"Because I have nae filter right now, princess. The demon that lives in my head and tells me what to say and what not to say is asleep. Ask me anything and I willnae lie to you."

It was an attractive offer, but…

"You would never forgive me if I took advantage of that, Valen. I would never forgive myself. If there's anything you need – want – to say to me, you can say it when you're sober or not at all."

He leant his head to mine. "You'll be the death of me, love." In his voice was an appreciation I didn't think it would be possible to put into words had he even been inclined.

"And why now?" I asked, finding humour in this Valen.

"Because you're the only who can save me…"

"If you let me," I finished for him.

He nodded. "If I let you."

The noise of an arriving celebration forced us apart. Under Valen's firm, watchful gaze, I put his cross back on and tucked it into my shirt. He gave me one nod, and then he was God's wolf for the rest of the night. Marco found me, with an earful about Apollo leaving me, and then made sure no one left my side for the rest of the night.

CHAPTER SIX

Unsurprisingly, Valen was no where to be seen on Monday, although Fender told me he was in the infirmary hopped up on that much morphine that he'd be seeing the fucking Loch Ness Monster dancing through his room.

On Tuesday, he was greeted at breakfast with a cheer from the majority of the dining hall.

"What did I miss?" Florence asked, having only got back late the night before.

I hadn't really filled her in on any of the weekend because I didn't know how to tell her some of it without telling her all of it. And Valen's express instructions had been to tell no one about Saturday. I didn't like keeping things from my best friend, but I felt, in this situation, maybe it was for the better. Especially when I didn't really understand it myself.

"Valk took down a fucking monster on Sunday," Fender said.

Florence blinked. "Literally…or?"

Marco grinned at her. "Almost. He won our God a good-sized bet."

Fender inclined his head at Marco. "Cundy saw more of the winnings than he would have had Peskov won."

Florence looked at me, but didn't lean over until the boys were distracted welcoming Valen in. Valen, who looked like he'd much rather everyone fucked right off.

"They don't talk about these things with us. Why are they talking about these things with us?" She leant away, gasped, then leant even closer. "Did you finally fuck God?"

I smirked. "Apparently I'm more invisible?"

She frowned. "How the fuck does that work?"

I shrugged. "Some weird psychological bullshit that lets the men-folk think we women don't know anything."

"Ah." She nodded. "Gotcha." She seemed to think of something and leant back in again. "*Did* you fuck God, though?"

I looked at the God in question, who was making a whole bunch of grand gestures about an increasingly angry Valen in front of the whole dining hall.

"No."

"Why does this piss us off?" Florence asked.

"Because it almost happened on Saturday, but instead he stormed off."

She frowned around the toast in her mouth. "What? Why?"

"I don't know, but I plan to get to the bottom of it."

Florence breathed out. "Honestly, I might not even go on the next retreat. Fuck Paris. I don't wanna miss the drama here."

I smiled, knowing her words for the attempted cheer-up they were. "You're going to fucking Paris."

She nodded. "I'm going to fuck in Paris," she said, as though repeating my words.

I laughed, feeling like the first time in a good few days. But I was still determined to find out why Apollo had left. Fuck Paris? Fuck this me and Apollo not talking bullshit. I wanted answers and I was going to get them.

So, I strode purposefully down the boys' dorm hall after lessons that day. Fender was at Apollo's door, presumably on sentry duty, and tried to bar my way.

"You do not want to fuck with me right now, Fender," I warned him.

I saw a new-found respect light his eyes, but he only said, "I can't let you in, Miss Vanguard."

"Can't or won't?"

"Both?" I appreciated the uncertainty in his voice.

I nodded. "Let me in."

He shook his head. "You don't want to go in there."

"Why not? Has he got a Magdalen in there?"

Fender seemed to rethink hiding things from me, but he stuck to his guns. "Just trust me, please."

I paused in my attempts to get by him and really looked at him. "Just tell me. Has he got a Magdalen in there?" I demanded.

Fender paled but did an expert job of holding his own. "Miss Van—"

"Don't 'Miss Vanguard' me, Fender," I warned him, my tone icy.

I saw his visibly gulp. "They…uh…"

"They?" I clarified and he nodded.

I felt anger boiling. If this was another one of Apollo's orgies, then I was going to… Well, I didn't know what I was going to do. I didn't feel betrayed by him, but I was feeling cheated that I was right fucking here, I wanted to have sex with him, and he was still choosing Magdalens over me.

I shoved Fender aside and threw open Apollo's door. Orgy was about as good a word for what it was going to be in a few minutes as anything else. There were a lot of clothes still on, but there were also a lot of cocks in mouths already.

"Luis!" I heard Apollo cry, then his muttered, "Fuck, Harlow?"

I finally found him. He pushed the Magdalen's head away from his crotch and I was gratified to see his zipper was still up. For now.

I didn't want a confrontation in front of all these deflating cocks. I didn't have the guts to order everyone out. All I did was frown at him like I planned to murder him in his sleep, turn on my heel, and storm right back out, slamming the door behind me.

"I did try to warn you," Fender said apologetically.

Like Valen and Marco, Fender had perfected the 'I'm saying one thing with my words and another with my tone' thing. He was apologetic that he'd not told me, apologetic he'd had to side with his God, but also not apologetic he would never waver from that. I had to give him credit for his loyalty, and he deserved it. I just couldn't decide if it was a more organic loyalty and less obsessive than Valen's loyalty to Apollo, or more so.

I took a deep breath, then trained a smile on him and ran my hand down my front like I needed to smooth my uniform. "Thank you, Fender. But if you think *that* affects my sensibilities, then you clearly don't know me as well as you think you so."

One corner of his lips tugged. "Even if it's your thing, doesn't mean you want to walk in on it without warning."

I nodded, feeling it useless to point out that he *could* have warned me. "No. There is that. Although, I'm not sure that is my thing."

Fender didn't seem surprised by that, but he did seem surprised I'd admitted it out loud.

The door opened behind me, and Apollo nearly ran into me in his hurry to come after me. "Babe."

"Oh, you came after me this time? Good to know," I spat at him. "Just go and sink your cock in whichever Magdalen spreads her legs the fastest. I certainly won't be lining up for the 'honour'." I used air quotes and everything.

He'd left the door open, so I knew a few people inside heard. Not that I was aiming to keep my voice inconspicuous or anything. Now, he closed it.

"What is wrong with you?" Apollo hissed, looking to Fender like he shouldn't be listening. In Fender's defence, he tried to look like he wasn't listening while still not leaving his post.

"What's wrong with me?" I hissed back. "I don't know, Apollo. You tell me. What *is* wrong with me?"

He looked like he had no idea what I was talking about, and I didn't blame him. "What?"

I shook my head. "Nothing. I'm sorry I interrupted your *party*.

You go in and have a lovely time." I threw my most saccharine sweet smile at him and turned to leave, making for the cheeky service stairs.

But, surprise, surprise, Apollo actually continued following me. I wanted to feel a little bit of hope at that. Was he actually choosing me for once instead of…absolutely anyone else?

We were halfway down the stairs when he caught my arm. "What is going on?" he asked me, his tone pleading with me to talk to him.

Well, that's exactly what I wanted to do, so I was going to.

I huffed. "Why?" I asked him. "Why won't you let me…reciprocate?"

"Reciprocate?" He blinked in confusion. "What?"

"Sex, Apollo! Why won't you have sex with me? Do you…? Do you think I won't be any good?"

"Not any…?" he breathed. He leant against me and nuzzled my nose with his. "Jesus, Harlow. No. Fucking… No. I…"

"What?"

He breathed out as he ran his hands over my sides. "I know our relationship is changing. It's not like we used to kiss or touch, I did notice. You weren't– *We* weren't like that. I want to give to you, Harlow, because you turn me on, and I think – hope – the feeling's mutual."

"It is," I assured him.

He nodded, more to himself than me. "But I feel like if I take, then…"

"Then what?" I asked, taking his cheek in my hand.

"I've spent my whole life taking. I take what I've been taught others owe me. I've taken from you even when… Even when my instincts told me not to. Dad said it was the thing to do, so I did it. I have taken from girl after girl after girl. So, if I let you touch me now – if I take from you now – then it's just the same as always. We're just the same as always." He looked me dead in the eye. "Then we're not different anymore."

"We'll always be different, Apollo."

"Will we?" he asked.

I nodded. "We will," I promised. "You're my best friend, Apollo. Buried under all that conceit and entitlement, you're still my best friend. We can't not be different."

He looked into my eyes like he really saw me. Not just the me who was showing a bit more skin lately that got his dick hard, but me. Inside. The real me that was still connected to the real him. Both had been buried and hidden and protected behind facades for what felt like so long, but we could still find them in each other.

Like we were still twelve and our worlds' hadn't changed, the moment seemed charged with all the potential we could have had. Those two naïve children with their whole lives ahead of them, full of wonder and excitement and promise. Except now we were in our final year of school, and we had someone else's life ahead of us. But together, living someone else's life could be bearable.

As long as we stuck together, we could get through it.

"Do you…do you really want to have sex with me?" he asked, a smile playing at his lips.

A smile tugged at mine as well. "Of course, I do. I want to be close to you. I want to give you as much pleasure as you give me. Did you really think I didn't want to?" I asked.

He shrugged. "I guess I… I don't know. I want to say I didn't want to assume—"

"But you had no problem sticking your face or your hand between my legs?" I teased.

His smirk lit up his sapphire eyes and all he was took my breath away. He was stunning. He was beautiful. He had the power to make you fall in love with him entirely, to give everything you were to him. He flaunted this power with everyone around him. Everyone but me. Well, that ended now.

He cupped my breast as he pressed me against the wall of the stairs. "I was scared," he admitted.

"I'm not asking for promises, Apollo. I'm asking for…equality?"

That didn't feel like the right word. "Give and take. I'm asking we give this a chance. I'm asking you give me a chance."

"What chance?" he asked as his nose ran down my cheek and over my neck.

I breathed in deeply as my body responded to his touch. "The same chance you give all your Magdalens."

"None of them compare to you."

I fisted his hair and pulled him up to look me in the eye. "No, they don't," I agreed pointedly.

His smirk was more rueful, and he stepped closer, pushing me a little roughly against the wall again, his body hard – in all senses of the word – against mine. It excited me.

"Do you want me to fuck you, Harlow?" he asked, his voice low in my ear.

My nipples responded to him, and I rocked my hips against him. "I want you to fuck me, Apollo."

His growl was all appreciation as he captured my lips with his. "Where's Flo?"

"Don't know. Don't care," I breathed against his kiss.

He ran his hand up my leg, coaxing it around his hip. He slid it up under my skirt and gripped my skin tightly as we rocked together. Our kiss deepened as his tongue swept in to claim mine, but I wasn't giving in without a fight. He was rock hard where he pressed against me, and I ached to know what he felt like.

"Fuck, babe..." he sighed. "Fuck..."

He pulled away, grabbed my hand and pulled me to my room. People noticed the speed with which we passed. I'm sure they noticed my flushed cheeks and quite possibly the rod in his trousers as well. They could no doubt guess what we were off to do. I didn't give a single fuck. As far as they knew, this wasn't the first time. We were all but engaged, what did it matter how often or when Apollo and I fucked?

We more fell than walked into my dorm room, lips and hands

roving each other's body.

"Well, I know when I'm not wanted," came Florence's sardonic voice.

I heard the question in her voice and gave her a thumb's up behind Apollo's back; yes, this was the first time and, yes, I'd give her all the goss when I was done.

"Thank you," I said, already reaching for Apollo's jeans button.

"Message me when you're done," she said on her way out.

"Will do. Thanks," Apollo answered, kicking the door closed behind her. "You?" he said to me as he ripped my shirt off. The heat in his eyes threatened to engulf me in a flame of passion.

"Me?" I clarified, breathing heavily.

He nodded as we climbed on my bed. "You're mine."

Apollo grabbed my hips and pulled me to him, lying over me in one decisive motion. I smiled up at him, surprised at his dominance. I'd guessed he was dominant with his Magdalens, it seemed to run in the whole Saint circles, but I'd expected he'd err on the side of caution with me. At least our first time.

"What?" he asked as he dropped kisses over my stomach.

"I'm just glad you didn't put the kid gloves on for this," I said as I grabbed his head and pulled him up to mine.

"There's only one glove I wear for this, sweetheart," he said with the sexiest glint in his eyes as he winked at me.

"For me," I clarified with a warm smile.

His return smile lit me up inside. "I never got to tell you all the things I wanted to do to you."

"I'm listening," I told him, settling into my pillows.

Apollo dropped his lips to my neck as he tantalisingly slowly ran a single finger up my thigh. "I'm going to touch you. I'm going to kiss you. Every single piece of you will be mine." He dragged his teeth across my skin softly as his fingers found their way to my centre. "I'm going to have you screaming my name." He slipped his finger in my panties and right into me. "I'll make you see stars."

I gripped his back and arched into him, and he pumped me gently.

"By the time I'm done with you, you won't be walking right for a week."

I smirked against his cheek. "Promises, promises."

He pumped me faster as he kissed my neck, and his teeth this time weren't quite as soft. My nipples tightened and everything zinged as pleasure shot around my body. My hands roamed his body, trying in vain to get him closer. I nudged his face, and he lifted it to look at me.

"Kiss me," I told him, my voice breathy as my orgasm built, but I didn't care.

Apollo dropped his lips to mine and kissed the ever-loving hell out of me as he worked me. When my orgasm finally washed over me, I took his lip in my teeth as I breathed through it, and I felt him smile.

Our kiss grew lazier as my hands went to his belt and, this time, I met no resistance in getting him undressed. There was a lot more laughing, and Apollo actually fell off the bed at one point when his foot got caught in his trousers. He looked up at me with the most tender expression, no sign of embarrassment or annoyance.

It was hard not to wonder if he was like this with the others, and hope that his mask wouldn't allow that. I'd always imagined – and the few times I'd witnessed, I was right – that it was more clinical, more about dominance and superiority and this sense of gravity that the Saints and Angels were expected to exude to maintain their aura of dark and dangerous fearsomeness.

But this wasn't that Apollo. He looked at me with a determination in his eyes that he was going to fuck me hard and rock my world, but he also looked at me like we'd just nearly broken something mattress surfing down the stairs at his father's estate. My heart swelled as I reached down to help him back onto the bed and I felt nothing but love for the man in front of me.

Apollo grabbed something out of his pocket, then took my hand and crawled back over me with a wicked smirk.

"Are you sure about this?" he asked me solemnly.

I nodded. "Very sure and, if you ask even just once more, I might change my mind out of spite and we'll both be incredibly pissy."

He laughed. "Noted. Thank you for your consent, ma'am."

I snorted as he reached down between us. "Thank you for your consent? Do you say that to all the girls?"

He shrugged. "Usually they sign a waiver, so consent is in writing."

He leant down to kiss me and I put a hand on his chest. "Hang on."

"What?" he asked.

His cock was hovering at my entrance and part of me really wanted to just tilt my hips and let him in. The other part of me needed some clarification.

"You have a…contract with your Magdalens?" I asked.

He looked like it was the most normal thing in the world. I guessed to him – to them – it was. On too many levels, it made sense. On the other hand, he was barely eighteen and already had who knew how many contracts with how many women, girls? Somewhere, there was a legitimate record of the number of people he'd fucked.

"How much of that is to please your father?" I asked him, my tone icier than I'd intended.

"What do you mean?" he asked.

"How much of your number of conquests is just to show your father you're playing your role?"

I didn't know why, but his answer felt very important. I wasn't even sure I wanted a specific answer. I just knew that I needed one.

Apollo looked down at me and I saw the concern in his eyes. "It's my life, Harlow," he said quietly. "How I was taught to be. I don't know how to be anything else, but…" He paused and ran his nose over mine. "But I hope I'll learn another way…from you."

Well, that was definitely not what I'd expected him to say, and I was going pay that. Yep. That was, hands down, unobjectively, a pretty good answer. I couldn't fault it.

"I guess I don't need to ask where my contract is," I teased, not wanting to delve any further into where his words had the potential to lead us.

He smirked. "I don't think there's a sex clause in our contract."

"Yet."

"Yet," he agreed.

"So, one could say that I'm…recreational?" I joked.

"Desired," he corrected me, and that desire dripped from his words as our bodies shifted against each other.

He throbbed at my centre, and I ran my hands slowly over his back as we looked into each other's eyes.

"Not an obligation," I ventured.

"Definitely not an obligation," he agreed. "I want *you*, Harlow."

He dipped his head and kissed me deeply. I tipped my hips to meet him, and he slid into me slowly. His hand went to my thigh, and he coaxed my leg higher around his hip as he slid strong and sure and steady into me. His lips never left me; my lips, my cheek, my neck. He held himself up on one arm, but the other trailed over my body until he dragged his fingers over my clit. My back arched in pleasure, and I felt his smile against me. His finger circled my clit as sure and steady as his thrusts.

The whole thing was slow burn, but it was no less amazing for it. I felt honestly closer to him than I ever had, not just physically. I felt worshipped and wanted and appreciated. My orgasm was slow building, the crescendo taking me by surprise and falling over me like a warm blanket. It filled me up and left me with this lazy feeling of happiness and softness. But Apollo didn't stop there.

His finger left my clit, and he palmed my breast for a bit until I felt the sensation building up again. My head fell back against the pillows as he lavished attention on my neck again. Apollo pushed my leg up, sliding into me deeper.

As my second orgasm started washing over me, I felt his thrusts gets harder and his pace increase just a little.

"Harlow." He breathed my name reverently, like I was really that goddess everyone expected me to be.

I felt him throb in me, his lips found mine again, then he tensed as he came. One, two more languid thrusts as we kissed deeply, then I felt his smile brush across my lips.

"Give me a minute," he said, before getting up and dealing with the condom.

When he came back to bed, he snuggled me up, his hands and lips all over me still.

"I wouldn't have called that hard and fast," I teased him. "I think I'll be walking fine, thank you."

He gave a rough, breathy laugh. "Who says I'm done with you, darling?" he asked me wryly.

By the time Apollo left my room, we'd almost missed dinner and we'd used up four condoms. It was good the man maintained a decent supply on his person at all times, but we still had to raid Florence's stash for the last one. I had a feeling she'd forgive me when I told her what went down.

Chapter Seven

After dinner, Florence and I had gone straight to our room, and I'd given her the play-by-play. Twice. She'd been impressed with Apollo's performance and decided that it seemed there really were men who lived up to the lofty expectations after all so, "Suck it, Romance haters," were her actual words.

As we got dressed the next morning, I felt buzzed. Happy buzzed. I looked forward to my day and the people in it, even if those people were Valen's grumpiness. Hell, just then, I felt like I could take on these Black Bloods all by myself.

"Fender?" I said as I saw him leaning on the wall outside our dorm room.

He pushed off it and gave me a short nod in lieu of a bow as he took his vape pen out of his mouth. "Morning," he said simply.

"What are you doing here?" I asked.

Florence bumped into the back of me and frowned. "Angel escort?" she asked.

Fender got a wicked gleam in his eye, but his lips barely lifted. "I don't usually take payment."

Florence shook her finger at him with a grin. "Well played, sir."

"But why are you here?" I asked.

"Marco sent me."

"And you always do as Marco tells you?"

He shrugged like that was a given and didn't deign to give me a verbal answer.

I was vaguely aware there was a hierarchy within the Angel's structure. Valen was, obviously, their leader. In theory the other three were equal. In practice, hierarchy depended on the length of your tenure. Fender was the last one to sign his contract, so he was on the bottom rung. He'd only become one of God's Angels after God had risen to power. It had been an impressive fight, only ended when Marco had pulled Fender off the other guy.

It wasn't the first time I'd wondered why Fender had been so keen to be an Angel that he'd nearly killed a guy, but then I also guessed that's what their world demanded of them; get what they need, what's expected of them, at any cost. It didn't have to speak to any particular underlying motive.

Sinners they were indeed, for they were all forced to be too soulless to be true Saints, before I'd even met most of them.

"Do we…?" Florence started. "Do we just go to breakfast, and you trail behind?"

Fender shrugged again. "Behind. In front. I'm easy."

Florence looked at me like she was wondering if he was still making innuendo, or whether he just didn't realise he was making innuendo. I could only shake my head and shrug.

"Okay." Florence nodded. "To breakfast then, I guess."

"God is detained this morning," Fender said as he followed us.

"Is that why you're here? You're playing messenger boy?" I asked.

Another of those almost apathetic shrugs. "I play whatever role I'm asked."

"Figures you'd be into roleplay," Florence muttered.

"We all get…job satisfaction different ways," he said, and I still couldn't tell if he'd intended the 'job' to sound like he was talking about something else, or if that was just who Fender was as a person.

We got breakfast and Fender sat across from us. I noticed that Marco, Valen and Gage were also noticeably absent.

"Where is everyone?" Florence asked in general.

I frowned. "Is this one of those times God and his Angels are up to shady shit and one of you is set to protect me?" I asked Fender.

"Couldn't rightly say," was Fender's answer.

"Can't or won't?"

He gave me a flash of a cheeky grin above his coffee mug. "Both?"

I leant towards him. "Fender?" I started.

"Mm?" he answered, mimicking my lean.

"Is it your mission to be terribly unhelpful?"

"I'm not unhelpful, Miss Vanguard," he told me as he sat back and pulled out his vape pen. "I'm doing exactly what I need to do, even if *that*…affects your sensibilities." There was a gleam of shit-stirring in his eyes, and I had to be impressed.

"Fine," I told him with an acknowledging nod; he'd won this round. "Is it *helpful* to keep from us how long we'll have your company?"

He shook his head as he blew smoke up over it. "They should be done by lunch."

By said lunch, I was starting to worry. Fender was the only Angel to be seen all morning and God was markedly missing. I didn't know why I'd expected whatever they were doing to mean they'd at least be visible on campus, but it was worrying me nonetheless.

Fender, as our shadow for the day, Florence and I were all walking into the dining hall, and I was telling myself that I wasn't looking for any sign of God or his Angels.

So, when Apollo's arms wound around me and his voice was in my ear saying, "Hello, gorgeous," I breathed a little easier.

I wrapped my arms over his and smiled. "Hi. You guys missed a spectacular morning break."

"Did we?" he asked as he put his arm around my shoulder, and we walked to our table.

Florence nodded for me. "Your heir's little cherubim decided to have a wee scuffle at their table."

"Exie got raspberry jam all over her face," I added.

"Tyson tried breaking it up and his top little cherub ended up accidentally punching him in the face," Florence continued.

"And Triss retaliated by kneeing Ryko in the crotch," I finished.

Apollo smirked, always amused by the younger Saints antics. "Sounds eventful. Ryko get a new challenger?"

I shook my head. "Don't think so. Looked like a fight over a girl."

"That'll do it," Apollo said. "Eh, boys?" He chuckled as he smacked Valen companionably and Valen audibly choked on the vape he was inhaling.

"That'll do it," Marco agreed enthusiastically.

As we walked to our table, Apollo couldn't keep his hands off me. Running them over my body, even when it tickled and made me laugh. And he was all smiles. Obviously, whatever they'd been up to that morning hadn't put a dampener on what had happened the day before.

As he sat down, he pulled me into his lap, and I couldn't help smiling at him. He was whispering things in my ear as we waited for the Saintling on duty to bring us our lunches. Even Florence made use of the Saintling delivery service, despite her protesting just the existence of the Saintlings in the same breath.

Someone cleared their throat behind us, and Apollo pulled his head out of my hair to see what they wanted. It was a Magdalen that I'd seen him with before.

"Macey?" Apollo said, an expectation that she state her business and move on quickly in his voice.

"Do you want me to meet you in your room?" she asked him.

I had to admire the audacity of this bitch. Here was his princess, sitting in his lap, and she just walked up and expected to lure him away. I admired her, but it would be a cold day in Hell before I let that happen.

Before Apollo could respond, I just shook my head at the Magdalen.

"We have a…date," she said to Apollo, clearly wondering at *my* audacity. "It's my time."

"Not today," I told her before he could reply.

She looked at Apollo like she expected him to leap to her defence. As though her pussy was so unimaginably extraordinary that he would drop everything just to get another taste of it. I couldn't help but be just a little impressed; I wished I had that much belief and conviction about any part of me.

Apollo kicked his head to indicate she leave. "You heard your princess," was his answer.

The Magdalen huffed. "Fine. Next week then."

I levelled my gaze at her. "We'll see."

There was a shrewdness in her eyes. It was dangerous. I knew it was dangerous to provoke the Magdalens. Me, who until now hadn't said boo to a fly. But then I was surviving attacks by Black Bloods and forging my own future for myself. Annoying a few little girls who had to sleep with men for power was the least of my worries.

And this Magdalen didn't argue with her princess. She walked away, head held high, like she hadn't just lost something she might never get back; namely her chance at being something better than she was. Unless she was one of the ones with daddy issues. But, in a lot of ways, weren't we all?

"That," Apollo murmured in my ear, "was fucking sexy." And he nipped my earlobe playfully.

I chuckled against the tickle and batted him. "Just testing my authority," I told him.

He wrapped his arms around me and groaned appreciatively. "Keep testing it, baby, and I might take a knee before you."

I liked the sound of that very much. If God himself thought I was worth his fealty, then our future was indeed looking like it was coming up Harlow.

On my way to the boys' dorm after school, I might have been on a high from my win with Apollo at lunch, but I was under no delusions that the Magdalens weren't suddenly watching me far too closely and talking to each other behind their hands whenever I passed. They didn't like me flexing my authority, especially over them. I was looking forward to seeing what they were going to do about it.

As I walked into Apollo's room, I found him sitting on the couch with his Angels, and they were all staring intently at something on the coffee table between them. They were all dour-faced and Valen looked particularly grumpy, with a steady stream of hazy smoke above his head. Then again, that could have just been Valen's face.

"Who are we killing this time?" I asked, aiming for a joke.

All five of them turned to me and the looks on their faces suggested that they might have actually been planning to kill someone. *Great* time for me to try to test out that new authority I'd been waving around.

"Uh…" I hurriedly tried backpedalling. "I will leave you to it."

Apollo sighed. "Gage, get the car ready. Valk, take Harlow back to her room and meet us at the garage."

Us? Apollo was going on whatever 'errand' they were running? Again?

"What's happened?" I asked.

"Let the men handle it, babe," Apollo said, his father coming out again.

I stiffened but knew better than to argue. "Fine."

Gage stood up and walked towards me, still standing in the doorway. He stopped next to me, crowding my space. I almost felt threatened by it, but this was one of Apollo's Angels and, if I didn't believe I would always be safe with them, then I didn't think I'd feel safe with anyone.

He looked me over intently and I knew I was still lacking in his eyes, still the little princess in her ivory tower. So separate and other to their world, yet so very firmly at the centre of it as well. I would almost say he hated me for it. Hated me for having a place he had to work so hard for, and yet he couldn't be sure I even wanted what I was being handed.

"We've all killed for our God, princess," he said, his voice low but

I couldn't tell if it was a warning or a threat. "But would we kill for you?"

Valen appeared behind him, a scowl on his face. "Get moving," he snapped.

Gage looked like he was going to argue, then just nodded his head and walked out.

"You, too," Valen said to me, flipping his hood up over his head and leading me to the service stairs.

He exuded anger and retribution, and I was worried about what they had planned. In the safety of the service stairs, when I put my hand on his arm, he whirled quickly and pressed me against the wall.

"What, princess?" he asked before I could say anything. "What information do you feel the unrelenting need to rip from my unwilling lips tonight?"

"Loquacious today," I quipped, and he snarled.

His hand snaked around my throat and fuck had I missed it. "What do you want?" he ground out.

"I just want you to be safe."

"Death will be my only safety, princess."

"Valen–"

"What?" he yelled, pulling away from me. "What, Harlow?"

"What is up with you?"

"With me? Nothing's up with me."

"Then why are you extra pissy right now?"

He slammed his fist on the wall opposite me, then stormed to crowd into my space. "You will be Apollo's. He will claim you."

Now didn't feel like the time to tell him it had already happened. There was too much swirling between Valen and me to think about Apollo and me. I could smell everything that Valen was, and it made my blood sing. I could feel his body humming with barely restrained fury mere inches from me and my senses awoke. His clothes brushed mine and my fingers itched to drag them off him.

I should have told him about Apollo.

"And what if I want you?" was what I said instead.

He paused. "I thought you fucked me out of your system?"

"Well, clearly I didn't," I snapped.

I was beyond pretending I was over Valen. That I'd ever be over Valen. I didn't know how I could be so drawn to two men at the same time, seemingly for such very different reasons and in different ways. All I knew was that I needed Valen. I wanted Apollo, but I needed Valen. Apollo was a rich Victorian Sponge cake. Valen was air and water.

He looked me over. "Why?" he asked quietly.

I didn't think he was asking about the current conversation. "Why what?"

"That Magdalen today. You let him fuck around for so long. What's changed now?"

"Because I didn't have a way out, Valen. I still don't have a way out and now Apollo's…complicating things." I lay my hand on his cheek. "But I need you. At least for as long as I can have you."

His jaw clenched. "Bad idea, princess," he said.

"I know," I said softly. "But I can't stop."

He dropped his forehead to mine with a gentle growl. "Neither can I."

"What are we going to do?" I asked him.

"You let him claim you. But," he said carefully and my eyes snapped to his, "the only cock you cum for is mine." He lay his hand over my throat again and a thrill ran through me. "Understood?"

Aside from the fact that I'd broken that rule already – more than once – I couldn't find it in me to correct him. It was wrong on so many levels, but I wanted him to feel that possessive of me. I couldn't help it. I'd tried to let him go and I just couldn't do it. I wouldn't do it. Not yet.

"I don't bow to you, Valk," I told him, and his lips curled in an unbidden smirk.

Fuck, but he was sexy. All dark and dangerous, gorgeous and

sinful, and with the singular ability to make me feel alive with nothing but a single look.

"I will have you on your knees," he promised me.

"We'll see who bows to who," I told him.

Triumph lit his eyes and I felt it in my clit. "Yes," he said slowly. "We will."

He dragged his lips over my face, so close but just not quite touching me. I leaned towards him for a kiss, and he pulled his face just enough away that, with his hand on my throat, I couldn't reach him. But somehow, I still felt the victorious grin at his lips.

"But my lord God is waiting on me tonight, love," he said, his voice low and gravelly. "And the good little princess needs to be locked away safe in her tower."

I thrashed against his hold. "I will not be–"

He silenced me with the quickest kiss I'd ever had, then left his face just touching mine. "Just for tonight, love. Please."

He'd said please. Was it bad that my instant instinct was to obey? I didn't think it wise to let him in on that Harlow-hack.

"All right," I answered begrudgingly. "But only for tonight."

"Thank you."

One more lightning quick kiss, then he was tapping my arse to get me going. I threw a questioning smirk back at him and he winked at me.

"Stay safe," he told me sternly.

"Stay alive," was my answer before hurrying to my room where, like a good girl, I made sure Florence was back and locked us in tight.

Chapter Eight

"Uh, can I help you?" I heard Florence ask while I was in the bathroom on Friday night.

The shower was already running, but I was looking for the bottle of conditioner I knew I'd squirrelled away in the cupboard under the sink.

"Okay," she answered whoever it was. "And how long do you need? Ten-minute quickie? An hour? Just so I–"

"Get out," I heard the unmistakable voice of Valen growl.

I tried standing up too quickly and hit the back of my head on the top of the cupboard.

"Ow!" I said pointedly and just a little too loudly.

The bathroom door crashed open. I whirled, landing on my butt on the cold bathroom floor, and looked up at the concerned features of Valen Kincaid. When he saw me, all concern was gone and all I saw was deep-seated lust.

I hadn't had a chance to really talk to Valen since Wednesday. Apollo had kept him busy, and I'd been trying to work out whether I cared enough about my authority to wage full-on war with the Magdalens. All that totally flew out of the window at the sight of Valen in my bathroom.

Valen. In dark jeans, a white long-sleeved tee, and a black jacket. He was a walking wet dream, and he looked particularly large, intimidating, and utterly scalable – preferably with my tongue – from my position on the floor.

"You okay, Harlow?" Florence called.

I nodded, even though Valen was no doubt shielding me from her view. "Yeah," I answered.

"Good. Great. Well, I have…absolutely nowhere else to be, so I'm going to go do that."

I nodded again, all thought taken up with Valen being in my bathroom. "Okay."

"You two need–"

"Leave," Valen growled.

"Okay, Mr Bossy! Text me when you're done, Harlow," she said, then I heard the bedroom door shut.

Valen and I stared at each other for too many heart beats.

I had too many questions fighting for space in my head.

"What are you doing here?" I finally asked him.

That seemed to break whatever spell he was under. "Why is the shower running and you're not wet?"

I scoffed and muttered to myself as I picked myself off the floor, "Trust me, I'm wet."

But he obviously heard. "You could be wetter." By the cheeky tone in his voice, he meant that in all the ways it was possible to mean it.

I looked at him. "How would you know?"

He stepped into the bathroom, shutting the door behind him all the while never taking his eyes off my face. He looked conflicted for the first time since I'd met him all those years ago.

"What?" I asked him, suddenly concerned he was dying.

"Apollo…" He didn't seem to be able to say the words.

I looked at the floor. "He told you?"

"Yeah." His scoff was anything but humoured.

"Oh," was all I could say.

"In his words, he had you screaming his name, seeing stars, and he doubted you'd be walking for a week."

The idea that Apollo had gone into that much detail, with Valen of all people, almost made me laugh. Almost.

The idea of what Valen would say – or do – now knowing I'd broken his one rule kinda put a dampener on my humour. No matter if I thought it was a stupid rule, that I hadn't agreed to it, or that it wasn't really any of Valen's business, I couldn't lie to him when faced with the…accusation. As it were.

"If you want me to say I didn't–"

He took another step towards me, put his hand under my chin and tilted my face to his. "He might please you, but I'm just going to have to do it better," he said gruffly.

Relief flooded me.

As he looked in my eyes, his softened.

"What?" he said gently.

I bit my lip, feeling suddenly foolish. "I thought you'd be angry."

He took a deep breath. "I'm not...angry."

I lay my hand on his chest. "You're…something." He wouldn't be here in my bathroom if he wasn't…something.

He nodded. "I'm something."

"Jealous?" I teased.

He huffed a rough laugh and looked like he was trying to repress a smile. "You just don't let me stop until I've beaten him, understood?"

"What exactly are you planning to do?" I asked, feeling my own smile threaten.

"Understood?" he asked, his voice taking on that commanding tone again.

"Understood," I answered, hoping he hadn't noticed that I'd already completely melted for him.

Valen slowly undid the tie on my robe, then equally slowly slid it off me.

But that was where the slowly ended.

He picked me up and pressed me against the wall of the shower as his lips claimed mine. I jumped against the chill of the tile, and I felt him smile against me.

Water rained down around us, me totally naked and him fully clothed, but he didn't seem to care. He just kissed me like the world was ending. Like I was the air he needed to breathe. Like I was his.

"You're getting wet," I laughed.

He pulled back only enough to look at me. "So?"

"So, what are you going to tell people when you walk out of the girls' dorm soaking wet?"

A wicked gleam lit his eyes. "I could say she was a squirter."

I bit my lip because I didn't know if I wanted to encourage that sort of thing. "Seriously, Valen."

His hand ran up my body to cup my breast as he nuzzled into my neck. "Seriously, Harlow. I'm not really thinking about leaving you."

My hand slid into his hair, and I rocked against him as he pinched my nipple lightly then nipped the skin under my ear softly.

"I thought this was a bad idea?" I breathed as pleasure shot around my body, awakening my senses in the most glorious anticipation.

"It is a bad idea."

"Yet here you are?"

"Yet here I am."

"Why?" I pulled his head away to look into his eyes.

"Why what?"

"Why now?"

"Because I don't fucking care anymore," he snarled. "I don't care it's a fucking bad idea. I want you." He shook his head. "I need you. And I'm fucking having what's mine. God be damned."

We searched each other's eyes for a moment. Like we were checking we both still wanted it. Like we both needed confirmation that this was bigger than his promise to Apollo. Like we needed one of us to walk away or neither of us ever would.

"Then take it," I told him.

His lips claimed mine hungrily again. Our bodies moved together against the shower wall. My hands were in his hair. His were running all over my body, which was being held up only by him pinning me, and my legs around his waist. He lifted me higher and nuzzled my breasts.

"Valen…" I sighed.

Having his hands on me, his lips on me, being able to touch him. It felt like the world had been off its axis for the last three weeks and was only now suddenly righted again.

"It's hardly fair that I'm naked and you're not," I told him.

I felt his smile against my sternum. "It's more than fair from where I'm standing."

"Yes, but you do have your face in my tits."

He looked up at me and he was all sinful cockiness. "Would you rather it was somewhere else?" he asked.

I bit my lip against a full-blown smile. "I'd like equality of the sexes."

He dropped me to my feet quickly but was there to make sure I didn't fall. "Equality, love?" he said as he pulled off his jacket. "Our world's not well known for equality."

"I'm *painfully* aware," I told him as my hand went to the bottom of his tee.

It was plastered to his body, and I took a second to admire the pattern of his tattoos showing bright through it before starting to peel it off him.

"This would have been easier if you hadn't got wet," I muttered as I struggled with the material.

Valen put his hand under my chin and tipped my face to his as he leant down towards me. There was a softness about him that I didn't associate with Valen Kincaid, but it was so subtle I wondered if I was imagining it.

"And where would the fun be in that?" he asked cheekily before winking and helping me pull the offending garment over his head.

I ran my hands over his body. I didn't think I'd ever be sick of it. The way his muscles twitched as I brushed my fingers over them. The way the shifted as he moved. I looked up at him and just wanted to savour the moment for a second.

"What?" he asked me, stepping closer and running his hands up my back.

"I'm just…" Did I dare to tell him? "I'm glad you're here."

"You are?"

I nodded. "Yes." I slid my hand up his body to cup his cheek. "I need you, Valen," I whispered.

Something changed in him, but I couldn't put my finger on exactly what it was. He kissed me, deep and strong, as he held me tightly. My arms wound around his shoulders and my fingers played with his hair.

My hands were the first to drop and search for his jeans button without breaking our kiss. Valen finally pulled away from me, looking down at me through the water of the shower with a smouldering intensity that threatened to set me on fire. Everything in me zinged at the mere thought of his touch, and he seemed to realise that. He flicked his wet hair from his eyes and made short work of getting his boots and rest of his clothes off before joining me back in the shower.

He lifted me up, positioning his cock firmly between my legs. The whole moment was swirling with a delicious tension that I'd never felt with him before. There was something different about it, about us. I just couldn't put my finger on it. And I didn't want to. Whatever it was, I embraced it right along with him.

He slid into me slowly and we held each other close as he thrust into me. It was slow and powerful as we kissed or just stared into each other's eyes. A message was being conveyed between us and I didn't need to know what the words would have been to know the way it left me feeling.

Water dripped off Valen's hair over his face as he looked at me through it, but neither of us paid it any mind aside from me thinking it just made him look incredibly sexy.

It was all slow burn and passion and something I came very close to calling love. The pleasure built in me slowly and only overtook me as finished with me. Still, he kissed me, like he didn't want it to be over, and I wrapped my whole body around his like I'd never let him go.

But eventually, he pulled away and gently lowered me to the floor again. Wordlessly, I reached for the shampoo, cognizant that I was actually in need of a shower, and he only gave me enough space to do my thing as he could while still keeping two hands on my body at all times. His touch wasn't fire. It wasn't seduction. It was connection. It was the kind of warmth that didn't fade when he left.

We washed ourselves and each other, sharing a smile when he got shampoo in his eye and surprised me with the wimpy way he handled it.

"You kill people and you're complaining about a bit of shampoo in your eyes?" I laughed as I helped him wipe his eye clean when we were out of the shower.

My laugh was mirrored in his eyes, a bright grey that shone so much it was almost silver. "Nothing – no blade or fist or bullet – hurts like getting shit in my eye."

"Are you all right?" I teased, pouting.

Valen wrapped his arms around me and pulled me close. "I'm fine," he growled, and it was almost in danger of being playful.

I brushed my fingertips over his cheek as I looked him over. "Are you afraid of being human around me?" I asked softly.

"Scared isn't the word I'd use," he replied, just as softly and I felt a smile rise at my lips.

"Will you ever tell me what the word is?"

"Hesitant," he said slowly.

I cocked my head in question and he sighed heavily.

"Humanity in our world can get you killed, and I'm no use to anyone dead."

Something twisted uncomfortably in my gut at the implications of his words. "So, I'm a liability?" I started pulling away, but he stopped me.

"No," he told me firmly. "But the more I let you in, the harder it is to let you go."

We were interrupted by his jeans buzzing on the floor. He gave a reluctant sigh, then bent down to answer his phone. "Yeah?"

He kicked his head towards the bedroom, and I nodded. He grabbed a towel to throw around him before he went into the other room. While he was on the phone, I wrung out his clothes as best I could and draped them around the bathroom in the futile hope they might dry before he had to go.

I got another towel out to wrap around me and leant in the doorway to watch him. He sat on the end of my bed and already looked exhausted by whoever was on the phone.

Valen scrubbed a hand over his face. "Aye," he said carefully, like he was actually disagreeing. "We had good intel, Da." He shook his head. "Kane wouldn't know where his own cock was if he didn't constantly have his hand around it."

At the sound of Kane's name, my hand slipped off where I was leaning on the door, and I nearly fell flat on my face. Valen looked up at me quickly and I know I didn't mistake the apology in his eyes.

He rattled something off into the phone that sounded like Scots, as much as I knew about anything other than the King's English, then hung up.

"Sorry," he said as he reached for me.

I shook my head as I went to him. He tugged my hand and helped me climb into his lap.

"Do you need to go?" I asked.

He kissed my shoulder as he shook his head. "Mm. No. Da was just checking in about a job I did for Archer. Conflicted with one o' his," he answered casually as his lips brushed over my skin, like he wasn't really thinking – or caring – about what he was saying.

My heart hitched as I remembered what Marco had said about invisibility and being special, but I tried hard not to read anything into it.

"I don't think I've ever heard you speak Scots," I said.

"No?" he murmured.

I shook my head. "I don't think so."

"I suppose I rarely say anything in front of you that I don't want you to understand."

"That makes sense. How else are you supposed to intimidate me into hating you?"

I felt his smile as he dragged his teeth over my neck. "How else was I supposed to keep my hands off you?"

"I wasn't aware it helped?"

He gave a rough chuckle, like it was unbidden. "I couldn't guess that hating me turned you on."

I slid off his lap as my hands went to the top of the towel. He crooked an eyebrow at me and I kicked my head to indicate he scoot up the bed. He scooted, leaving his towel behind. I dropped mine to the floor and crawled back over him.

"A lot about you turns me on, Valen," I told him as I lowered myself over him, taking him in slowly, bracing my hands on his chest.

He put his hands on my hips and seemed perfectly happy to watch me ride him.

"Everything about you turns me on," he said, his voice husky and low, like the words had ripped out of him against his will, or perhaps just his better judgement.

I leant down so our faces were close and looked at him shrewdly as I rolled my hips over him. "Until you walk back out that door, you're mine," I told him. "You're mine, and I'm yours."

"You think me walking out that door is going to change that?" He touched the cross at my throat. His cross. "We are bound, Harlow. You will always be mine. His ring – his name – won't change that."

My gaze pinned him as we moved together. "It's a good thing Kincaids never marry."

"Why is that?"

"Because you will always be mine."

He wrapped me in his arms and whispered in my ear, "For once, I approve of the double standards."

"Does the big, bad wolf like that?" I purred in his ear as I rode him faster.

He sucked in a breath. "I love it."

He captured my lips with his and our previously lazy pace grew frenetic. I sat up to give me better leverage and watched with increasing pleasure as the big, bad wolf came undone for the little princess.

Valen sat up to hold me tight as he thrust into me powerfully.

"Valen…"

"Harlow…"

I came hard and he wasn't long behind me, his head on my shoulder and his hands splayed on my back. We sat there, his head on my chest and I kissed his temple. I felt a small smile on his lips before he toppled backwards, taking me with him. I rearranged to lie beside him with my leg over his and my head on his chest.

As I leant there, I thought about Apollo's words from weeks ago. "Would you change anything if you could?"

He kissed my hair. "You deserve the world, but I can't give it to you."

"You don't want to—?"

"I can't, princess. I'm a trained killer. You should be taken on…last-minute dinner dates in Paris, or dancing in Spain. Apollo can give you the world. I can't."

My hand cupped his jaw. "Apollo's never thought about giving me the world."

"Not yet, but he will."

He seemed very sure about that. I wasn't. I didn't doubt Apollo would end up giving me the world, but I couldn't be so sure that it would be for the right reasons. He hadn't been raised that way.

All I knew just then was that Apollo hadn't thought about giving me the world when he easily could. But Valen *had* thought about it.

Even if he didn't think he could give it to me, he thought I deserved it. And that counted for a lot.

Valen sighed. "I should go, princess."

"Do you have to?"

He sat up and stretched his neck. "Yes. Or I won't leave at all, and Florence would fucking kill me for leaving her out in the cold all night. Let her know she can come back." His phone buzzed again, and he picked it up to deal with it. "Yeah?" he answered.

I grabbed mine and went to check on his stuff in the bathroom under the guise of giving him some privacy, and shot off a text to Florence before picking up my bathrobe and pulling it on.

"I'll sort it," I heard Valen saying. "Sure. What else am I gonna do on a Friday night? Have a life? Don't fucking start, Marco. I said I'll be there. Just save some of the fuckers for my blade, yeah? Cheers."

"Your stuff's still kinda wet," I said from the bathroom, trying to gauge whether that meant his call was done or not.

He came up behind me and wrapped his arms around my stomach, planting a kiss on my neck. "I can sort that before I go?" he offered cheekily as one hand danced down my leg to play with the hem of my robe.

I laughed and span in his arms. "As tempting as that offer is, Florence is on her way back already and I would feel very shit if I asked her to wait a minute."

"Minute?" he asked, all affronted. "Have I not performed to her highness' standards?"

I smirked. "We both know you have. And we both know there's barely enough time left in the night for all the things you could do to me."

His eyes were dark, and I got the feeling he was so close to asking me if I wanted to continue this in his room. His room, his bed, where we wouldn't be disturbed. And I was so close to saying yes.

But it was dangerous enough that he was here, that we'd spent as long together as we already had. I didn't owe Apollo anything, but Valen's life was literally in his God's hands. Plus, Marco was waiting on him for something that sounded important.

"Besides, there are only so many times I can feel guilty for getting Marco injured," I said quickly, before either of us said or did anything we might regret. "It sounds like he needs you."

He dropped his forehead to mine. "Aye, but what if I still need you."

I felt myself smile. "I'm not in any danger tonight."

He sighed like he wished I'd stop making so much sense. Before he let me go, he pressed a kiss to my temple and then started reaching for his clothes. I left him to it, sure that my willpower would go out the window if I was with him a second longer. Instead, I pulled on my pyjamas and plopped onto my bed to wait.

While Valen was still getting dressed in the bathroom, Florence poked her head in the room.

"Safe?" she asked.

I shrugged. "Sure."

She came in and dropped on her own bed just in time for Valen Kincaid to walk out of our bathroom in damp clothes. His jeans looked like they chafed, but it was the long-sleeved tee that clung to every single ridge and contour of his marvellous body that I was sure Florence was gaping at as slack-jawed as me. His tattoos were stark through the wet white fabric, sending off very Rockgod Darcy vibes.

Valen paused, his eyebrow quirking as his eyes darted between us. "My grandmother would ask ye if ye're trying to catch flies."

"Nope," Florence answered. "Just having a right old perv."

"I've warned ye how far my restraint goes, Miss Walton."

"Och, aye," she said, teasing him about the thickness of his accent. I snorted. Valen frowned. "But you're also standing in my dorm room in a tee that leaves *nothing* to the imagination."

"What do you want me to do?" he asked her.

She shrugged. "I could run out and get you a change? I've always wanted to see the great Valen Kincaid's dorm room."

"I'll be fine, ta."

Florence crossed her legs. "We do not doubt that."

Valen's frown deepened in a way that warned her yet again about his restraint, but he said nothing. Instead, he just walked over to where I sat on my bed, bent down to give me a quick peck on the lips, then nodded to her.

"Good night, Miss Walton." A nod for me. "Princess."

"Good night, Valen," we chorused like good little schoolgirls welcoming the Sister to lesson, much to his displeasure.

He walked out of the room, with his head held high, like he owned the bloody place.

Florence and I sniggered and hurried to the window to wait for him to appear at the bottom of the building. When he did, people were already staring at him in surprise. But he strode across the quad like it was the most normal thing in the world for him to be walking out of the girls' dorms more than a little damp.

"The balls on that man," Florence whistled.

"The arse on that man," I countered.

"The mouth on that man."

"The cock on that man."

We dissolved into a puddle of laughter on her bed, and she insisted I tell her about every single second of the last couple of hours.

CHAPTER NINE

Did I feel conflicted sleeping with two guys at the same time? Yes. Did I feel like, if those guys got to do what they wanted without anyone batting an eyelid, then I should be able to as well? Also, yes. Did it complicate matters that I was contractually obliged to marry one of them and it was hard to maintain the other was only casual? Yeah. Very much so.

Still, I was an independent modern woman carving a future and a life for myself despite my world's insistence I do neither, so I was going to roll with it until it all came to an unavoidable head.

And it was all so much easier *and* harder to do when we were all heading back to the Callahan Estate for the Christmas holidays a few days later. Something I wondered if Apollo was thinking about as well that Saturday before we left.

"Do you want to live at the Callahan Estate?" Apollo asked me suddenly as we lounged on the sofa.

I spluttered my drink. "What?"

"She basically already does," Valen offered from the other couch where he was busy comparing something from a map to something else on a tablet. He gave no indication of what he thought about the matter, if he even should have an opinion.

"Nah," Apollo said. "I meant after the wedding."

I didn't know where to look, and I chastised myself for feeling foolish in front of them. All three of us knew I was marrying Apollo. Or else. It didn't do me any good thinking I could pretend otherwise in front of Valen in case it hurt his feelings or something ridiculous. It was ridiculous to imply Valen *had* feelings to hurt in the first place. At least ones he'd admit to.

"I just assumed we're expected to," I answered.

"No. I mean, I know. But did you *want* to?"

"Where else would we live?" I asked.

He shrugged. "I don't know, but I'm not sure it's the place I wanna raise the kids. You know?"

A noise made us look over to Valen and I noticed he'd dropped the tablet on the floor.

"Butterfingers," Apollo laughed.

Valen nodded to him but said nothing as he went back to whatever he was doing.

"Dad will freak, but I was thinking we could get our own place for a while," Apollo continued.

"Is 'our own place' code for the old groundskeeper's cottage on the other side of the estate?" I asked.

Apollo smiled at me. "Maybe. But it would still be somewhere we could call ours. We can have it redecorated and brought back to its former glory. You'd still want to take a car between it and the main house, so Mum wouldn't be dropping in every five seconds. What do you think?"

"I think it sounds like you've thought about it a lot."

"I *have* been thinking about things lately," he admitted, sounding quite proud of himself. "The future. What it looks like. I'm looking forward to it."

I noticed, in all his talk about the future, he didn't mention anything about the present. Nothing about promises to each other. Nothing more than what we were at face value. As far as I knew, he was still hooking up with Magdalens. It made me slightly apprehensive about what that future would actually look like, but at the same time it meant that, in the practical sense, nothing had changed, and I didn't have to feel bad about Valen.

Apollo nuzzled my nose with his and I smiled at him.

"I'm glad," I said.

"Are you…not?" he asked.

"I'm not…not. I guess I just haven't thought about it as much."

He grinned. "I was thinking that we could call our daughter Amelia Florence and our son Harrison Valen."

My throat threatened to constrict, but I hid it by widening my smile. "Were you now?"

He nodded. "Cliché I know, but I like it."

"I need to meet Marco," Valen said quickly as he stood up.

Apollo untangled himself from me and nodded. "Yeah. All good. I'll see you later?"

Valen gave him a single nod in return.

"And cheer the fuck up," Apollo added. "I'm naming our son after you!"

Valen gave him a withering glare. "Can ye not just get me an expensive bottle of Scotch?"

"I'll do that, too!"

Valen sighed and rolled his eyes. "Good afternoon, Miss Vanguard. Apollo, I'll see you later. Plans are on the table."

Apollo waved to Valen as he walked out, closing the door behind him.

"Right moody fucker he is. I was sure naming my firstborn son after him would crack at least a tiny smile."

I nodded. "You'd have thought so."

"But," he said, dragging me fully into his lap. "We can worry about that later."

"What are you planning on worrying about right now?" I asked, amused by his playfulness.

"The fact you've given me a raging boner and we're finally alone."

I ran my slit along said raging boner. "Did you want me to do something about that?"

He breathed in deeply as his hand slid between us and he circled my clit. He wasn't the only one breathing in deeply.

"Not before I do something about this," he said against my lips before kissing me hard.

He rubbed me until I was dripping for him, then plunged two fingers into me. He seemed inpatient to get me off, but I wasn't complaining as I came hard and fast in his arms. Then I was reaching for his belt buckle, and we laughed as he started reaching for his pocket as our arms collided. He pulled out a little silver square and winked at me.

Now I was the impatient one. Impatient to have him inside me. We did the least amount of work required to get the condom on and him sliding into me. We both sighed as I rocked my hips, grinding against him. There was nothing slow and steady about it, it wasn't connection for connection's sake. It was for pleasure, pure and simple. Carnal pleasure. And neither of us were apologising for it.

As Apollo's movements got jerkier and I felt him throb in me, his finger found my clit and it was enough to bring me to satisfying orgasm just as he finished as well. I pumped him a couple more times as we both rode the high down, then slid off his lap and we both breathed heavily.

We caught each other's eye and laughed.

"And that couldn't wait until we got back?" I asked him.

He shook his head, stole a quick kiss, then got up to deal with the condom. "No. It couldn't."

I sighed. "I suppose I'd best go and pack."

"You could put it off for another half hour or so…" Apollo said suggestively, and I smirked at him.

"You're going to run out of condoms if you keep this up."

"It's a good thing I had a fuck tonne delivered to the estate then, isn't it?" he said cheekily.

"You don't half have high hopes, do you?"

"I never do anything by half, babe."

I smiled as I hauled myself off his sofa and rearranged my panties.

"Nevertheless, I need to pack some shit and spend some time with Floss."

He nodded. "Yeah, fair. I'll see you later?"

"Yep. Garage at five?"

He gave me another nod. "Garage at five."

I threw him a wave over my head as I wandered out of his room and headed for mine.

As I jogged down the main stairs, something hit me. Something that really should have hit me earlier. Something that had me wondering where I might find Valen. Apollo always used a condom, even with me. Valen and I had never used one. And I had to wonder what that meant.

My head was totally up my own arse when I ran into Fender.

"You okay, Miss Vanguard?" he asked.

I blinked. "Uh, yes. You don't know where Marco and Valen are do you?"

He nodded. "You're in luck. They're training in the gym."

"The Saint Benedicts' gym?"

He snorted. "Fuck, no. The Angels have their own. Basement."

I nodded. "Great. Thanks, Fender."

"No worries."

I turned and headed for the lift.

"I'll need to let you down," Fender said, and I turned back to him in confusion. He kicked his head toward the lift. "The elevator. The basement needs a code."

"Oh!" I said. "Oh, okay."

Fender smirked at me like he'd forgive my ignorance just this once, then led me to the lift. He called it for me and then nodded for me to get in when the doors opened. I stepped in and he leant towards the control panel.

"No looking now," he warned me with a wink. I dutifully looked away until he said, "There you are now."

I smiled at him. "Thank you, Fender."

He touched his hand to his head. "My pleasure, Miss Vanguard."

Anxiety gnawed at me the whole ride down, despite it being a short trip.

I stepped out of the lift and saw Marco and Valen sparring. Neither of them was in anything more than a loose pair of shorts with their hands taped. They were both sweaty but, as physically pleasing as Marco was to look at, I couldn't take my eyes off the sheen on Valen's body. The muscles rippling. The barely constrained force he could wield.

"Next time, hit me like you mean it," Marco was saying sarcastically as though Valen had just hit him quite incredibly.

"You *wanna* visit the doc again?" Valen asked, with a sexily wry smirk to his lips.

"Wouldn't mind an excuse. Always wanted a go with an older woman."

"She'd wipe the floor with you."

"More'n can be said for your piss weak love pats," Marco said, clearly goading Valen.

Valen swung his hand back and, "We need to talk," exploded out of me.

They both looked at me as Valen's fist crashed into Marco's face.

"Oi!" Marco said to him, and he shrugged.

"What do you want?" Valen asked.

"Is everything all right?" Marco asked, worrying about me now.

I nodded to Marco. "Yes. Everything's…okay. I just… Can I talk to Valen? Alone?"

Valen's nostrils actually flared as he looked at me, as though how dare I come into his house and make demands. And more to the point, how dare I make demands in front of Marco.

Marco nodded slowly. "Sure. I'll just be…upstairs if you need me."

"Lock it on your way up," Valen said sternly.

Marco obviously realised that his boss wasn't in the mood for jokes, so he just gave me a teasing grimace of 'oh dear, we're in trouble now,' and slipped into the lift behind me.

Once the doors were closed, Valen and I just stared at each other for the longest time. My heart thundered in my chest, and I saw he was breathing heavily as well.

"Valen..." I started, not at all sure how to continue.

"Princess?"

I took a few steps towards him. "Just... We've never talked about..."

"About what?"

"Contraception."

His eyes widened "If you're about to tell me you're pregnant..."

I frowned. "Then, what?"

"Then I'm a dead man."

The way he said it, it didn't sound like hyperbole, and a shot of panic ran through me. "Really?"

"Really."

The way he didn't seem to care made me want to show him I didn't care either. Even if I cared more than I should. "Well maybe you should have thought about that before you fucked me bare?"

"Maybe," he said slowly as he took a step towards me, "I thought the risk was worth it."

My nipples tightened. But it was not the time to beg him to throw me against the nearest surface and take that risk right now.

"Now," he continued before I got my thoughts together. "Am I a dead man or not?"

"Not," I said quickly. "A doc in Bieityn gives me an injection four times a year and I don't even get a period."

He nodded like that was the end of it. "Okay."

"But that..." I petered off at the look he gave me. Somehow humoured and yet daring me to test him by continuing. It had to be done. "Pregnancy's not the only reason to use...protection. There are other reasons that a contraceptive shot doesn't cover."

He nodded again. "I'm aware."

"So?" I pressed, annoyed with myself that I'd never really thought about it before now. Or maybe I'd just never *wanted* to think about it before now.

He sighed. "I can give you the flippant answer, or the deeper answer, love. Take your pick."

"Since when do I get to choose what you say to me?"

"Since I'm in a giving mood. I get like that when I have a brush with death."

Had he honestly thought he was a dead man just now? Who would kill him if he knocked me up – his father, Apollo, Archer? What exactly had gone through his mind at the idea of me pregnant with his child? And why was the idea not entirely unappealing to me?

"Which one's true?" I asked, ignoring all my other questions.

"They're both true," he said carefully.

"Fine," I said. "Then, I want both."

"Both isn't an option."

"I say it is."

He growled and surprised me when he didn't argue further. "You are mine, Harlow. I won't fuck my own woman with a barrier between us."

The possessive streak did something to me, even if I did think it a bit of a caveman mentality. Had I not agreed with the sentiment, I would have told him where he could put that barrier. As it was, he was still going to need a better excuse.

"Uh huh," I replied, my tone telling him to keep going.

He sighed and ran his hand over his jaw. I knew the full truth was coming and it was going to cost him an effort. With each sentence, each word, he walked closer to me. "I am forced to be tightly controlled and vigilant in every aspect of my life. I fight. I fuck. I protect Apollo from whatever stupid shit he gets himself into. I've killed people, and not always when it was the plan." He looked at me like he was checking I was still with him. "Then there's you. You make me not just the fists for hire, or a son of the Kincaids, or Apollo's tame wolf. You are the closest to freedom I will ever get and..." Here, his voice softened, and he reached for me. "And I forget myself. I forget propriety. I don't just forget but ignore everything that's been beaten into me; never lose, never love, and never make an unworthy kid. I–"

I lay my hand on his chest, knowing how much he was revealing and thinking he didn't need to reveal more. "If you ever give me anything..." I warned him.

The corner of his lip threatened to tip. "What are you saying, love?"

"I'm saying, as long as you promise me you're clean, I don't want to change a thing."

"I deal in blood, Harlow. You better believe I get checked regularly. And I'd never fuck anyone else bare," he added, like it was both an afterthought but also the most important point.

"You mean that, don't you." It wasn't a question. I didn't need an answer.

I could see it, in his eyes. It was the closest he'd come to telling me I meant something more to him. It was the closest he'd come to saying this could be more to him. Because it couldn't last forever. I didn't know how it would ever – could ever – end, but I knew that one day it had to.

"You should go," he said softly.

"Why?" I asked.

"Before I feel the urge to remind you who you belong to right here."

I took a deep breath and ignored my own urges. "I'll see you at the garage at five."

He inclined his head, almost like a bow. "I'll see you then, princess."

I turned to go, couldn't help throwing him a small smile, which he very nearly returned, then waited for the lift yet again.

"Send Marco back down when you find him," Valen said as I stepped in.

I gave him a nod. "Will do."

"And Harlow?"

I looked up from pressing the button for the lobby. "Hm?"

"I—"

The doors closed and I debated the sense in going back. There was no sense in going back. I knew where that would lead and, while I was embracing this whole multiple sexual partners thing, I wasn't sure I wanted to embrace it quite so back-to-back like that.

Chapter Ten

Christmas holidays at the Callahan Estate that year were much like the previous four Christmases at the Callahan Estate.

Valen had been in and out – of the estate – with his father and brothers. Apollo had been mostly locked in his father's study under intense apprenticeship. Which left my days free to spend blissfully alone, or hanging out with Frenella as she helped Mrs Mack run the household. I tried not to think too hard about the fact that this was an apprenticeship of my own; learning how to run the Callahan Estate as I'd be expected to do once Apollo and I were married.

My nights were taken up with both Apollo and Valen, when he was there, in the rumpus room. I wasn't sure if Apollo was trying to make sure Valen didn't feel left out if Apollo just locked us in his room all the time, or whether he was agitated about what Valen was up to when he wasn't there. I felt the connection between them, and it felt to me like Apollo was worried it was fraying. I just hoped it wasn't anything to do with me. Luckily, our world was so convoluted that there were plenty of reasons other than me that it could be.

"Your parents are getting in on Friday, yes?" Frenella asked me as we were walking through the dining room.

I pulled my head out of my arse and nodded. "Yes. I think their flight's at around midday."

"Which will mean they get here at…" She did the maths, then smiled. "Just in time for pre-dinner drinks."

"Mum will like that," I commented and Frenella smiles

knowingly.

"Won't we all. Now, I want all the presents under the tree by Christmas Eve," she said as she consulted her list. "Christmas morning, it's church, then brunch in the parlour with the tree. Presents. Lunch at the rectory. Then back here for drinks and dinner."

I nodded. "Okay."

"And we must remember it will be the seven of us for Christmas day," she said, and I frowned. "So, we'll need two drivers."

"Seven?"

At that moment, Kane Kincaid walked into the hallway, and I actually froze mid-step as it felt like my whole body went cold. Kane had seemed to be at the Estate too much lately. More than usual. And he always found me. Anyone else might have thought it was simple innocence that he found himself in the same place as me. I was trying to believe it and ignore the stalker vibes.

"Oh, Kane," Frenella said pleasantly, much more used to this world to hide her discomfort around men like Kane.

"Mrs Callahan. Miss Vanguard."

Kane's gaze didn't just linger over my body. His words lingered over my name. Like a caress, but one that made my skin crawl. I repressed the shudder and inclined my head to him.

"Archer and your father are out the back," Frenella said as though he must have been looking for them.

I wished I thought that's what he'd been doing sneaking around the hallways.

He nodded. "Ta, I'll go and find them."

He left and I wasn't the only one breathing an audible sigh of relief.

"That one sends a frozen shiver down your spine, doesn't he?" Frenella said.

I nodded. "Yes."

"Anyway," she said like it was that easy for her to shake it off. "Yes, seven for Christmas. Valen's staying this year and Apollo refuses to let him work. That will be nice, won't it?"

Something about it was very nice. Something else about it was horrible.

But I smiled. "Lovely. I'm sure Apollo's looking forward to it."

"Oh, he is," Frenella said happily. "He's got a big surprise planned."

She winked at me, and I felt like maybe the big surprise wasn't for Valen, but that didn't seem to make sense. Why would she have brought it up like that if the big surprise wasn't for Valen?

Later that night, the men-folk were still busy and the women-folk had retired to their rooms to do whatever it was we did when the men-folk were away. I busied myself finalising my presents, all of which would be delivered in the next couple of days, so plenty of time for Frenella's Christmas Eve deadline to be under the tree.

I hadn't had a chance to really speak to Valen since we'd all arrived at the Callahan Estate so, when I happened to pop my head out of my room and he was walking by, I grabbed him and tugged him to my room.

He looked down at me as I used his body to push the door closed. "Can I help you?"

I nodded. "You can."

His eyebrow quirked. "God doesn't need his princess?"

I stepped back at the tone of his voice. The excitement I'd felt at having him all to myself, in my room, crumpled at my feet.

His face softened. "I didn't mean… I mean, I did… Fuck!" he muttered, then reached for me.

I went to his arms, and he held me close. "How…?" I started, not sure how to continue.

"How, what, love?"

"How does it make you feel?" I asked him slowly.

"What?"

"Me…sleeping with Apollo."

"I have to be okay with it because you're his, not mine."

"That's not what you've told me before."

He held me only far enough away so he could look at me. "You cannot be my princess."

"No," I admitted. "But I am your goddess."

The smile in his eyes was small, but it was there. "I suppose you expect me to bow to you now?"

I ran my hand over his chest. "Do you wish things were different?" I asked him, not sure if I wanted to know the answer or not.

His eyes narrowed as his fingers played with my top at my waist. For the space of a heartbeat, I was sure he was going to say yes. He brushed an escaped strand of hair away from my face, his touch tender. Then he'd fisted my hair in his hand, and he tugged gently.

"There is only one rule, love," he started, his voice deliciously low.

"Really?" I sassed. "I seem to have forgotten."

He pulled my hair a little more. "Do ye need a reminder?" he asked, and I nodded. "You only cum for me, princess. Understood?"

"You don't tell me what to do."

"Understood?" he repeated, pulling just a little more.

"I don't answer to you, Valk" I teased him.

The heat in his eyes told me he liked that. The way he tugged my hair and pulled me closer to him suggested he was still going to punish me for it.

"And what makes you think I answer to you?" he asked, his voice all warning.

"I *am* your goddess, Valk, and you *will* bow to me," I said.

A ghost of a sinful smirk lit his lips. "I'd like to see you make me."

I batted at his arm, and he obliged by letting go of my hair. Then I brought that hand back and laid it over his throat, a sinful smirk of my own at my lips and a demand in my eyes.

"On your knees," I commanded him.

His lip quirked, along with his eyebrow, but he very slowly dropped to his knees in front of me. He looked at me like he was saying 'I'll do it, but just this once'.

That surprised me.

"Why now?" I asked, fighting a smile.

He spread my legs and pushed my pyjama shorts aside. "I came undone, princess. You're in charge."

As his tongue brushed over my clit I sucked in a breath. My hand went to the back of his head, fisting in his hair, and mine fell back as I breathed against the shooting pleasure. His hands gripped my arse firmly, just in case I had any ridiculous notions of getting away, and I was not complaining…

Until he pulled back and swore. He pulled his phone out of his pocket with a grumbled, "Always fucking interrupted," before answering with a mighty pissy, "What?"

He sighed as he leant his head against my legs and nodded to whoever was on the phone.

"Right now?" he asked. "Fucking hell, Creed. No. Do *not* tell my da," he ordered. "Shit." He pulled himself off the floor and wiped a hand over his face. "No. No. Yeah. I can be there in…fuck… It'll be an hour. Earliest. Fender's off duty. I *can* drive, ye ken?" he snapped. "I'll take the hit."

He hung up and swore again.

"Is…everything okay?" he asked.

He shook his head. "No. Vinnie Rossano's killed…" He gave a humourless laugh. "Fuck! He's a fucking dead man."

"You have to go?" I said more to try and get him focussed.

He nodded. "Aye. That fucker's begging for a shallow grave."

"Just be careful," I whispered.

He looked at me and I saw his eyes soften. His hand reached for me, and I went to him. "I'll come back," he promised.

"You'd better."

"I've got a reason."

The 'now' at the end of that sentence was heavily implied, and I counselled myself against feeling too much about it. So, I just nodded.

Valen pressed a kiss to my lips, then slid wordlessly out my door and off into the night.

I went to look out my window to watch as he peeled out of the garage a few minutes later. The speed at which he left kicked gravel up behind his precious Viper. As I watched him go, a part of me wished he didn't have to. Wished our world didn't expect him to go and deal with assassinations and cleaning up other people's kills.

Whoever Vinnie Rossano had killed, it sounded important, and I couldn't help but feel a flare of hope that it might have been Kane.

I stayed on my window seat for a while longer as though me just sitting there could bring Valen back safely. Then, I realised, it wasn't up to me. It couldn't be up to me. It shouldn't be up to me.

Did I *really* wish things were different? The tiny part of me who wanted Valen and wondered about that other life was awfully quiet on the matter. It was enough to make me think that, maybe, it was safer to not wish things could be different. If things could be different, then this thing with Valen had the power to be real and, if it was real, it had the power to destroy me when it ended. When he rejected me.

A Kincaid never marries.

It was so ingrained in our world that it may as well have been a foundation block upon which the rest was built. It was like a mantra. A Vanguard always rules. A Callahan does not lose. A Branch eeks vengeance. An O'Malley will always fight. A Fife will never waver. A Walton counts the coffers. A Kincaid never marries.

If Valen and I never had any hope because I had to marry Apollo, then it couldn't be my fault when it ended. Even if the idea of Valen was wrapped up in the idea of the freedom that small part of me still craved, Apollo was my destiny – my fate, my future, my security, the security of other people's lives.

Valen.

Apollo.

Freedom.

Destiny.

I wanted both of them for very different reasons. One was little more than a wish that warmed my dreams, the other was the path I had no choice but to tread yet I would do so willingly. And both of them were so very entwined into who I was now that I couldn't see a way of untangling either of them.

Chapter Eleven

Valen did come back safely, but not for a few days and even Apollo could be found pacing in agitation. Gone was the man who was enamoured with our new relationship and in his place was only the man who worried for his friend and servant.

It was enough to have the anxiety eating away at me even when I wasn't watching Apollo's endless pacing and handwringing.

I didn't know much about Vinnie Rossano except people's reactions to his name and the fact he seemed to have it out for Archer. Not that I blamed him. I suspected a lot of people had it out for Archer. Vinnie was unlikely to be special in that regard. What was special was the way even Florence has reacted to his name.

And that had me terrified for the state Valen would return in.

But a couple of days after he'd left, a knock came at my door and I went to open it to see Valen standing there looking exhausted and bruised, but no worse than I'd seen him after his fight with Peskov.

"You're alive," was the first thing I decided to say to him.

He nodded. "I have to go and speak to Archer, but I wanted ye to know I kept my promise," he said.

I smiled at him. "Thank you."

He inclined his head. "Later."

"Later."

He slipped away and later turned into Christmas Eve, and I still hadn't had a chance to talk to him. The looks we shared as we passed each other in the hallways felt like my feelings were on display for the whole world to see, but no one seemed to pay me any undue attention. No one except Kane when he was there.

I was heading back to my room to get dressed for dinner when I finally had a moment alone with him.

"Princess," Valen said as we passed each other in the hallway, like he wanted something, and I would have been quite happy to give him everything…had time allowed.

I looked up at him expectantly. "Yeah?"

He looked around like he was checking that we were alone. "I have something for you later. Not really the sort of thing you can put under the tree."

I looked down at his crotch, then back to his face and raised my eyebrow in question.

He gave a huff that looked like it was trying to hide a very real smile. "Uh. No. It's the kind of something with ribbons–"

"I mean, you *could* put a ribbon on it…" I suggested playfully.

The ghost of a smirk lit his lips as he kept talking like I hadn't interrupted. "–and paper and sentimental bullshit."

"Aw," I cooed, and he waved his head as though it was the last thing he wanted to be admitting.

"Yeah. That sort of thing."

"You got me a present," I said, actually reaching out to tickle him.

He gave another of those huffs as he batted my hand away. This one might have been hiding a laugh. "I did. Don't make a big deal out of it."

Okay. I wouldn't. To him. Florence would be hearing all about it. "I didn't get you anything," I told him.

He shrugged. "No one ever does."

"Harlow?" came the barked tones of Archer Callahan.

I stepped away from Valen just as Archer rounded the corner. He looked to Valen with a short greeting, then turned his attention on me.

"Ah, there you are. I need to steal you away for a moment."

I nodded to him. "Of course." I inclined my head to Valen. "Valk."

"Miss Vanguard," he said smoothly, all propriety when it was necessary.

By the time I was done for the night, it was far too late to find Valen, so I went to bed not knowing what his present was, but looking forward to finding out the next day.

† † † †

The six of us were in the parlour on Christmas morning. Copious mimosas had been drunk by the women. The men's coffees were more whiskey than they were coffee. And it was all cheer.

"All that's missing is Valk," Apollo said to me, literally like a little child on Christmas morning in a man's body…on Christmas morning.

"Speak of the devil," my mum said happily, and we all turned to see Valen walk in.

Apollo snorted in a very undignified manner.

"What?" Valen asked as though he wasn't wearing a black jumper with a great big red bow on it that was very close to being Christmas cheer. My dad passed him a 'coffee' and he took it with a nod of thanks.

"Oh, you wore it!" Frenella cooed.

Valen looked at Apollo like that was all the explanation needed.

"Stand together. Stand together," Frenella said as she got her phone out.

Not one to disobey the woman who let him sleep on her nice linen, Valen took his place at Apollo's side for a photo. Valen with his present jumper and Apollo with his Christmas tree jumper. They were light and dark, but somehow made total sense.

"Harlow, dear, hop in the middle," Frenella said, waving me in.

I paused, then my mum was agreeing and even Archer told me good naturedly to hurry up.

I slid in between the guys and Apollo put his hand around my

114

shoulder instantly. My right hand hung perilously close to Valen's left behind my leg. His fingers brushed mine imperceptibly.

"Oh, lovely smile, Harlow," Frenella said, and my cheeks heated. "All right. Wonderful. Done."

The three of us moved awkwardly away from each other, and Apollo started handing out presents like an over-exuberant Father Christmas. I half expected to see one from Valen sitting in my pile, but it never appeared. I wondered even more what it was that he hadn't wanted me to have it in front of others.

"And Valk," Apollo said finally. "This one's from the lot of us."

"To say thank you," Frenella offered.

"A token for your service," Archer added.

"I knew if we got your more than one present, you'd kill me," Apollo finished.

Valen frowned as he took the large box from Apollo. Inside was a set of black and white marble inlaid guns, with black leather holsters decorated with silver. And a matching hunting knife and sheath.

"It's fucking beautiful," Valen said, looking at them. "Thank ye."

Archer inclined his head. "We can hardly expect you to protect our son with substandard weaponry."

Valen clearly had thoughts about Archer's summation and shot a look to Apollo, whose answering look suggested he leave it alone.

"If you want to try them out, Cortas has set up the shooting gallery," Archer told him.

Valen looked like he'd take him up on it if only to get out of an awkward situation. "I might just do that."

The rest of us set to opening our presents. I got the usual tat of expensive perfume, another strand of pearls I'd never wear, a book on home maintenance like I was a fifties housewife with a normal life, and two tickets to Scotland.

"For Cousin Darcie's wedding," Mum said, smiling.

Dad seemed to think the idea of going to Cousin Darcie's wedding was a stupid idea. But of course, he did. It wasn't his family.

"You'll be taking Apollo, of course," Mum said.

I forced a smile. "Of course." I mean, I *had* been planning to take Florence, but sure.

I went to give her a hug, because I wasn't going to be ungrateful, even if she'd only given me the tickets to force my dad to let us go. Not that he would have physically restrained us or anything, but he'd have tried something on to keep us home. But then Scotland had never been a Vanguard thing, it had been a my mum's family thing.

Turning to go back to my seat, I realised Apollo was standing up as well. I gave him a questioning smile…that didn't stay on my face long.

"Harlow…" Apollo started as he reached into a pocket and dropped to one knee in front of me.

Mum and Frenella made appropriate coos of excitement and clapped their hands, and our fathers were already murmuring their obligatory congratulations. Because it was inconceivable that I'd say no. No one in the room except me had any idea that 'no' was even a remote possibility.

Apollo held a ring box out to me and opened the lid. On his face was the hazy smile of the besotted and utterly contented. In his eyes was a depth of adoration and a teasing 'I know it's just a formality for the parents' glint that I didn't share in. My heart was pounding in my chest, and I suddenly felt very hot. My cheeks burned and I felt like I was going to throw up.

Movement from the door caught my eye and I saw Valen stop dead in his tracks, his eyes pinned on me and, more importantly, Apollo on his knee in front of me. The mince pie he was in the process of lowering from his lips dropped from his hand. Without taking his eyes off me, he caught it, after a single fumble, and he seemed to choke on the pie he had in his mouth.

Apollo looked back at him with a smirk. "First time eating?" he asked.

"Apollo!" Frenella hissed, reminding him he was in the middle of something important.

I wanted to tell her that it was totally fine, and she needn't have worried on my account. If Apollo was otherwise distracted by Valen choking, then maybe I could sidle out of there and avoid giving Apollo – or our parents – an answer, as though that could stop it from being yes.

"Harlow Regina Vanguard," Apollo said slowly, showboating again and my smile was the most forced I'd worn in a long time. "Will you do me the honour of becoming my wife?"

I took a breath in the hopes my voice came out calm. "Of course. Yes."

The parents had a lot more cheering to do as Apollo slid the huge diamond onto my finger. It sat there, heavy and foreign, but I smiled as the others came to hug us.

Apollo got to sidle away and went to Valen. I saw them exchange words. Apollo smiled and laughed and Valen clapped him on the back. I didn't know what the words were, but Valen's eyes didn't leave mine.

More champagne was poured, and I was starting to wonder if any of our parents would be in a fit state for lunch at the rectory. But then, for people like them and the parties they threw, being able to hold your alcohol was as important for the women as it was the men.

As soon as I could, I ran to my room and the flood of emotion hit me as my shaking fingers looked for Florence's number in my phone.

"Merry Christmas!" she cried drunkenly in answer.

"Floss," burst out of me along with a huge sob.

"Fuck." She sobered up quickly. "What happened?"

"He… Apollo proposed."

"Yay…?" she offered weakly. "Not yay, obviously. Why not yay?"

"I don't know," I sobbed. "Why isn't it yay?"

"How did he…? How did he do it?"

"In front of everyone. Floss, I couldn't say no. I had to say yes. I was always going to have to say yes, but I couldn't say no. And Valen walked in, and I couldn't say no, Floss!" just poured out of me along with all the tears.

"Okay," she said. "Okay. Shh. It's okay. You couldn't say no. Got it. Shit," she seemed to mutter more to herself than me. "Okay. It's fine. Mrs Callahan was the endgame and here we are."

In lieu of words, I blubbered at her.

"Nope. Okay. Wrong tack. Babe, I'm here for you. But you've taken a bit of a detour from the road I thought we were taking, and I need a signpost."

"I couldn't say no!" burst out of me again.

"Yep. That'll do it. Is it the way he proposed? Is that the problem? The fact he didn't really give you a choice? No," she answered for herself. "Stupid Florence. You didn't have a choice anyway."

I felt like I was hyperventilating. "I just... I don't... Floss..."

"Shit," she said, then she got quiet. "Just hang on, babe. I've got you." Then she got louder again. "Harlow? Just breathe, okay? In and out. In and out."

"I'm not in fucking labour," I snapped.

"Not going to take that personally," she said. "Just hold on for a couple more minutes, babe. Okay?"

I blinked, looking around the room like she was about to walk into it. "What? Why?"

She didn't walk into it, but Valen did.

I stumbled back, knowing I probably looked just a little crazy.

He walked towards me carefully and I kept backing up. My legs hit the window seat and I dropped into it. He took the phone from my hands gently and said to Florence, "She's safe."

I didn't hear Florence's reply, but Valen hung up and threw my phone on the bed.

"What are you doing here?" I asked him, more like an accusation.

"When Florence messages me to say you're in danger, I come."

"Is this another rule?" I sneered.

"It's a fact," he said simply.

I sniffed, feeling everything in me fall. "What do I do?" I whispered, ashamed of how pathetic I sounded.

Valen looked torn but, when he spoke, his voice was cold. "What you were always going to do. Marry Apollo."

I felt tears leaking from my eyes and gave up even considering what my eyeliner looked like now. "He didn't give me a choice, Valen." Why I said it like I thought Valen would give me one, I didn't know.

Unhelpfully or not, he didn't. "There wasn't one," Valen reminded me.

My heart felt like it was throwing up and breaking and dropping and trying to escape out of my mouth all at once. "I had to say yes…" I muttered, more to myself than him.

"What did you expect, princess?" he asked snidely. "Rose petals adorning your bed, a soft romantic fuck on the rug in front of the fire, him proclaiming his everlasting love for you, then a glass of Champagne with a ring at the bottom? Something sweet and special and private?"

Gone was my sadness and, in its place, Valen had sparked white-hot anger. "Do not talk to me like that," I commanded as I stood up. "Don't talk to me like me wanting a different fate is disgusting. Me wishing for a choice is wrong."

"Why?" he asked as he came to stand as close to me as he could get. He looked down at me and almost dared me to leave my head in the clouds. "None of us have a choice."

"Does that mean I can't spend a few moments wishing there was?"

"And what would you have chosen? Huh? If you had this miraculous choice? What would the perfect Harlow Vanguard choose?"

To tell him now seem farcical. To not tell him now seemed like the coward's option. So, I told him.

"You," I said as my heart seemed to crack in my chest.

Suddenly, everything I'd thought about that other life with Valen being possible seemed…ridiculous and irrelevant. He was a mighty Angel, above the wishes and desires of mere mortals like me. We may have joked I was a goddess, but I was nothing of the sort. I was a pawn in someone else's life. This wasn't my story, it was theirs.

"I'm not a choice, Harlow."

"Does that mean you wouldn't?" I asked softly, my voice threatening to crack along with my heart. "Choose me."

"No amount of wishing, love," came his strangled reply.

"But if you could, Valen," I pressed.

It felt like maybe I could continue, I could get on with my life with Apollo, as long as I just knew that it wasn't all me. That I wasn't the only one dreaming about a different future.

Yes, I loved Apollo, and I would make it work with him because I had to. I'd thought it was going to be easier now we were getting closer, but my reaction to his surprise proposal told me we still had a way to go.

"Valen?"

"Take a minute to get cleaned up." His voice wasn't unkind, but it wasn't warm. "The pastor is waiting on us for lunch."

He walked out and I felt my heart go with him. I tried to make it stay, but it wouldn't. Or couldn't.

The ring on my finger felt like my chains were back, and this time they tied me directly to Apollo with no question. I was living someone else's life again and the walls were closing in. And I couldn't talk to the one person who was supposed to make it all bearable…because it was his life I was living.

Chapter Twelve

I woke the next morning and the first thing I felt was the weight of the ring on my finger where it hadn't been before. I lifted my hand and breathed out heavily.

It wasn't overly garish, not compared to the crown I wore on the other hand. I couldn't complain about that. Apollo had obviously taken into account what he thought my tastes were when choosing it. What I wanted to know was why Valen had seemed so surprised. Valen had known about the crown ring, but not about the engagement ring? Why?

So many questions and no answers.

And I'd keep getting no answers if I just lay in bed all day and avoided my problems.

I got dressed and told myself to buck the fuck up. I was newly engaged to a man I loved. I should be happy.

Right?

But I wasn't.

I was back to 'fake it until I made it' mode and I wasn't sure why.

I kept seeing Valen's face, choking on his mince pie, with Apollo on his knee in front of me. I kept thinking it meant something. I kept wishing it meant something, but it couldn't mean anything. This was where my life was always heading and...

No amount of wishing could make it otherwise.

No amount of wishing, love.

I sighed as I pulled open my bedroom door and forced a smile, ready for the first person I saw. My eyes slid to Valen's door down the hall, firmly closed with no way of knowing if he was on the other side or not. I made my feet take me in the opposite direction, reminding myself Mrs Callahan was the endgame. And here we were.

Hooray.

"Here comes the bride!" I heard Frenella coo and my mum's laughter.

I took a breath and widened my smile for them. "Good morning," I said happily as I dropped into my chair at the breakfast table with them.

Fake it until you make it.

"Good morning," Mum said.

"Where are the boys?" I asked, looking around.

"Nursing a bit of a hangover," Mum offered, sharing a knowing smile with Frenella.

"Yes," she agreed. "Archer insisted on opening some terribly rare brandy last night in celebration and none of them went to bed until they'd gone through two bottles and couldn't see through the cigar smoke anymore." Her words suggested she disapproved. Her tone suggested she was amused.

I nodded. "Fair enough."

"Mrs Callahan," came Valen's voice from the door.

He looked like he was still deep in the hangover, but he was showered and dressed. I saw the flash of his new holsters and sheath under his clothes.

"Valen, dear," Frenella said. "What can we do for you this morning? Bacon? A little hair of the dog?"

Valen inclined his head, as polite as I'd ever seen him. "Nay, ta," he said, his accent thick. "My da needs me. Will ye tell Apollo and Mr Callahan for me when they're up?"

Frenella nodded. "Of course, dear. You'll be gone all week?" she asked, and he nodded, but it looked placating rather than agreeing. "Apollo will be terribly upset if you miss the party."

the sand. A point at which I said 'enough' before I crossed lines that I wasn't willing to cross, even if no one else had any qualms about it.

By the time we went in for lunch, the men were up. Archer and Dad were going for a hair of the dog approach to the hangover, and Apollo was downing copious amounts of bacon, but he spared me a warm if tired smile as I sat next to him.

"Sorry we didn't wait," he said.

I grinned at him, all my hesitation and uncertainty put aside with him right in front of me. "You look like you need it."

Dad put his hand to his head. "I don't think I even remember going to bed."

"Valen basically carried you in," Mum said, with a knowing smile to me.

"Where *is* Valk?" Apollo asked.

"Cillian needed him."

I wasn't surprised Apollo dropped his fork at that. Frenella said it with such finality that everyone at the table knew how big a deal it was.

"Fucking Rossano…" Archer muttered.

"When will he give up?" Apollo huffed.

"When the Kincaids do their fucking job and put him down," Archer growled.

"They're doing their best," Apollo said.

Archer stood up quickly, slamming his hands on the table. "Then perhaps their best isn't good enough!" Then he stormed out.

Apollo threw his napkin on his plate, muttering incoherently, and ran after him with a snide, "What do you want me to do? Rig a fight so he loses lieutenant?"

I didn't hear Archer's reply, but I heard a door slam. I didn't know whether Apollo was in the same room as his father or not, and Apollo's continued absence didn't answer that question.

"Frenella," Mum said quietly, and they both made their excuses to leave.

He inclined his head. "Aye. I'll try to be back. In time," he added, as though there was a question that he'd be back at all.

Frenella's eyes darkened as though she knew more about what Valen was off to do than she probably should. "I see. Well, you be careful, dear. The roads are icy this time of year."

He inclined his head again. "Aye, I will. Mrs Vanguard."

"Goodbye, Valen," Mum said. "It was nice to see you again."

"The pleasure was mine, ma'am. Thank ye for including me in the festivities." He finally looked at me. "Congratulations again, Miss Vanguard."

I swallowed hard. "Thank you, Valen."

He gave a short nod, then turned on his heel and walked away. My throat constricted to watch him leave, but this was our life. This was our world.

"Have you thought about your dress?" Frenella asked, and I wasn't the only one who could feel the forced joviality in the change of subject.

We made small talk about the wedding while we had breakfast. Nothing decisive, just ideas for flowers and music and colour schemes and themes. Nothing was said about where or when. I guessed that had a lot to do with the mothers knowing they'd have differing opinions and we women-folk were nothing if not good at maintaining the pretence that everything was lovely and wonderful and we all got along. Not that our mothers didn't get along, but an argument about the location and date of the wedding surely would have ruined the image.

I spent the rest of the morning just with Mum. We rugged up and went for a walk in the grounds. I'd always loved the Callahan Estate in winter. Everything covered in a blanket of snow. So clean. So full of hidden promise. Like a blank canvas upon which you could write anything.

"Are you happy, sweetheart?" Mum asked me as we sat on one of the benches, her with her arm around me and me snuggled into her side like I was still small.

I nodded against her. "Of course."

She sat me up and made me look at her. "Are you sure?" She searched my eyes like she was really asking.

I felt the tears threaten again. "I don't know," I said honestly. "But it doesn't matter, does it?"

Mum hugged me. "It matters, Harlow. We can't do anything about it. There's a difference."

I breathed deeply in an effort to keep the tears at bay. "I know what's expected of me and I'll do my duty."

"A lot is riding on this contract," she said, as though that was an answer. "Apollo's not that bad, though, is he?"

I wasn't quite sure what answer she wanted me to give her now. She seemed almost prepared for any.

Was he that bad? In many ways, yes. In others, no.

He's been swept up in our relationship changing. He'd fallen for the ruse that had become something more but just not quite enough. Yet. He was still everything our world had made him. He was still the God of Saint Benedicts, ordering his Angels to kill with as much regularity as their fathers. He still – as far as I knew – kept appointments with Magdalens, even if it was barely once a week.

And yet, things *were* changing. He was more attentive. He was sweeter. He'd taken me off that pedestal, like I was a real person again. We were closer than we'd been in years. We talked. Freely and openly with no barriers – real or imagined – between us, except when we had sex. There were more flashes of the boy I cherished growing up, of Frenella's little boy, the one I'd vowed to keep safe.

"We're…closer," I said carefully. "But we're just not…" I sighed deeply as the tears threatened again. I looked down at my ring. "I wasn't ready for this. We weren't ready for this."

"He certainly thought you were."

"I worry that Apollo hasn't separated the expectations for us versus the reality of us. Not really. Things are going okay between us,

but this wasn't for us. This was for you and Frenella."

Mum nodded. "I understand that." She took my chin and made me look at her again. "But it *was* for you as well, sweetheart. There are worse men to be bound to than Apollo Callahan. He truly cares for you, even if your relationship isn't quite as…normal as other people's."

"What would Dad do if I honestly didn't want to – couldn't – marry Apollo?" I hedged.

"Is there someone else?"

I dropped my eyes again and shook my head.

There wasn't. Not really. There was the dream of another life. But even then, the man I'd choose wasn't the sort of man to give me that other life. And, if he was, then he wouldn't be him and I might not have wanted him anymore.

"No, there isn't. But what if there was?" I asked.

"I don't know," she said slowly, like she was actually considering it. "I don't know that it would make a difference, unfortunately. Are you that unhappy?"

"I'm not unhappy," I assured her. "I'm just not sure that I'm happy either. I think I could be though, with time. I think Apollo and I can be truly happy together."

With time.

"It's better than nothing," Mum pointed out.

I nodded. After all, I'd spent so many years believing that my future was going to be completely miserable. Probable happiness was a huge step up from that. And I did love Apollo. No matter how much I longed for Valen, I loved Apollo. And I wasn't opposed to our engagement in theory. It was the fact that it had felt so theatrical.

That fact and that I didn't know what it meant for Valen and now.

By rights, this was the end. There was a ring on my finger. It may not have been a promise beyond the one our fathers had already made for us, but it was a line in the sand. And there needed to be a line

I froze not sure what I was supposed to do now. I was all-but one of the women, so I should probably go with them. On the other hand, I very rarely got to spend any time with my dad and, after the emotional drain of the last day, the little girl in me wanted a few minutes with her daddy.

I couldn't tell him anything I wanted to. I couldn't be anything other than perfect and accepting and pliable for him. I couldn't talk to him about my reservations and my fears. But I could get some comfort at least from his presence and the knowledge he did love me.

"How is Florence?" Dad asked, as though he could read my mind and was telling me to stay.

I nodded as the staff brought me my lunch, obviously also getting the memo that I was staying. "She's good."

"Good. I saw her father the other week. He said she's got a shot at Paris…?"

I appreciated him trying. After all, what did he and I have to talk about otherwise?

"I don't really get it myself," I admitted. Maybe because I'd been quite hung up on my own shit lately and not given her the time I should have. Or maybe because she knew I didn't understand Art and didn't waste time explaining it to me. "But it sounds like some swanky art school. She's been working her butt off."

"Good for her."

Dad didn't ask me what I was working my butt of for because it wasn't expected that I go to university or pursue an interest outside flower arranging or fashion parade organising or managing my household. It was unfathomable that I, with my life mapped and set and secure with the contract of a good marriage, could want anything differently. A woman wanting an actual life? How absurd.

It was so absurd that *I* hadn't even considered what I might do if I'd had any other option. I didn't have any interests or hobbies or anything I was good at outside the persona our world expected of me. It was pretty sad when I stopped to think about it.

"And work's…good?" I asked, more for the act of asking than anything.

He nodded. "Fine. The usual."

I nodded as well. "Good."

"Are you…all right, Harlow?" he asked, like the question wasn't customary for him. Which it wasn't.

I forced a smile for him, the one I'd always worn for him. "I'm fine," I answered as I tucked into lunch. "Why do you ask?"

He shrugged as he, too, ate. "I just want to make sure my little princess is happy. I'm sure I can have Apollo get you a bigger diamond."

I had to laugh, or I might cry. That Dad actually thought that could be the most pressing issue at the moment. What I wouldn't give to change the men in my life. Show them there was another way from the one their fathers told them it had to be. That we women weren't as vapid and useless as the previous generation told them we were.

"No. I love it. But thank you," was all I said to him.

He gave a curt little nod, but I could tell he was happy.

I just wished I could be as well.

My parents left the next day and I wished I cared more, but Valen was gone and I didn't know when he was coming back this time.

Chapter Thirteen

I felt like I lost a lot of myself over the next week. At least the person I'd spent the last few months fighting to become. Back was my mask. The pastels and the pearls. The demure smile and the forced cheerfulness.

And there was no space for Apollo to notice because he was clearly worried about Valen, which only served for me to layer the mask on thicker because I couldn't be worried about Valen *and* my future at the same time.

Valen wasn't mine to worry about.

My future was all I had.

Apollo was my future and he needed me.

"I need to go to him," Apollo said fiercely, on the phone to someone as he paced yet again. "You don't tell me what to do, Gage." Apollo's voice was iced venom. "You will know your place, or it would be my pleasure to remind you with whatever force necessary."

There was a part of me, who still lived outside the mask, that thought it would be nice if Apollo's ruthlessness would come out for me like that. It sounded like he'd go to the end of the universe for Valen and kill everything and anything in his path if he had to. Anything to bring Valen back safely.

I loved that Apollo cared that much about something, but I'd be lying to myself if I said I didn't wish that, for once, that something was me.

The Kincaids weren't helping. There had been no sign, that I'd seen, of Valen. But Kane and Neo made appearances. A little more bruised and battered each time. And each time, Kane's eyes stayed on me longer, like the worse things got for them the more he looked at me for…what? Comfort? Relief? I didn't know what he wanted, and I didn't care. All I cared about was that Neo never left his side while the two were there.

While Apollo was busy threatening Gage's manhood, I slipped out of his room and took up my usual random wandering around the estate to try to just get a moment's peace where I wasn't pretending. Where I could be sad or lonely or angry or scared, and it didn't matter because there was no one to judge me.

Florence was coming for the Callahan's New Year's party, but it was the soonest she could get to me, and I didn't want her to feel guilty for that, so I kept from her exactly how bad my mood was getting. There would be time enough for me to sob into her lap. There was nothing she could do yet so I wouldn't worry her unnecessarily.

Pretending, though, was harder than it used to be. Back when I knew there was no way out of my cage, that was just what life was and I didn't know any other way. I saw other people have a different life, but it would never be mine. Now I'd tasted freedom and my heart railed against the bars. It crashed. It threw itself against them in the hopes that we could find another way out.

By the day before New Year's Eve, I felt bruised and broken on the inside and looked the perfect porcelain trophy wife on the outside. When I deigned to be with others. With Apollo and Archer busy with whatever shitstorm was raging with Vinnie Rossano and the Kincaids, I withdrew entirely.

I was slipping through the servants' passages, hoping to avoid…well, anyone.

Before my mum had left, she'd made Frenella promise that she would get as many wedding details out of me as she could before I went back to school, and Frenella had been making good on that promise. I'd only just escaped a particularly cheerful session that morning that I hoped was Frenella trying to offset my moodiness of late.

It wasn't any different really than the previous five years, though. Our mums had been excited about the wedding in lieu of anyone else being excited about it. Because, after all, *someone* had to be excited about it. What did make it different now, and exceptionally irritating, was that Apollo was just as excited and used that as an excuse to not worry about Valen.

He was chaffing at the bit, going on about how we could get married as soon as school finished. And I had to smile and nod and hope to all that was holy that Apollo and I would have the time to actually have a serious discussion about the whole thing before we found ourselves down the aisle already. Actually, we'd had the time. If anything, Apollo had been making sure he made at least an hour a day for me. So, time wasn't the issue. It was a significant lack of balls on my part that was the issue.

Suffice to say, my head was a literal mindfuck. Whenever I was alone, it was a frantic mess of bullshit, and I couldn't sort anything from the noise. So, to say I wasn't watching where I was going that day would have been an understatement; I was just trusting my feet to take me along the roads that they'd been taking me for so many years.

I felt a hand on my shoulder roughly and fear pool deep in the bottom of my spine. I was shoved back into the wall and blinked at the sudden pain in the back of my head.

"Little princess," came a voice that made my skin crawl.

I swallowed. "Kane."

He planted his right hand next to my head like it was a threat against even the idea of moving, as his hips pinned me to the wall at my back. I couldn't look at his face, so I stared at his arm and wished to any power above that someone would come down this rarely used passageway.

He had what looked like a fresh tattoo on the inside of his arm. It was a black rose, but the bottom of the stem looked like an upside down cross, and there was a pentagram behind it. By the time I dared to breath, I think I'd committed it to memory.

"Brave of you to be out and about alone," he hissed in my ear, and I tried to repress the shiver than ran through me at the feeling of his breath on my face.

"This is to be my house," I said, forcing a courage I didn't feel a shred of. "I should be free to be wherever I like."

"I've been waiting to get you alone, little princess."

I took a deep breath, my chest inadvertently pressing against his and he grinned. I didn't know if he was more pleased about the closeness of my tits, or the fact I was terrified and doing a piss poor job of hiding it.

"You can fight me all you want, but I'll have you screaming in pleasure before I'm done." He took my face in his hand and forced me to look into his eyes. "There's no one here to save you now."

Kane's hands were on the skin of my legs, scrabbling to get into my pants. His breath was hot in my ear. I squeezed my eyes shut and tried to unfreeze enough to get him off me. To say something. To fight back. To scream for help. But I couldn't. Fear gripped me. I knew without a doubt that Kane Kincaid was about to ruin my life and I wasn't doing a single thing about it. Except maybe surviving.

"Kane," came a barked voice. A voice the recessed consciousness in my head knew.

"Get out of here," Kane said lazily to him.

A hand grabbed the back of Kane's collar and wrenched him away from me. I recognised who was attached to that hand and he had no qualms throwing his brother violently against the floor.

Neo Kincaid was the heir to the Kincaid family business. Like his younger half-brothers, he was built for damage. At twenty-nine, he was taller even than Valen and had similar colouring; dark hair but pale blue eyes in place of Valen's grey ones. He exuded a quiet fury that surpassed even his father's mastery. He was the spitting image of what I imagined Valen would be in ten years. Neo knew he was the most powerful force and most violent man in any room he walked into.

Although, I wondered about this particular room because Kane had always had an air of insanity about him that I was convinced made him more dangerous than any other man I knew.

"What?" Kane laughed – actually laughed – as he held up his hands and looked up at Neo.

Neo's eyes narrowed on his brother. "What the fuck do you think you're doing?" he asked, his voice quiet.

Like Kane, Neo terrified me. Like Valen, I knew that Neo would never hurt me. He was cold and detached but had never once given me the creeps. So, as far as Kincaid men were concerned, Neo was far favourable to Kane.

"Just having some fun," Kane said, pulling himself off the floor.

He took a step towards me, and Neo slid between us, as fluid as a dancer. "She is off-limits to you, Kane."

"The Callahan brat will be busy putting it into whatever whore he could get his hands on. He won't mind me having one taste."

Neo took a step towards Kane, towering over him with more than just height. "You do not touch her."

I could almost mistake Neo for caring, but he just sounded bored. I didn't know why he'd bothered stepping in, because he clearly didn't give a shit about what happened to me. Then again, Kincaid family obligation was real, and I guessed he was doing Valen's job where he thought Valen had failed. A failed contract on the part of any Kincaid would no doubt be considered a failure by all of them, and I didn't much like to think about what Cillian might do if he ever found out one of his sons had failed a contract.

"You can't babysit me every hour of the day," Kane taunted Neo.

"No," he admitted, a taunt of his own. "But someone *can* babysit Miss Vanguard every hour of the day."

Kane's face fell, but he rallied like a fucking pro. "You going to tell little bitty Valen how close I came to defiling his God's new fiancée?"

Neo took another step towards Kane and *I* fucking trembled. "Valen would kill you for so much as looking at her. Thank me for sparing your life by walking the fuck away. Now."

Kane seemed to know that he'd lost this battle, but it felt like the war was just starting. Neo seemed to think the same. After Kane had left, Neo whirled on me.

"*Never* be alone when Kane is around."

Like Valen, Neo seemed to say a lot with few words. Neo also seemed to realise what Kane was capable of and now it was clear what he wanted as well. I think I'd always known what Kane wanted from me, but I'd never wanted to acknowledge it. Now I had to. And now I knew he'd take it at any chance he could get, and it wouldn't matter what I thought about it.

I nodded quickly when Neo's eyes widened like he was waiting for an answer. "No. I won't."

"And do not breathe a word of this to anyone. Especially Valen."

I wasn't sure, but it felt like Neo knew something that no one should. "I won't," I promised.

Neo took a step towards me, and I instinctively cowered away, the memory of Kane as hot as his breath in my ear had been. Neo swayed away from me again like he was trying to be as unintimidating as possible.

"Stay vigilant, Miss Vanguard." It was the most emotive he'd been. He was practically begging me. "Even for the sake of fulfilling a contract with the Callahans, killing our own blood is a fucking mess."

I nodded. "Thank you, Neo."

He shook his head as he started to leave. "Thank me by making sure he can never touch you again."

And then he was gone.

I waited for a few moments, scared of leaving in case Kane was hovering around. But then, I was also terrified that Kane would come back to look for me. It was a conundrum, and it wasn't so much fight but flight that was battering on my ribcage.

Finally, I gave into it and let my feet carry me to my room. I forced a smile and slowed my pace for the few people I saw, then I was barricading myself behind my door, telling myself that it was safe. That, at the Callahan Estate, I was safe.

But no amount of reminding myself could make me feel clean again. I spent far too long in the shower, first just sitting under the scalding water and letting myself cry out all my feelings and then scrubbing at every piece of skin Kane had touched. When I finally walked back into my room, my skin still crawling and a bright shade of pink, I screamed in surprise to find a body waiting for me.

"Missus!" Marco said and all panic in me subsided.

Emotion overwhelmed me at the sight of not just a familiar face but a comforting one. I ran into his arms, and he wrapped me up unhesitatingly.

"Shh, ye're all right now, missus," he said, and I pulled away from him.

My mind was whirring. "What are you doing here, Marco?" I asked him.

He shrugged, pulling away from me and trying to play nonchalant. "I'm here early for the New Year's festivities. God was worried he hadn't seen you for a few hours, so I offered to break into your room to check on you."

I frowned as I looked him over. "Why are you really here?"

"I told ye," he said, sounding very defensive.

Pieces were falling into place.

Kieran O'Malley and my father having a meeting before we all started at Saint Benedicts.

Valen's cryptic words about double duty the night Marco and I had gone shopping in Bieityn.

The way Marco had spoken when we arrived at the underground fight club.

I didn't know if I was very clever or very stupid for coming to the conclusion I came to.

"Who owns your true allegiance, Marco?" I asked slowly, not sure I wanted the answer.

"What do ye mean?" he asked, trying to laugh it off.

"Who do you answer to, Marco?" I asked, putting as much of my new force and authority into my voice as I could. "Let's not pussyfoot about this any longer than necessary, eh?" I suggested.

Marco swallowed. "It's you, missus," he admitted. "My allegiance is to you. First. The week before we started at Saint Bens, my da and yours had a meeting. They made a deal that makes me, for all intents and purposes, your Angel first. I made sure to become one of God's Angels to help keep you safe. Lotta work that was, I'll tell ye. Talk about a business expense. That shite was…" He petered off at my unimpressed raised eyebrow. He inclined his head. "I am loyal to my God, but my Goddess comes first."

Well, that answered that question.

I took a deep breath. "Did Neo call you?"

He nodded once. "Aye. He did."

"He said I couldn't tell anyone."

"Ye can tell me, Harlow. Ye can always tell me."

I nodded now. "And I suppose no one is supposed to know? About you and me, not just…Kane." I told myself that saying his name out loud took his power away. It didn't.

"Aye, missus. You weren't even supposed to know."

I gave him a nod, wondering how that was supposed to work. "Okay. So, nothing needs to change going forward."

"Except I need to find an excuse to be here every time you are without making the wolf suspicious."

"I could just never leave my room," I offered, and he smiled.

"I think that would make him more suspicious."

"You're probably right."

"I'll leave you to get dressed. Neo's escorted Kane off the Estate and I'll be here until we go back to Saint Bens."

"Thank you, Marco," I said, not sure how I could properly show him my gratitude.

He shrugged. "It's my job, missus."

"A business expense?" I joked.

He laughed. "If you want me to take you out to dinner again, yes."

"I'll try to come up with every excuse for you to have business expenses to claim."

He tipped his head and touched his hand to it. "I appreciate that, missus." He turned to leave then stopped. "Oh, and congratulations, missus."

All the lightness he'd managed to give back to me was doused in a bucket of icy trepidation. "Thank you, Marco."

He gave me a nod and left me to myself.

I dropped on my bed and sighed heavily. "Floss is here tomorrow," I reminded the tears that burned my throat and pricked my eyes. "We can lose it tomorrow."

Chapter Fourteen

"Could Mrs Kincaid-Callahan be the new endgame?" Florence asked gently as we lay on my bedroom floor late the next afternoon.

We were half-ready for the party later and both hugging our own half-empty bottle of liquor. I'd cried and laughed and thrown pillows and hugged her tightly for a good few hours. Now I was feeling much better able to cope with my life, to put on that unwavering brave face, even if I was still sad and angry and scared.

I huffed a humourless laugh. "Mrs Kincaid-Callahan?" I asked. "You're suggesting I keep them both?"

She nodded. "I *am* suggesting you keep them both. Yes."

As attractive as that idea was… "I'm not sure I'd be allowed to keep them both."

"Says who? Shouldn't the Goddess of Saint Benedicts get to dictate if she wants a harem of men?"

Now I snorted, very much humoured. "Just how many men am I having in this harem? I asked.

"As many as you want."

I looked at her with a fond smile, feeling like maybe life wasn't quite as sad as it felt just then. Not when I had a friend like her by my side. And I knew that, no matter what contracts were drawn up for me, Florence Walton would always be by my side. And she was going to be with me now until we went back to school the next week.

"Just them," I answered softly. "I just want them."

Because I did. I still wanted them both.

Since the proposal, I was starting to doubt how much of me wanting Apollo stemmed from the knowledge I had to have him. But I clung to the way he'd made me feel in the month and a half leading up to Christmas. The way we'd honestly grown closer and been happy. I reminded myself I did love him. Even if our lives wouldn't be what we wished, I did love him.

Florence took my hand and held it tightly. It was the closest she knew I'd let her come to giving me sympathy now. In our world, we were only going to survive by being strong, and that meant no more meltdowns on my part. I had to tread my path and I had to survive it. I wasn't against a life with Apollo, but I had hoped everything would progress a bit more organically.

By the time the Callahan New Year's Eve party was in full swing that night, I'd almost convinced myself and Florence that everything was okay.

I was fine with the ring on my finger, and I was over the incident with Kane. Not that Florence knew about the Kane incident. Neo had been very specific, and I'd been a very good girl at obeying his instructions. I ignored the vague thought that Kincaid men had a habit of having a singular power over me, for good or bad.

The kids were outside under heaters and fires, and the adults were inside. It was hard to tell which group was drinking more, or who was pretending their function was fancier. We were all certainly dressed up to the nines in our best gowns and suits and acting like we weren't all years away from real adulthood. And I wasn't having a terrible time as Florence and I talked with Exie and Triss.

Then Valen walked out onto the patio, and I realised that nothing was okay, and that maybe it would never be okay again. I took a step towards him involuntarily. Florence grabbed my arm and coughed. I nodded to her and forced a smile.

"Holy shit. He looks like terrible," Exie said. "Where's he been?"

He did look like shit. Not his clothes. They were impeccable. He wore a black suit, black shirt open at the collar, and black shoes. His tattoos peeked out at the collar and sleeves. There was a grazing of stubble over his jaw that served to make him look even sexier than usual. But his colour was paler than usual. Ashen somehow and haunted. I hadn't seen him like that since he'd disappeared from school six weeks ago and come back a shell of a man. Apollo had been worried about him then as well. I hated to think what he'd been forced to do, this time or that.

"Harlow?" Exie pressed.

"Hm?" I asked, forgetting what her question was.

Triss laughed. "Harlow's been too busy with her new fiancé to keep track of who the tame wolf's been paid to kill now."

I forced my smile widen. "Of course. Leave that to the men," I said, and we all tittered.

The women stick together.

"Darling," Apollo said as he came up and put his hand on my back. "Can you make sure Valk gets a drink?"

I wondered why it was suddenly my job to get Valen, who was well known for his ability to find the booze if he wanted to, a drink. Then my hand shifted on my glass, I felt the weight of my ring again, and I realised why it was my job. I was officially our mothers. I was the host here and it was my job to see to it that everyone was having a good time and being taken care of.

"Of course, Apollo."

He smiled at the others, kissed my cheek, and then got caught up in Luis' attention.

"Excuse me," I said to Florence, Triss and Exie.

Florence looked a little bit like she didn't want me to leave her with the others, but then she might have just been worried about me going to talk to Valen. I gave her a nod, encouragement regardless of what her look had been, and swept away.

By the time I got to him, Valen had found himself at the bar no problem.

"Valen," I said, and he turned to me.

"What?" he asked.

I was supposed to be the good host, but I was going to make use of the moment I had. "Where have you been?" my voice was too plaintive. There was too much in it. And he noticed.

Suddenly on alert, he asked, "Why? What happened?"

Neo's words were loud in my head, and I shook it to clear them. "Nothing. I just… You just left."

He set his jaw hard. "I don't owe you anything, princess."

I took a step back. "No. I… No, you don't."

He looked over my head at the party going on around us. The night was at the tipping point between refined social gathering and raging kegger. Everyone was just drunk enough that the volume of each song that played was being turned up incrementally and soon we'd put aside all pretence of social acceptability and just be horny, drunk teenagers.

Unthinking, I brushed a piece of hair away from my face with my left hand and the movement caught his eye. I couldn't tell what went through his mind at the sight of the great, honking diamond on my finger.

When he spoke, his voice was choked and gravelly. "You asked about protection, princess–"

I was going to stop that right there. "I only have no barriers with you, Valen."

That didn't look like it had been the answer he was looking for. He set his jaw again and nodded shortly.

"Barriers," he scoffed, picking up a bottle of whiskey and pulling out the stopper.

I frowned, not sure what he was doing. "Valen–"

He kicked his head behind me. "If you'll excuse me, princess, there's a Magdalen over there begging for a taste of my cock."

What?

Given our situation, it wasn't him being with someone else that I objected to. I didn't have that right and I tried not to be jealous. It was the fact that he'd said it in such a way that his only intent could have been to hurt me.

"What?" I spat and he turned a truly spiteful grin on me.

My heart wasn't the only thing in me that sunk as his eyes went cold.

He looked me up and down like I didn't impress him, then shrugged as he took a swig. "What?"

"You…" I breathed out heavily. "What?"

He gave me a humoured huff. "What's wrong, princess?" he asked snidely. "You forget there are people in this world who don't live to please and congratulate you?"

I was torn between feeling upset at his behaviour and just plain angry. "You're the one who told me you weren't a choice, Valen. You're the one who told me to marry him."

Valen's face was blank. Bored. "I don't give a fuck what you do. You're not my problem."

Anger won out. "Fuck you, Valen." I started to leave, then turned back to him. "Like your life isn't yours, my life isn't mine. I… You know what I would have chosen." I turned on my heel and stormed inside, needing a moment to myself before I risked falling apart entirely.

But Valen wasn't done with me yet. He and his bottle followed me inside, boxing me against the wall in a darkened section of corridor. My run in with Kane flooded me but, as angry as I was with Valen just then, I didn't feel in danger with him, and I stamped down the fear.

"How much does it kill you?" he asked, his lips turned in a malicious smirk.

"What?" I breathed, not liking where this was going.

"Wanting quite possibly the only person in the entire world you can never have?"

How dare he turn my words back on me! And now? After everything? With such scorn and hate in his voice, in his eyes. Well, two could play at that game.

"Do not test me, Valk," I warned him, feeling the full force of the courage and power that flowed through my words.

If he was actually going to go through with this, then he had to know that was the end of it. For real this time.

"What are you going to do, princess?" he asked, begging me to try my worth against the mighty tame wolf, against the strongest avenging Angel of God. "I have the power. Not you. Every step we've taken, I've had you right where I wanted you. Now I'm done. I've had my fun with the little princess, and I'll move on."

A part of me threatened to crumple at his feet and never get back up again, but I refused to give him the satisfaction.

"I mean that little, do I?" I asked him, daring him to tell me it was true.

"You mean nothing to me other than an obligation as Apollo's princess. And now I don't have to pretend you're any more than that."

"Pretend?"

He ran his nose over my face as he whispered, "You were just some fun, Harlow. A joke to see if I could corrupt the princess. You did challenge me to do it, after all. What we had? Meant nothing to me. I just wanted to see if I could break the future goddess." There was such vicious glee in his voice that I found it hard to believe the tiny little voice in my head that said he had to be lying.

"What?" My voice was a broken rustle of leaves along the street in autumn.

He shrugged, still up in my space. "Consider it insurance for the next time I'm getting my arse kicked for him," he said simply. "I'll know I had his goddess first."

He pushed off the wall behind me and made to leave. My hand shot out and grabbed his wrist. He turned back to me, and I was sure I wasn't imagining the sizzle of sexual tension that wrapped around us. It wouldn't have been the first time that hating him had made me want him nigh uncontrollably.

There went a flicker of something in his eyes. Something that made me sure his words were a lie. I just didn't know why. What I did know was that, if he was enough of a dick to pull that shit with me, then I'd be more than happy to walk away. I knew my worth, as little as others seemed to think of it, and I knew I was worth more than that.

"You think you're good enough to break me? To ruin me?" I scoffed, levelling him with a fierce stare. "Don't flatter yourself, Valk."

Fury marred his features. "Still that delusional princess," he said scathingly.

I kicked my head behind him and threw his arm back at him. "Walk away, Wolf, before I tell your master you've been a bad dog."

Valen snarled at me, and I glared right back. He wouldn't break me. I wouldn't let him. I would give no one the power to break me. So, I stood my ground until he finally conceded defeat and walked away.

I'd been lying to myself the first time I'd walked away from him. Thinking I was okay with it, that I could walk away and just instantly, miraculously be over whatever insane attraction I had to him.

I knew now I was wrong. I could never walk away from Valen Kincaid.

One of us has to walk away...

Shamefully, I'd let him be the one to do it. I'd forced him to do it. I'd hung on to him long past my welcome and he was done with me and whatever sick and twisted game he was playing with me.

I told myself it didn't matter.

I told myself it didn't make me less just because he was an arsehole.

I told myself that I might love him – I might love him for the rest of my life – but I didn't need him. I was Harlow fucking Vanguard, the Goddess of Saint Benedicts, and I needed no man to survive.

And, after I told myself a couple more times, I started to believe it.

Chapter Fifteen

Florence came and found me in my room later, full of drunken swagger and a false belief that I'd spent the evening being ravaged by Valen.

"You know, the Callahan Estate might not be so bad if Marco keeps making me forget about those ghosts–" Then she saw my face. "What the fuck did he do?" she sighed.

I took a breath as I sat in my window seat. It was late but the parties were still raging. I had to wonder if the adults were having as much drunken sex as the kids were. I had no doubt that Apollo was in his room, probably with a Magdalen.

"Valen set me to rights about what I am to him."

"Ugh," she sighed. "Why can't that ever be said in a good way? Like, 'he fucked me raw, ripped off Apollo's ring, and replaced it with one of his own, and now he's going to war for me'. Why is it always a bad thing?"

"I don't know, Floss."

"You seem…okay. Considering."

I nodded. "I am okay. Considering."

"Babe…" she said slowly as she came to sit with me. "You're scaring me. You're way too calm right now."

I nodded again. "I am calm. So, what if I tasted freedom, Floss? My life is just the same as it's always been and there's no point wishing otherwise or fighting back. I won't survive and I won't thrive that way."

"Tell me what happened," she said kindly.

And I did. I was a little less calm at the end of it, though.

"I just… I can't believe it," I told her.

"I can," she said simply, and I looked at her for an explanation. "What?" she asked. "You might not have been cheating on your prince charming, but his tame wolf sure was."

"Valen was cheating on Apollo?" I huffed, thinking it sounded ridiculous.

"Yeah. Think about it. Apollo was off doing the dirty all this time, so he can't be angry with you for doing the same. But Valk's his best mate. If he knew Valk was doing his girl behind his back? Fuck, I wouldn't want to be the lawyers involved in that divorce."

Now she'd brought it up, it sounded eerily like something I'd said to Valen. How I'd promised Apollo nothing, but Valen had promised him everything. I saw the truth in that, in theory. But that was nothing like what Valen had actually said.

"Then why not just say that?" I huffed. "Why not just tell me he's doing it for Apollo? Why be suck a dick about it?"

"Have you met these boys?" Her eyebrow rose above her glasses frames. "They have the emotional range of a pebble." She shrugged. "Idiot probably thought he was doing the right thing."

It made a kind of sense. If I let myself believe that was what he'd been doing.

"I almost love him more for that," I whispered.

"Almost?" Florence asked.

I nodded. "Almost. But anyone who'd say those things to me, even if they *thought* they were doing the right thing, doesn't deserve me."

I expected cheering and agreement. But for once, Floss wasn't immediately in my corner.

"You disagree with me?" I asked her.

She shook her head. "No. Not at all. I'm just sad it all went down this way. I kinda had my bets on Valk being worthy of you after all."

I sighed as I leant my head against the coolness of the window.

"Yeah. Me, too."

"And what about your fiancé?"

I still hated that word – that title – for Apollo. It meant nothing. It had the power to mean a lot. It should have meant everything. But, just then, it meant nothing more than living someone else's life on someone else's timeline. And I hated him all over again for it.

"What about him?" I asked sullenly.

"Is he worthy of you?"

"I don't know yet."

"Well, why don't you go and find out?"

"Are you suggesting I go all Khaleesi on his arse again?"

"I am suggesting…" She nodded vigorously. "Yes. Go and do that."

I sat up, feeling a smile on my face. "Okay."

Florence blinked. "That took less convincing than I expected. I had a whole speech planned and everything."

I shrugged now. "There's no point wasting my life on a guy like Valen. He had his shot. He fucked it up. We both knew it had to end sooner or later. Now I can get on with my life."

"Do you…" she started carefully, then cleared her throat. "*Do* you want to get on with your life?"

I sighed. "I can't dwell on what might have been, Floss. I'll go mad if I do. In another world, maybe Valen and I would have been a romance for the ages. But I was promised to Apollo long before Valen claimed me. I have to look forward if I want to survive this. Besides," I added, "I do love Apollo."

"As well," she seemed to add for me.

I couldn't help giving her a grin. "As well."

I got up and checked myself over in the mirror. I hadn't cried so my makeup was no worse than the usual end of the night state. I was still in my tight-fitting silver dress. One I liked; I hadn't worn it with anyone else's admiration in mind than my own. I was thinking about someone else's admiration now.

"Are you not going to change?" she asked me.

I caught her eye in the reflection. "Why would I?" I replied, all sass. "I don't plan on being in anything for long."

"Ooo," she crowed. "I love you."

"I love you, too," I told her, blowing her a kiss as I slid out the door.

I scurried down the hallway, and straight to Apollo's door. If he wasn't there, I'd go looking. I didn't see anyone until I pushed open his door. There was indeed a Magdalen in there with him, though they'd only just started by the look of it.

"Harlow!" Apollo said, clearly surprised.

I didn't bat an eyelid. "Get the fuck out," I told the Magdalen, my voice calm and steady. No animosity. No jealousy. Just bored indifference to her inconvenience.

She looked like she was going to argue for the space of about a second, then I frowned, and she ran out of the room, clutching her dress to her body like it was covering anything as she left. Leaving Apollo gaping at me from his couch.

"Harlow, I—"

I shook my head as I closed his door and locked it. I stalked towards him; the woman Valen had given me room to become. I was confident and sexy, and I was going to claim my fiancé. By the time I walked back out of his room, there was going to be no confusion about who he belonged to.

"Babe?" he asked. He was currently confused but didn't sound worried. I wasn't in the mood to assuage him one way or the other.

I stopped in front of him and, in one smooth motion, I ripped his shirt open. Buttons popped everywhere, and I slid it off his arms with no bothers. I ran my hands down his body as I claimed his lips with mine. As we kissed, I deftly undid his trousers and slid my hand into his pants.

He breathed deeply as I stroked him, and his hands went to my hair.

"Babe–" he started again, but I shook my head.

"You're not in control here, Apollo," I whispered against his lips before trailing mine down his body.

When I got to his waist, I settled on my knees and pulled down his trousers and pants. I looked up at him coyly, through my lashes, as I ran my hand over his length and licked my lips. He looked like he was going to say something, but I just raised one eyebrow as though daring him to open his mouth. Like a good boy, he didn't.

But I did as I took him into mine.

It was the first time I'd gone down on Apollo but what better way to demand his submission than to offer my own first? This wasn't the battle for power that I played with Valen. This was to be a proper relationship of give and take. I couldn't just demand Apollo's obedience and know he'd give it to me. I had to show him he had mine and trust that he'd pledge his in return.

Apollo's hand rested lightly on my head, a connection rather than guidance. "Holy shit," he breathed.

I looked up and saw him with his head back on the couch, a look of intense pleasure on his face. I was under no delusions about the quality of my blowjobs, this being my second and all, but all indications suggested he didn't have any complaints.

With my hand at the base of his shaft, I blew him fast. My goal here was to quite literally blow his mind, then make him spend the rest of the night making it up to me. If my plan worked, I could walk out of his room again with some idea of where we stood.

I felt him start to throb. He started rocking his hips in time with my movements, pressing himself deeper into my mouth.

"Harlow, shit…" he murmured.

I couldn't help my smile as I worked him. I didn't care what the Magdalens did for him, I was just going to have to give him something they couldn't.

"Fuck," he groaned as his body twitched and he came in my mouth.

Not really knowing what to do with it, I swallowed before I gagged on it. Not that I was thinking about the consequences of a blow job for long.

Apollo pulled me into his lap and kissed me hard.

"Just give me…a couple of minutes," he said, breathlessly, "and I'll be ready to go again."

I quirked my eyebrow at him as I slid off his lap and stood up. I walked backwards, biting my lip at him as I did.

"Babe?" His tone was playful, excited. He wanted to know where this was going to go next.

I reached to my side for my zip and started undoing it. "I have an idea how you can fill those…few minutes…" I told him.

It did take him a second, then he was grinning. As he stood up, he discarded the rest of his clothes. He helped get me undressed as he kissed me, palming my breast in his hand like a man possessed. Then, in one fluid motion, picked me up and threw me onto his bed.

He looked down at me with a deep-seated heat in his eyes.

"You going to scream for me, baby?" he asked, and a thrill ran through me.

"You going to make me scream, baby?" I countered.

He huffed a rough laugh as he settled between my legs at the foot of his bed. "I'm going to make you fucking scream, babe."

He grabbed my thighs and pulled my centre to his face before burying it between my legs like there was no where else he'd rather be. Like I'd just done to him, his aim was to get me off hard and fast. The benefit of being a woman was that it was far easier for me to cum twice in quick succession.

After my second orgasm, he pressed a kiss to me and said, "Stay there for two seconds."

He got up and grabbed a condom from his bedside before resettling between my legs. I rested up on my elbows and looked at him quizzically. In answer, he just dragged me off the bed and into his lap, straight over his cock. We both looked at each other as he settled in me.

"Fuck," he moaned appreciatively as he nuzzled his face over mine, then started thrusting. "Shit, Harlow. You feel amazing."

We held each other tightly. The angle meant he really had to do most of the work, but it didn't stop the pleasure building up in me. Our foreheads rested against each other as we stared into each other's eyes, and he drilled me deeply. As my orgasm built, I wrapped my arms tighter around his shoulders and rested my head over one side.

As I came in his arms, he whispered in my ear, "It's only you, Harlow. It was always you and I've just been too fucking blind to see it. It's only you."

We kissed deeply as he came hard, and I felt a singular sense of satisfaction. He breathed hard, a wide smile on his face as he tipped sideways, and we lay beside each other, his head by my chest. Apollo kissed my breast tenderly.

I put my finger under his chin and made him look into my eyes. "Just remember who you belong to," I warned him.

I saw the smile in his eyes and the love that emanated from them. He looked at me with the very definition of puppy love. "Always," he promised.

I might have lost Valen, for good this time, but I had the means to build a happy life for myself. Apollo and I still weren't perfect, but we were working on it. And now it wasn't just a ring on my finger, but a promise in our hearts as well.

We spent the next two days basically locked in his room. It was probably a good thing Marco was there to distract Florence for the majority of the days and nights. Not that Florence was complaining at all. Apollo all-but told Archer to get fucked when Archer demanded his attention on something, and it was the first time I think I'd seen Archer have a shred of respect for his son. Trust it to be because Apollo was more concerned with fucking his fiancée than learning how to run his father's empire.

Back at school the next week, I committed myself fully to being

Apollo's fiancée. And I wasn't the only one. Apollo's eagerness for the perfect engagement didn't dissipate when there was a horde of onlookers or people who might consider romance to be a weakness.

As Florence and I walked into the dining hall at lunch on Monday, Apollo was faced with a Magdalen, his hands up and a haughty smile on his face. She had her body rather up close and personal to his and was shoving her tits in his face as much as she could.

"Well, here we go," Florence muttered to me as we walked towards them.

I tried not to expect the worst from him, but I knew him too well. He rose to the occasion and actually surprised me, though. Seems that he remembered the lesson I'd been rather literally pounding into him for the last few days about who he belonged to.

"Sorry," he chuckled to the Magdalen. "I'm a one-woman man now, Chloe."

"*You're* playing the monogamy card?" Chloe asked sceptically.

Apollo shrugged like he wasn't sure what she expected him to do about it. "I've been given my orders and I'm a very good boy."

Chloe stepped up even closer to him and ran her finger over his chest. "There's nothing *good* about you, Apollo," she purred.

I saw on his face that he liked the attention. How could he not? He'd been groomed for five years to enjoy the attention. To expect the attention. To know it meant that he was at the top of the hierarchy where he had to be.

Florence took my hand and Apollo's eyes just happened to flicker to me.

The smile that crept across his face was vastly different for me than the one he had in the face of the Magdalen trying to seduce him. It was deep in his eyes. There was a softness to the desire in his smirk. It was tender. It was special.

At least, that's what I told myself with another woman with her hands all over my fiancé.

I shook my head, telling myself to get over my reticence at

thinking of Apollo as my fiancé. Me feeling weird about it wasn't going to change the fact and wasn't going to help me go all-in here.

I gave Florence's hand a squeeze before sliding my hand free and stepping up beside Apollo. I draped my arm around him and looked the Magdalen over as though she meant very little to me. For the most part, she did mean very little to me.

"Can I help you?" I asked her as Apollo put his arm around me.

She looked at me like she couldn't believe I had the audacity to stand between her and my man. If the Magdalens thought I wasn't going to fight for Apollo, then they had another thing coming. New Year's Eve had told me one thing about myself; I did care enough to go to war with them if I had to.

"Can I help *you*?" she countered.

I leant towards her conspiratorially. "Walk away now," I told her gently. "And you might retain *some* dignity."

"You have your place, and we have ours," she seemed to be reminding me.

I smiled at her pleasantly. "Yes. My place is with my fiancé and yours is to stay as far away from him as possible."

She had the balls to be affronted. "Who do you think you are to tell us what to do?"

"Do not test me," I said to her, my voice quiet fury. "I am your goddess, and you will bow to me."

There was a flicker of respect in her eyes, then she remembered everything I was taking away from her with my authority, and she glared at me. But she seemed to know a losing battle when she was faced with one. She turned on her heel, a parting glance to Apollo as though trying to make anyone watching believe she didn't think he was all that.

In answer, Apollo didn't watch her walk away, he pulled me to him and kissed me hard. His hand found the bottom of my skirt and I very nearly forgot that we were in the middle of the dining hall in front of most of the school and I was about to let him stick his hand in my pants.

I pulled away from him, both of us breathing hard. "Behave," I warned him.

"For now," he agreed.

As we sat down, I realised that Marco and Valen were both gone. I didn't see Valen again except in the very vaguest passing in the corridor or in class until Apollo had bundled me into his car with the promise of a very wicked night out.

I told myself my heart didn't flutter at the sight of Valen getting into the front seat. Since he'd come back for the New Year's Eve party, he'd continued sporting the stubble on his jaw. It made him seem so much older, more dangerous, sexier. He looked like the man I'd always pictured him being in ten – twenty – years' time. The things he'd be able to do a woman by then…

I forced my focus to Apollo and kept it on him until we got to *La Freeze*.

"Miss Vanguard," Valen said smoothly as he opened my car door, the picture of hostile professionalism.

I nodded and took the proffered hand the way I was supposed to. "Valk." I climbed out of the car and released his hand as quickly as required. No slower. No faster. I would not give Valen the satisfaction of a single doubt in his mind that he'd affected me.

Then it was back to ignoring each other again as Apollo reached for me. I took his hand happily, quite content with turning my back on Valen.

Apollo took me inside where he'd hired out the whole of the ice creamery and made sure they stocked a heavy supply of rainbow.

"An ice cream date?" I laughed.

He shrugged. "We won't be able to go mattress surfing, but I calculated the shop should be long enough for sock sliding."

"You're lucky I wore stockings," I told him.

He pulled me to him hard. "Just so long as they don't hamper my access later."

I smirked at him. "Oh, trust me. They won't."

Valen was noticeably outside for the whole date. Not that I cared because I beat Apollo at sock sliding after he ran into a table and fell over complaining he'd broken his pelvis.

Chapter Sixteen

As nice as it was that Apollo and I were living the dream, a girl did need an escape to breathe without the whole world of Saint Benedicts watching her every move.

And I was quite lucky that I had a friend like Florence to help with that escape.

She snuck me out of Saint Benedicts and down to the next town over from Bieityn, where there was a club that we could get lost in. Not just figuratively to forget our – my – problems, but where there was very little risk of someone recognising us.

We had a few too many shots. Our dresses were just a little too short and a little too low. We danced like absolutely no one was watching. And we had a fantastic time.

No one bothered us. No one looked twice at us beyond appreciating our very fine figures and carefree attitudes. We let a couple of guys buy us drinks, but they didn't try anything else on.

"Do you think they knew they had no chance?" Florence yelled at me, aiming to be heard over the thumping music.

"Why would they? That doesn't usually stop the self-entitled arseholery that is the male species."

Florence snorted. "Maybe men actually respect a taken woman these days?" she asked as she nodded to my engagement ring.

I thought about it. For about two seconds. "Nah. I think we're just way too fit. They know we're out of their league."

We laughed, threw back our drinks, and headed back out to the dance floor.

We'd driven into town and had rented a hotel room so we could get as trashed as we wanted and not have to worry about driving back to school. Our room also let us get dressed and primped and primed without worrying that anyone at school would see us leaving with the clear intention of partying.

As it was, Gage had run into us on our way to the girls' dorm garage and I wasn't sure if he actually believed we were doing super-secret art shit for Florence's next retreat. He hadn't held us up though, and neither Marco or Valen had come running like they knew we were flying the coop, so I didn't consider Gage a problem or an obstacle to my night of escape.

In the wee hours of Saturday morning, Florence and I felt like we'd danced our feet off and we were heading back to our hotel room to put those feet in a nice hot bath while we drank some more wine and pretended that this could be our lives after we graduated high school.

"I still think a jacket wasn't worth it," Florence said, with a nod like she was convincing herself, as we huddled in on ourselves and waited for a car to pass so we could cross the street.

The town was pretty much deserted, just a few odd people here and there. They were the sort who wanted to keep their errands to themselves, those whose errands were best left in the darkened alleyways, or who just had better places to be than standing half naked in the snow.

"I'm beginning to regret my life choices," I huffed a laugh. "Looking good is so not worth sacrificing warmth."

"I totally thought we'd drink enough not to feel the cold."

"Sensible of us," I laughed.

"I don't feel that pissed. Do you feel pissed?"

I shook my head. "Not really."

"Maybe we danced all the alcohol off?"

"Is that how it works?" I asked.

She shrugged. "I'm an artist, not a biologist," she said, then my blood ran cold.

"Somewhere," a voice said sinisterly from behind us, "God's missing a princess."

Florence and I grabbed hold of each other and whirled to face the voice.

A guy walked out of the shadows, and we started backing up. Until we felt hands on our arms and then we were wrenched apart. All the better to control us, one would presume.

"What do you want?" I asked, embarrassed by the tremor in my voice.

"What we Black Bloods always want," he said. "To fuck with your God."

They were Black Bloods? Shit.

"He's not my God," I told them, as though that was going to make them say, 'Oh, terribly sorry. Our mistake. Have a pleasant evening,' tip their hats at us, and let us go on our merry way.

"There's no O'Malley here to save you tonight, goddess," the guy holding me sneered and fear shot through me.

I'd become complacent. I'd been told not to leave school grounds without Valen or Marco, and I'd wilfully disregarded it. After two weeks of – relative – safety at the Callahan Estate and no mention of the Black Bloods, I'd forgotten they were a threat. If I was stupid enough to forget about a bunch of arseholes clearly giving God and his Angels a hard time, then it seemed that I was probably not cut out to be a Goddess after all.

"No, but there's a Walton," Florence offered, then stomped on the foot of the guy holding her.

He swore and let go of her. Just when I thought she was out of reach, he flung a wicked backhand into her head, and she went down hard on the pavement.

"Floss!" I yelled, straining against the guy who held me. I looked down at his arms like that was going to help me get out of them.

That's when I saw something.

I recognised that tattoo as one Kane had. The one that had looked new. The rose with a cross stem and pentagram. I wondered what it meant. In our world, tattoos were messages, labels. It could be as simple as Angels getting matching tattoos after a particular fight or getting drunk and randomly picking something out of the tattooist's book, or it could mean affiliation. Sinister or otherwise.

Then I felt a blade at my throat, and I gave zero shits about anyone's ink. "The same fate doesn't await you, Miss Vanguard," the guy behind me said into my ear.

The first guy walked towards us, and I realised they were all wearing the same jacket. A black bomber with 'BB' in red on the left chest side. They probably had 'Black Bloods' scrawled across their backs like they were trying to be some motorcycle club.

"I'm going to enjoy making you bleed," he said with an evil smirk.

"I've been more scared," I told him harshly.

"Oh, I'm not done with you, yet," he said.

He stopped in front of me, and I squirmed against the guy holding me. I felt his knife slip and slice my right shoulder.

"Idiot," the first guy snapped. "Get them to the nest."

Then something hit me in the side of the head, and everything went black.

† † † †

I woke up with a pounding headache and tied to a chair back-to-back with Florence. At least, I hoped that was Florence behind me, trying to loosen her bonds.

"Floss?" I whispered.

"Harlow?" There was a flood of relief in her tone.

"How long was I out?"

"I don't know."

159

"Where are we?"

"Don't know that either. They put our phones on the table over there."

I looked around and saw what looked like an abandoned warehouse or factory. It was dirty and dusty and incredibly poorly lit. Some wan moonlight filtered in from outside and I could just make out pillars and boxes dotted around. There seemed to be some old machinery lurking in the semi-dark, but I was definitely not the person to ask about identifying shadowed machinery.

"I like what they've done with the place," Florence said, matter-of-fact.

"I hear hobo chic is making a comeback," I replied.

"Nice interrogation tactic, leaving us alone to shit our pants for a while."

"Very O'Malley-esque," I said, pretending I knew anything about it.

"From the school of Kincaid," Florence added, clearly picking up the joke – such as it was – because it was better than either of us acknowledging we might actually be in a bit of danger here.

"Of course, handed down from the Volkovs."

I felt her chuckle, then we sat in silence for a little while.

"So…" Florence started, and I felt her testing the bonds at our backs. "Is this the kind of escape you had in mind?"

I sighed and leant my head back against hers. "Yeah, not so much."

"We really should have told someone where we were going."

"Yes, thanks. I'll just go back in time and do that, will I?"

"That would be helpful, thanks."

"Helpful to who?" came a voice from the shadows. "If no one knows where you are, then all the more time for me to play with you."

My heart thudded. For all my newfound sense of confidence and sass, it didn't seem to extend to kidnapping situations. Thankfully, I had Florence as my backup.

"You lot seriously need to get over yourselves," she said. "It's been fucking weeks. Apollo will get his for being a total git but holding us hostage is not the way to get back at God and his Angels for a dodgy car race. Besides, he gives zero shits about me, and his retaliation is just going to be way worse if you do anything to Harlow here. Do you idiots not realise she's Reginald fucking Vanguard's heir?"

"You think this is about a dodgy car race–?" another voice asked, humoured.

But the first one cut off the rest of what he was going to say. "I've heard Callahan's inheriting everything anyway and that bauble on Miss Vanguard's finger is just a fucking flimsy attempt to make the claim legit in the eyes of the Council."

I blinked. "Council?

Florence seemed equally confused. "What Council?" she asked.

"The Nameless have rules, ladies," the first speaker said, all ominously.

"And who are they, then?" Florence asked. Her voice was as chipper as it ever was, and I was sure it was a tactic of her own.

"There's naiveté and then there's just plain idiocy," the first speaker said.

"Pretend I'm *really* stupid, then," Florence begged.

It was obvious he didn't believe we didn't know who the Nameless was. It wasn't the first time I'd heard it – them? – mentioned, but I still didn't really know who they were. I could take a few educated guesses though.

"Merging two of the most powerful families into one borders on breaking the Law against Legions. Vanguard and Callahan had better have something pretty fucking epic up their sleeves if they expect to get away with it."

I heard a crash to the left and looked over to see a door burst open.

"It also technically breaks the rules to waffle on about business to the women-folk, as nice as these two are," came Marco's voice.

"O'Malley," came the first voice.

"Two against five, eh?" That was Fender.

"Well, let's fucking go, then," Marco said.

"Get down," Fender yelled and suddenly bullets were shooting over us.

"Fucking hell!" I heard Florence yell, then we were tipped sideways, and my shoulder hit the cement floor with a crack. "How's your head?" she asked me, concern marring her voice

I winced. "Better than my shoulder." The cut stung against who knew what kind of dirt and grime my body weight was crushing it into.

"Good."

I didn't really know much about what happened after that. When my eyes weren't shut tight against whatever horrors I might accidentally see, flashes of gunshot cracked through the darkened warehouse. There was a lot of noise, and a fair amount of shit-stirring courtesy of Marco.

Finally, "Fall back!" cried a voice I didn't recognise.

"Take your dead with you and consider this fuckery done," Marco commanded.

There was muffled footsteps followed by silence, then finally I felt someone drop beside us and I curled up as tightly as I could.

"There now, missus," I heard Marco say calmly as Fender murmured something to Florence.

The two of them got us free and standing.

"How did you find us?" I asked. "Not that I'm complaining."

"I might have stuck an app on your phone that day we spent shopping," Marco said, but he sounded odd as he looked around like he thought they might come back. "When you'd been hanging out in a warehouse for a little too long, I figured something was up."

"You know you've made this worse?" Fender asked him.

"Of course, I did," Marco snapped, his accent sharp. "But they fucking started it."

Then he buckled, his hand to his side.

"Marco!" Florence gasped.

I dropped with him, looking into his eyes. "You have a habit of bleeding for me," I said softly, more in my tone and eyes that only he, my own Angel, would understand.

He gave me a weak grin, but the glint of mischief I knew well was in his eyes. "It's me job, Harlow," he said as firmly as the wound let him.

"He's not the only one bleeding," Fender said, touching his hand to my shoulder and I grimaced.

"I'll be fine," I told him, but still imagined a long antiseptic shower. "What can we do for Marco?"

"We need to get him to the car," Fender said, getting under one of Marco's arms. I took the other. "I can manage, missus," he told me pointedly.

"I know you can," I told him just as pointedly. "But so can I."

Fender gave me a nod. "He told me about the last time."

"Someone's going to kill me for bringing him back like this again," I quipped and, despite the situation, Fender grinned.

"Aye, missus. Someone will."

"That someone will be me if we don't get him to a fucking hospital now!" Florence yelled, bordering on hysteria.

Fender and I smiled at each other, and we got Marco to the car with no more incident.

Florence climbed in the back with him, and I got in the front, with Fender in the driver's seat.

"You might want to hold on to something," Fender warned.

I could hear Florence and Marco muttering what could have been mistaken for sweet nothings to each other as Fender took us up the mountain with the skill of a man who did it a lot.

"You're a very good driver, Fender," I commented dryly.

"You've definitely made this world your home if you're more concerned about my driving than Marco's belly," he replied, just as dryly.

I smirked. "Marco has a way of surviving. And I wouldn't say I'm worried. It was merely an observation.

As he expertly drifted around a corner, he threw me the biggest shit-eating grin I'd seen in a long time. "Who do ye think wins all God's races for him?" He punctuated the statement with a rather dramatic gear change.

"I don't care if it's your job!" Florence cried at Marco in the backseat.

"I'm fine," Marco told her. "Nothing like a knife to the gut to wake a bloke up in the middle of the night."

"Marco!" she snapped, clearly not impressed with his flippancy.

"How many contracts did you break tonight?" I asked him. "Potentially failing your God."

"All of them," Marco said, his voice weak. "But I fulfilled the most important one."

Warmth spread in me to know someone like him was so firmly in my corner. That warmth didn't last long.

"Marco!" Florence's cry this time was full of concern, and I looked back to see her shaking him. "He's passed out," she informed us, and I heard the hysteria rising in her voice again.

"Can you go any faster?" I asked Fender quietly.

"I'll do my best. But I'm not explaining to Valk why I put you in so much danger."

I frowned, not caring what Valk might whinge about now. "If Valen has a problem with it, he'll have me to contend with."

"A year ago, missus," he started slowly, "that wouldn't have been nearly as terrifying as it is now."

I chose to take that as compliment. "Thank you, Fender."

"An Angel swears fealty to his God," he said in answer. "An obligation. My loyalty to you is a choice."

Chapter Seventeen

This time, I wouldn't be sent to my room while Marco was seen for wounds that he wouldn't have had if not for me.

But I did send Florence to hers with Fender as protection, promising I wouldn't leave Marco's side until he was given the all-clear. After a few stitches and a couple of bags of blood, he *was* given the all-clear, but I still wouldn't leave until he woke up, and I refused any medical care until he did.

Which is why Apollo and Valen ran into the infirmary the next morning to find me bruised and finally being stitched myself.

"Babe," Apollo breathed as he took my hand.

"Give her some space, Mr Callahan," the doctor said. "You can paw at her once I finally get these seen to."

"How long have they been here?" he asked her.

"All night. But Miss Vanguard refused treatment until now."

"What?" Valen roared, and I didn't care for his audacity.

"I would have done something about it, but I was otherwise indisposed," Marco said sardonically from the bed behind me.

"I will deal with your fucking useless arse later," Valen snarled at him.

I frowned at Valen, heedless of the needle still attaching my shoulder to the doctor. "You can calm down or fuck off," I told Valen sternly. "You don't get to blame Marco for this."

"No?" Valen asked. "And who *do* I get to blame? You?"

"Yes."

"My fucking pleasure."

"Why don't we talk to Marco about what happened and leave the good doctor to finish up with Harlow?" Apollo suggested, throwing his authority into the mix of mine and Valen's swirling around the room.

Valen's lip rippled, but he let himself be led over to Marco.

The doctor sighed as she finished up with my stitches. "They pay obscenely well for my services, but they don't make it easy to do my job."

I didn't doubt that. "I'm sorry."

She smiled at me softly. "It's not the way of the women-folk to make excuses for the men," she said softly.

My eyes widened. "You're one of us?"

"Some of us," she explained, "make the money and the deals. Some of us make alliances. Some of us make the next generation. Some of us bleed for our betters. My family puts those who can be back together again as best we can. We all have our parts to play in the great machine that is the Nameless."

I frowned. "I keep hearing that. Who are they?"

She looked over to the men deep in conversation. I saw Valen and Marco keep sneaking looks to each other like they were hiding something from Apollo. I'd caught something about 'black blood', but the doctor distracted me.

"It's not my place to speak of them. I shouldn't have said anything." She put a final bandage over my stitches and stepped away from me. "If you need anything more, I'll be in my rooms."

Apollo waved a dismissive hand at her, but I smiled in thanks. She ducked her head in acknowledgement and hurried out. I slid off the table and went to sit by Marco.

"…and they thought taking Harlow would put an end to it?" Apollo scoffed.

Marco shrugged. "I don't know what they thought."

"It's been weeks since the car race. Why now?"

Here Valen and Marco exchanged another glance. Marco included me in it this time. I understood; we still weren't telling Apollo that this wasn't the first time I'd been put in jeopardy.

"Opportunistic?" Marco guessed.

I could tell he didn't think that at all. I was very interested in what he did think it was, but I doubted he'd be forthcoming in front of Apollo, let alone with me.

I looked up and saw Valen's eyes trained on me like he didn't dare take them off. I felt utterly naked under that gaze, but I tried not to be affected by it. He'd made his choice. Whether he thought he was protecting Apollo or whether he had been playing me this whole time, I didn't care. The choice was the same.

"Why wasn't Valk there?" Apollo asked Marco.

I was pretty sure it was because Valen was avoiding me and gave zero shits about what happened to me. But Marco's answer was just as valid.

"Because Valk would have just killed them all. Then we would have had five dead bodies instead of one to escalate the problem further."

"Of course, I would have. No one touches God's princess and lives."

A memory floated to me unbidden. *I'd kill any man who touches you.* But I shoved it away.

Had I been in a forgiving or forgetting kind of mood, I might have thought that his words were a bit emphatic. I might have thought there was too much emotional vehemence in his words to be from a man claiming I was nothing but a game. As it was, I didn't give a fuck what his motives were. He could just as easily have been acting the way Apollo wanted him to.

They argued some more about my safety and what they were going to do about it. Making extrapolations I neither confirmed nor denied with my insider knowledge of my experience. I was tired. I was numb. Emotionally. Physically, I ached in places I didn't even know existed.

My hands shook unless I held them firmly in my lap. My head still pounded and felt fuzzy even though the doctor had pumped me as full of pain meds as she felt safe.

I just wanted to go to my own bed and forget that the horrors of my world even existed.

"You're awfully quiet, Miss Vanguard," Valen said smoothly, and I realised there'd been a lull in their conversation for a for moments. "Care to tell us just where you've been in that get-up?"

Oh, I was getting mighty sick of the impudence of this jerk. 'That get-up?' I looked gorgeous. At least, I had before I'd been beaten and bruised and cut and covered in dirt.

"Leave her alone, Valk," Apollo said gently. "She's obviously tired and hurt."

"She's obviously been somewhere she shouldn't have been," was Valen's retort.

"What are ye?" Marco asked him. "Her keeper, now? Miss Vanguard has a right to go where she wants when she wants. She's nobody's prisoner."

There was a shadow hanging over Apollo and I didn't know what was going through his head. Was he just worried about me? Did he believe the insinuations in Valen's voice and think I was out with another guy? Although, mighty bold of Valen to suggest I was out with another guy when we'd never had to leave campus to be together before.

"Harlow," Apollo said firmly, "has a good explanation, I'm sure."

They all looked at me expectantly, but what did I have for them? I was too tired and wired from too much alcohol and adrenalin and medication to come up with an excuse. The only thing that played across my head was 'escape, escape, escape', and I couldn't tell any of them that Florence and I had sprung my cage just so I could have one night where I could be anything other than Apollo fucking Callahan's fiancée.

"Or she's hiding something," Valen said, crossing his arms.

"Harlow?" Apollo pressed, like he was entertaining the notion I was hiding something.

"Is there something you'd like to share with the class, Miss Vanguard?" Valen accused.

"Leave the woman be," Marco snapped at him. "Can't ye see she's been through a tonne of shit last night?"

"And who's fault is that?" Valen snarled. Apparently now, blaming just me wasn't enough and he was back to blaming Marco as well.

Marco and Valen squared off as well as they were able with Marco lying in a hospital bed, hooked up to an IV, and Valen standing imposingly beside him.

"If she has nothing to hide, she'd tell us what she was doing," Valen said firmly, as though that put an end to the matter.

"Do not mistake my silence for anything other than tiredness, Valk," I warned him, my voice low and even. "Florence and I went out. Is that a crime?"

"You have been warned—" Valen said quietly.

"About what?" Apollo asked pointedly as he looked between us all.

I raised my eyebrow at Valen, the corner of my lip going with it. If Valen wanted to truly reprimand me, then he was going to have to tell Apollo that this wasn't the first time I'd had a run-in with people wanting to use me to get to Apollo. The ball was clearly in my court because, for whatever reason, Valen and Marco seemed loathe to do that.

When Valen didn't answer, Apollo sighed, "All right, we're done here, Valk. This isn't an interrogation. Harlow's done nothing wrong."

Valen turned a steely glare on him. Valen clearly though someone had done something wrong, and I was done with him throwing his weight around after everything he'd said to me.

"If you've got something to say, Wolf," I said to him scathingly.

"Say it plainly. I realise monogamy is a new concept for the likes of the Saints, but that doesn't make it a myth."

Valen's eyes narrowed. "I would watch who you provoke, Miss Vanguard," he said, his tone dripping venom. "We pledged loyalty to our God, *not* his bride."

And with that, everything that was the hulking form of Valen Kincaid swept out of the room and it felt like everyone left behind breathed slightly easier.

"You need sleep, missus," Marco said kindly.

I felt a smirk rise unbidden. "Says the man who got plenty."

He shrugged. "Maybe you take the blade next time and get the sleep, eh?"

I smiled. "Maybe I will."

"I'll take you back to your room," Apollo said to me.

I nodded wearily and let him help me out of the chair. He said nothing as we walked to my dorm room, up the stairs, and to my door where Fender was still on duty.

"How is she?" I asked him.

He inclined his head. "I pop my head in every half hour or so. She's getting pretty sick of me waking her up, but doc's orders were to make sure she hasn't got a concussion and that's what I'm doing."

"Thanks, Fender," I said as I walked into the room and dropped onto my bed.

"I'll send Gage to take over," Apollo said to Fender.

"You're not staying?" I asked him.

He shook his head. "No. I've... I'm so glad you're safe, Harlow. I...need to go and debrief with Valk, though."

I felt like that wasn't the real reason, but I decided not to push him. I was too tired to bother anyway. It felt like, whatever it was, it could wait until I'd slept.

† † † †

When I found them all later that day, God and his Angels were regaling anyone who would listen with stories of Marco and Fender's bravery. They were in Apollo's room and the door was open and it seemed like people were streaming in and out for the story.

Based on their usual adventures, I didn't believe this could be their most exciting, but Apollo was acting like it was the most amazing and daring rescue in history. I smiled to see him, thinking this was what he felt for me. To him, it *was* the most amazing and daring rescue in history because they'd rescued me for him.

As I made my way through the crowd to Apollo, a Magdalen stepped in front of me.

"Yes?" I asked.

"Rumour is you've got a pussy made of gold," she sneered at me. "To keep him so enthralled. But those of us who know better know it's not your pussy, but Daddy's bank account."

I stiffened. I'd expected the Magdalens to fire back at me for cock-blocking them lately, I just wished they hadn't decided to do it the day after I'd been kidnapped by insane wankers.

"Either way, he's still enthralled," I shot back. The only way to win here was to not let her words get to me. I could agree or deny whatever I liked, and I'd keep the power as long as I remained uncaring and above it all.

"Is he?" she asked, cocking her head in question, like she knew something I didn't.

I looked to Apollo, who hadn't yet noticed I was in the room. No one else was paying the Magdalen and I any particular attention at all.

"You're an obligation," she said. "We are enjoyment. We are freedom." Her smirk grew. "We don't bruise so easily when he gets rough."

My jaw clenched in anger. "Well, no. But then he's only rough with toys he's going to throw away. The things he keeps are precious."

She grunted in fury. "You think he won't throw you away when you've outlived your usefulness?"

"I'm not so weak as to *let* him throw me away," I told her carefully.

Her hand flew out before I could register it and her fist collided with my lip. People noticed us now and the room was suddenly full of movement as Apollo and the Angels started heading for me.

"You what?" I asked, full of my own fury that she had dared touch me.

I balled my fist and smashed it into her face with my best swing behind it. I didn't think it was very impressive, it felt wayward and weak, and I felt my stitches pulling in protest. But she stumbled backwards. She screeched at me in anger and lunged for me again.

Valen stepped towards her with an arm raised like he was actually going to hit her, but Marco caught him before his fist could fall. It gave Fender and Gage enough time to strongarm the enraged Magdalen as Apollo finally appeared at my side.

"You will get yours, *whore*," the Magdalen sneered at me. She had blood dripping out of her nose, and I really hoped I'd been the one to make her bleed.

I nodded. "Yes. I will. I'll get *my* husband. You will not touch him again."

"You don't make the rules," she said.

Apollo stood firm by my side. "Harlow is my Goddess. If she lays down a law, treat it as though it came from me."

The Magdalen shrieked and lunged for me again, but Fender and Gage held her tightly as Apollo led me into his bathroom.

"Are you okay?" he asked me.

I huffed. "What's one more bruise? One more cut?"

He looked me over carefully. "Let me go and make sure she's dealt with and then I'll be back."

I nodded. "Okay."

He kissed my cheek and left me in his bathroom feeling like it didn't matter where I was because nowhere was safe now that I wore Apollo's ring. And, after he'd just proclaimed me the official Goddess of Satin Benedicts, I didn't think that was going to make it any better.

Chapter Eighteen

While Apollo, Marco, Fender and Gage were dealing with damage control and a screaming harpy of a Magdalen, Valen found me in Apollo's bathroom.

"Are you okay?" he asked me as I checked my bleeding lip in the mirror.

I frowned at him. "Last I checked, protecting Apollo gives you no obligation to pretend you care about me. I'm in no immediate physical danger, so you can kindly fuck off."

His fingers crossed around my arm, but the pressure was soft. Tender. "I can't fuck off, because I do care."

My frown became a glare. It had to. My heart was threatening to completely shatter. I couldn't deal with the knowledge he cared. Not when he'd discarded me. Not when I was bound to Apollo.

"Stop playing games with me, Valk," I snapped, ripping my arm from his.

He shook his head. "I'm not playing games, princess. Don't you understand?"

I blinked at him, uncomprehending.

He dropped his forehead to mine. "I will love you, Harlow Vanguard, with my dying breath. But until then… Until then, I have to hate you."

"What?" I breathed, my heart beating out an erratic panic in my chest. Like it was trying to skip for joy and sink in sorrow all at once.

He pulled away to look at me again. "I had to do what I did to protect you. So, I could keep protecting you. Because if Apollo ever finds out–"

"If Apollo ever finds out what?" the man – or God – in question asked, appearing in the bathroom with us.

Valen and I turned to find him standing with a quizzical raise of an eyebrow and his arms crossed. By the look on his face, Apollo knew or at least guessed the very thing he was to never know.

"Don't read anything into it," Valen said, feigning nonchalance scarily well. "She's had a few threats from a few places before now and we weren't going to worry you."

Apollo's eyes narrowed further. "You went to him?"

I swallowed hard, but I could tell Apollo the truth. "I went to Marco," I said, and I saw his eyes widen. He hadn't known that I'd found out about Marco's true alliance. Or maybe God didn't know everything after all. "Marco decided not to worry you, but…couldn't deal with every threat alone."

Apollo raised an eyebrow at his closest friend. "And you've been going behind my back for how long?"

"Ever since you started parading her around the school like a fucking target," Valen snarled, taking a step towards him. "Look where it's got her."

"It's barely bleeding, Valk," I snapped. "It's fine. I'm fine."

Apollo took a step towards Valen, and the two men glared at each other.

"And how long have you been fucking my fiancée?" Apollo asked Valen, his voice so low even I almost missed it.

"You watch yourself, *God*," Valen said, equally quietly. "We've got through a lot of bullshit, but there are some things even we won't come back from."

"And now you're lying to me," Apollo accused him.

"Not since you put that ring on her finger," he said, as though that was meant to mean something.

Apollo roared. Actually roared at him. All red-hot anger. He whirled on his heel and screamed at the others in the room, "GET THE FUCK OUT. NOW! OUT!"

I shivered. I'd never heard Apollo with that much absolute fury before. He'd been angry, but that had been calculated and calm. He'd been a man in control. The Apollo who was waiting in his room for his best friend wasn't calculated and he wasn't calm. He certainly didn't have a single shred of control.

"KINCAID," he yelled.

"Fuck," Valen muttered, resigned like he'd known this day was coming.

He spared me one, almost apologetic, glance before he went and faced the music.

"I will kill you," I heard Apollo say to Valen.

"Fine," was Valen's response.

I swayed forward and back, trying to get up the courage to go and watch two men I loved beat each other up. Fuck this for a joke. I steeled myself, reminding myself that this world would have me see far worse as Apollo's bride. I left the bathroom and was greeted with a torrent of emotion facing an immovable mountain.

Apollo's fist crashed into Valen's cheek, and Valen just took it. Hit after hit.

"Hit me back, motherfucker!" Apollo roared at him.

Valen's lip curled, and he spat blood. "I hit you and you're going down. Then you won't get to hit me anymore."

I didn't doubt it. Valen had taught Apollo how to hold his own in a fight, but that was a last resort tactic. If it ever came to that, the assumption was that Valen was dead, and Apollo would probably follow soon after. There was no way Apollo could hold his own, let alone beat, Valen in a fair fight. Thus, Valen would make sure Apollo had any advantage Valen could give him.

"This is all your fucking fault!" Apollo yelled at Valen.

"Really?" Valen scoffed back. "How the fuck is it my fault, *my liege*?" His voice was heavy on the sarcasm.

"That Magdalen wouldn't dare touch her if you weren't constantly distracting her and drawing her attention from me," Apollo said.

I thought that was rich. Apollo acting like he'd seen anything between me and Valen before now? Before he'd basically been told outright? I called heavy bullshit on that.

"No," Valen said sarcastically. "The Magdalen had no reason to think your relationship was anything but solid, especially not with your cock buried in her last night while Harlow—"

"Excuse me?" I spat, my head trying to wrap itself around all that.

Both boys froze and I knew that wasn't supposed to have slipped out. Whatever Valen and I had done or been, he'd kept Apollo's infidelities from me. And this time, they were actual infidelities. We'd been exclusive. We'd made promises. His ring was on my fucking finger after all!

Suddenly, all the push pull that I'd been feeling for the past five months felt like nothing.

All the guilt I'd felt over wanting Valen just melted.

I had a sudden blanket of clarity descend over me, accompanied by a chill of freedom.

Every tie I thought I had to Apollo. Everything I thought I owed him for all the reasons I thought I owed them, real and imagined. The unspoken promises I'd made to Frenella to save him from himself. The guilt for coming between these two friends. It all just…disappeared.

Apollo hadn't seen the real me. He hadn't let me shed my princess façade and look forward to a future where we were the only ones who could make living someone else's life bearable. He'd just made me exchange one façade – one set of masks – for another. Not intentionally, at least. He had that going for him. But I'd been so intent on making things work, keeping the Apollo I used to know, that I'd been whoever and whatever I needed to do that. I hadn't been myself, not fully.

Not the way Valen let me be, a small voice said inside, and I threw it away from me in disgust.

No, Apollo had talked about monogamy and marriage, and still been off wetting his dick in any idiot who'd spread her legs for him. And, this time, I was well aware I was one of those idiots.

I didn't like that.

I wouldn't have that.

"Harlow…" Apollo said carefully. The way you'd talk to an injured wild animal.

I shook my head, and I strode over to him. I pushed Valen out of my way, and poked Apollo in the chest as hard as I could. "Be very careful," I spat, "about what you say next, Apollo Callahan. Be really sure about what you say next," I warned him.

He actually had the fucking audacity to look to Valen for help. Unsurprisingly, none was coming. God might have called for aid, but the Wolf wasn't answering. Not this time.

"Enough, Apollo. We're done." I pushed him away from me and held my hands up in defeat. "Enough is enough."

"Why was it okay before and it's not okay now?" he asked me.

I gawped at him like the idiot he was. *Seriously?* "Because you lied to me. You told me it was only me. And I was stupid enough to believe you. Before, we'd never made promises to each other, it had all been our fathers. But then you made a promise, and you broke that trust. I knew I was making the wrong choice when I said yes. I knew it. We weren't ready. I know now we'll never be ready. But I let fear guide me, not love."

"Fear?" Apollo breathed, like it had been the worst thing I could have said to him.

"Fear of our fathers' retribution if they ever found out that I'd choose someone else if I could. Because you'd be blamed just as much as me. They'd blame you for being stupid enough to lose me, and I'd be blamed for being unfaithful. But no more. You were never worth me, Apollo Callahan." I looked at Valen and felt my heart hitch. "I'm not sure you were either. Which sucks because I think I'm in love with you anyway."

Apollo scoffed, obviously looking to gain back some of his composure. "You hate Valk."

I looked very pointedly at Apollo and reminded him, "I hate you, but that doesn't stop me loving you."

Apollo's eyes softened. "Then let's give it another go. I'll be better. I'll do better."

I shook my head. "I do love you, but I'm not in love with you and I never have been. I know now I never will." I pulled the crown ring off my finger and threw it on the carpet at Apollo's feet. "You can keep that ridiculously overpriced bauble," I told him.

"What about your engagement ring?" he asked, obviously confused.

I glared at him. "Unlike this," I waggled the fingers of my left hand in the air, the ring facing him, "that actually means something. Meant something," I corrected.

"Harlow..." he started, but I shook my head, not letting the pleading in his voice make a dent on my heart.

"Besides, I'll need it to keep up the charade," I said icily.

He looked at me like he didn't know who I was.

Good, I thought. It was about time that Apollo Callahan realised that not everybody loved him, his actions had consequences, and I was done bowing and scraping to his perceived superiority.

It was time I acknowledge that I'd lost Apollo the day that Valen had come into our lives. The day his father took him from me. I'd lost him and I would never be enough to help him find his way home. That wasn't a failing on my part, I wouldn't let myself ever believe it was. He wasn't ready and I wasn't waiting for him. He'd already shown me that my all wasn't enough to change him. Maybe one day, he'd find someone he could love enough to find his way back. But she sure as shit wasn't going to be me.

"Because we will be keeping up the charade, Apollo," I continued, my voice full of an authority I'd rarely fully flexed. "You and Valen will go on as you always have. Friends. Confidants. Partners in crime. You and I will do what is necessary to keep people thinking we're still engaged. Somehow, we'll work out how to either live this lie or get out of it without killing anyone. But I'm not in the mood for that right now and I'll let you know when I am. Until then, it's back to faking it until we're forced to make it. Understood?"

Apollo looked like he was going to argue, but something was holding him back. He didn't look to Valen. He kept his eyes on me and I saw the resignation hit him. He knew he'd cocked up royally. He knew it and he was owning up to his mistake.

Finally, he nodded and sighed. "Okay. Yeah. I agree. As much as I want to be, I'll never be able to be the man you need me to be. We're just not…"

"Like that," I finished with him, and he nodded again.

"You're in charge, Harlow," he said, his tone promising more than his words ever would. "We go at your pace, your instruction, everything."

I nodded. "Good."

Apollo did now look at Valen. "What about Valk?" he asked.

I glared. "What about him?"

"You said you're in love with him–"

"I say a lot of things about him that he doesn't deign to comment on," I said harshly.

"Well, are you going to give him another chance?" Apollo asked.

I wanted to ask him if he was seriously playing wingman right now. As much as a part of me was proud of him for trying to mend the cracks between them in the only way he could see right now, that wasn't in my best interest, and I didn't want to be between these two men any longer than I had to.

"Another chance?" I scoffed. "After the way he threw me away?"

Apollo was clearly at DEFCON 1 wingman mode. "He was thinking of me, of the contract between our fathers–"

"Yours and mine, or yours and his?" I asked, sceptically.

Apollo nodded. "All right, fair. He was just trying to do right by you–"

"If Valen wanted to do right by me," I said, looking at Valen but continuing to talk to Apollo very pointedly, "then he'd speak to me. He'd be the one championing his chances–"

"Would it make a fucking difference?" Valen growled, his arms crossed over his massive chest.

"Weirdly, Valen," I said, all sarcastic awe, like it was a novel idea. "Yeah, it might."

We all looked between each other like we were waiting for anyone else to speak. Apollo was making eyes at Valen like he was telling him he needed to say something.

"Well," Apollo finally cried. "Fucking say something!"

"What do you want me to say, princess?" Valen snarled. "You want me to say I'm in love with you? You want me to say I want the world to know you're mine? That my heart could never belong to another? That I'll die with your name on my lips and your smile in my mind?"

He spoke sarcastically, scathingly even. Like it was all a joke. Like he could never possibly think any of those things. I should have said I knew better. I should have said I knew he just didn't know how to talk about it and that was the only way he could. But they'd both hurt me, and I didn't want to know better just then.

"I've heard enough lies from the both of you," I told him, feeling my heart breaking all over again.

Valen's scowl deepened. "Because all our kind are liars."

"You've shown me I can't trust your words. You tell me you're done with me, that I was just fun, a sick game. You tell me you'll love me until you die. I've got fucking whiplash from whatever high and mighty ideals you think you're following, and I deserve better! I did nothing but give you everything I could, Valen. I gave you both everything I could give you. I gave Apollo what I thought he needed to save him from this path of destruction our fucking world has set him on, and it wasn't enough. I gave you – Valen – I gave you all of me. Everything I was it was yours. And you threw it back at me. You told me it wasn't enough. So, I'm done with both of you. Only absolutely epic levels of grovelling could save you now, Valk, and, even then, I don't know if I can forgive you." I took a deep breath as I realised how much my voice was trembling. "Although I doubt that I'd ever be enough for you to even apologise, let alone grovel."

I looked at them both one more time, took a deep breath, and started walking to the door.

"Harlow…" Apollo started.

I shook my head before I walked out. "No, Apollo. I deserve better."

I walked away from both of them. Two men who held different pieces of my heart. And no amount of knowing I deserved better made it easier to walk away without them. It hurt. It fucking hurt so much. I couldn't remember anything hurting like that.

Not when Valen had discarded me; I'd been in serious denial about my feelings for him and the depth of my need for him.

Not when I'd heard Apollo had cheated; I'd been relieved because it meant I was free. Emotionally at least.

I suddenly viscerally knew what the phrase 'heartbroken' meant. I was sure I could feel the pieces of my heart actually breaking. It wasn't so much shattering as it was fraying and dissolving into nothing, like ashes blown away on a mournful wind.

I made it back to my dorm with my head held high and my eyes dry.

But once the door was closed, I fell to the ground. The dam crashed open, and I was floored with the weight of the flood that battered me. My world felt turned upside down, over and over like I was caught in a riptide and couldn't find my way to the surface. Every part of me felt bruised and I wept until I felt like nothing more than a hollow carcass on the carpet.

Florence finally found me in the foetal position in the middle of the floor.

She bundled me up in her arms and I cried again. She had no questions. She let me get it all out until I didn't think I had any more to give and kept going still.

When the tears finally subsided and I felt like I wasn't going to start again…just yet, I looked up at her and saw nothing but support. Well, support and a desire to hurt whoever had done this to me.

"Do you want to talk about it?" she asked softly.

I knew that cost her quite the effort. Florence was the nosiest person I knew. She was dying to know what had happened, who had hurt me, and where to aim her fist, or whose jewels to aim her foot at. But she wouldn't make me if I didn't want to or couldn't.

I shook my head, but not because I didn't want to talk about it.

"That's okay," she said, holding me close.

"No," I sniffled. "I mean…" I took a deep breath. "It was both of them. It was me. It… It's all over. For good."

I could feel the questions buzzing in her, but she didn't press.

"This Magdalen attacked me–"

"What in the actual fuck?"

I gave her a damp smile that suggested she keep her mouth shut and she'd find out.

"Sorry," she said, trying to hide a smile of her own. "Continue."

"She full on came at me. To the point even Valen lifted his hand to her. Marco grabbed him before he could hit her, and Gage and Fender grabbed the Magdalen, but Apollo noticed. Apollo noticed Valen was going to hit a woman. For me. Then Valen comes up and asks if I'm okay–"

"After everything he said?"

I nodded. "After everything he said. And while he's *defending* caring, Apollo overheard him say that he can never know. So naturally, Apollo's putting more pieces together. Then! Fuck, Floss…"

"What?" she asked. "Don't end there!"

I took a breath. I wanted to tell her, but I also needed strength. "They fought. Well, Apollo hit Valen and got mad Valen wouldn't hit him back–"

"Valk would have fucking killed him."

I nodded. "Right? Anyway, they're both blaming each other for the Magdalen attacking me…and Valen lets slip that Apollo fucked her–"

Florence rolled her eyes. "Was she feeling sour about being replaced?"

"Last night," I finished, and Florence's eyes bugged out of her head.

"The actual fuck?" she said, her voice dangerously low.

I nodded again. "Yeah. So, words were said. I told them both to basically fuck off and neither of them were worthy of me, and I walked away. Apollo tried to get me to give Valen a second chance and agreed to continue faking this bullshit until – if – we can get out of it without killing anyone. But the worst part, Floss?"

"There's a worse bit?" she whispered.

"Valen said…" Tears threatened again, but I held them back. "He said he'd love me until his dying breath, but until then he had to hate me…"

She gave me a sympathetic smile and brushed the newly falling tears from my cheeks. "What did you tell him?"

"That I was in love with him, but even epic grovelling might not make me forgive him."

She laughed.

"What?" I asked.

"Good," she said. "Make him work for it for once."

I shook my head. "He won't."

She shook her head as well. "You don't know that."

"We are talking about the same guy, right? The one you accused of having the emotional range of a pebble?"

She nodded and brushed my hair off my face. "Yeah. We are.

Apollo's not standing in his way anymore, babe. The four of us are the only ones who know beyond a shadow of doubt that you and Apollo aren't for real. If Apollo's in Valen's corner, do you think he's not going to try to make amends with you by getting you and Valen together?"

I took a deep breath. "That sounds exactly like Apollo."

"Well, the Apollo you tell me is in there."

She might refuse to see that Apollo – and maybe she was right that he didn't exist anymore– but I noticed she didn't argue with me about his existence anymore.

I smiled despite myself. "Yeah."

"So, just give them time."

I shook my head. "I'm not waiting for my life to start anymore, Floss. If Valen proves himself worthy, then fine. But I'm going to live my life."

"Fucking-A," she laughed.

Then reality squashed a little of my newfound strength. "Although, if I do forgive Valen, I don't know how I'm supposed to be with him while I'm still faking being with Apollo."

"Look," she said carefully, and I knew something big was coming. "If Valen manages to prove himself worthy and we forgive him, I will double date with you and 'Apollo'." She even did the air quotes. "Between the four of us, we'll find a way for you to be together."

I shook my head, this time smiling. "You and Apollo. Between you, you'll make it work."

"You better believe it."

"You might find you two make a good team."

She actually shivered. "Ew. No. Apollo and I will never be a team."

I didn't really believe they would, but I did believe they'd put their differences aside for me if they had to. But then, that all hinged on Valen making an effort and me forgiving him. So, thus far, Team Apollo and Florence was nothing more than a moot concept.

Chapter Nineteen

On Monday, life went back to the way it had been at the start of the year.

Apollo and Valen were indeed thick as thieves, they planned their kidnappings and car races and fights and whatever else the men decided needed doing, side by side as our world intended. They were seen at the Saints' shenanigans again – polite way of talking about their drug- and alcohol-fuelled orgies. There were no obvious signs of fractures between them as they lorded over the school the way they always had.

I was miserable without them both. Even knowing I was better off that way, I was still miserable. So, I did what I used to do as well and stuck with Florence, letting Apollo do what – or who – he wanted when he wanted it. In public, Apollo kissed my cheek and I smiled at him politely. We even went to a faculty dinner together and played our parts perfectly, as decorum dictated. But that was the extent of our contact.

There was, though, one major difference; no longer was I seen as the meek and mild Princess Harlow.

Saints gave me due deference, even the guys.

Magdalens didn't dare put a toe out of line.

And, according to Marco, Apollo spent the next week celibate, despite going to every orgy. I hadn't told Marco all that had gone down, but he certainly guessed.

"Missus, can I ask ye something?" he said while he joined me on a stroll around the grounds the next weekend.

I might have been ignoring Apollo and Valen, but that wasn't going to stop the Black Bloods if they chose to come for me again. Or Kane. I'd been an idiot once. I wasn't going to be an idiot again. About my safety or my heart.

"You can ask, Marco," I said.

He nodded. "Fair. I just… Valk's posted up in the infirmary," my heart lurched, but I said nothing, "after hunting down some Black Bloods, you're suddenly talking a daily constitutional, and God's nary even looked at a Magdalen for over a week now…"

"Get to the point, Marco," I snapped, and was thankful he was a good enough friend and confidant not to take it personally.

"What the fuck happened?"

The fact it had taken him a week to ask showed his restraint, but he wouldn't have missed the fact that his God had ordered everyone from the room, then turned up with bruised knuckles to match the new ones on Valen's face. He might not have known the intricacies, but he knew something had happened between the three of us.

I stopped and he pulled up hard. "What happened?" I asked, as though he was going to have to be more specific.

"I'll put it a different way, what did Valk do?"

I swallowed hard. "Why do you think he did anything?"

Marco reached for me, and I let his hand trail down my arm to take mine gently. "I know, Harlow. I know it all."

Okay, so maybe he did know the intricacies after all. "How?"

He shook his head. "I saw you and Valk coming like a fucking derailed train since your birthday. The way you looked at each other. The way you didn't. Valk's been hard for you since the day he first fucking saw you. And you were no better."

I scoffed. "So? We hate each other."

"There's a fine line between love and hate, Harlow."

Of that, I was well aware. I sighed. "It doesn't matter, Marco. It's over."

"I see that, missus. It's written all over all three of your faces. It's all over the deep shade of blue of both God's and Valk's balls. What I want to know is why."

I didn't know about their blue balls, but I hadn't seen it written on Apollo's or Valen's faces. There were other hints they weren't as happy as they acted, but to everyone else they looked just like their usual level of tomfoolery and fuckery. Valen had even cracked a smile or two in the last week. It might not have reached his eyes, or counted for a smile on anyone else, but it was there.

Not that I'd been staring at him every time I saw him to have noticed.

"I *could* tell you it's none of your business," I told Marco.

"Aye, you could."

I sighed. "But I won't."

He grinned. "No, you won't."

So, he may as well know it all.

"I fell in love with Valen," I said with a pathetic shrug. "I *thought* I'd fallen in love with Apollo. Valen threw me away. And Apollo broke my trust. I'm still in love with Valen. I do love Apollo but only like a friend, or maybe a really annoying brother now I think about it. And I hate them both."

Marco blew out heavily. "Phew. That's a lot."

I nodded. "You asked."

"No. I know."

"Does Valen know…that you know?" I asked him.

Marco nodded. "He does. We've had words. We'll be having more now. God, too."

"You don't need to. Not on my behalf."

"I *am* going to tell you that's not your business, missus."

"I'm not sure I'll ever be your God's 'missus', Marco."

"Maybe not," he agreed. "But then we both know he's not just my God, is he?"

"And what else is he to you?" I teased.

"The man who broke my Goddess' heart."

I nodded, finding less humour in that than I wanted, but it warmed my heart to hear it. "My heart's not quite as broken as I thought. Not unmendable, anyway. It hurts. They both hurt it, but I did have a part to play in it."

"You can't help who you fell in love with."

"No," I agreed. "But I can help how I deal with it. I might love Valen for the rest of my life, but I don't have to let it cripple me. We never would have worked anyway, so it's better left in the past. I might still have to marry Apollo and, at some point, I'm going to have to deal with that."

"Do you think you can break the contract?"

I shrugged. "I don't know everything about it. I refuse to give up all hope, but it's dim and, I suspect, futile."

"I don't know everything either, missus, but I'll stick my ear to the ground and see what I can do."

I nodded. "I appreciate that, but that's not your battle."

He winked. "That's the best part, missus. It is. I'm contractually obliged to fight for you, to put you first. But I'm concerned that only another offer of marriage will possibly be enough to break the contract."

"Are you offering?" I asked with a smirk.

He laughed. "Fuck, no. I'd be a piss weak option. I'm a confident man, I've got a lot going for me, but not nearly enough to make Reginald Vanguard rethink his debt to Archer Callahan."

I didn't think I'd ever heard it called a debt before.

"There's a debt?"

Marco paled. "I quite possibly shouldn't have said that."

"Marco…what do you know?"

He sighed. "Only what me da told me. That Callahan saved Vanguard and the price was his empire. I don't know how or why God's dad saved yours, but if Vanguard gave up his empire in payment, it must have been big."

Dread settled in the pit of my stomach. Marco's words had brought back a memory. A memory that had faded until now. On the eve I was promised to Apollo. My mother and I sitting in my room at the Callahan Estate, her worrying about what had happened and what was going to happen.

"This whole thing is far bigger than just signatures on some paper, isn't it?"

"It seems that way. But I will always be by your side, missus."

I sighed heavily. "I'd say thank you, but I'm sure you'd just say you were contractually obliged," I tried for some humour.

He smiled, wide and warm. "Aye, I would. But you have more than earned my loyalty, Miss Vanguard," he said solemnly. "I would die for you because it's my job, but it would also be my honour. You have grown into a remarkable woman, and it is my privilege to be in your service."

I felt tears threaten and huffed a laugh to keep them at bay. "Marco, who knew you were such a soft-touch at heart?"

He wrapped me in a hug with a huffed laugh of his own. "Take that to your grave, miss."

I noticed the change in moniker, but I didn't bring attention to it. I took it and appreciated it for the gesture it was.

We pulled away and I wiped my eyes dry.

"What is it Florence says, miss?" he asked me cavalierly. "Tea and cake?"

I smiled. "That she does, but I'm paying."

"But my taxes, miss," he whined jokingly as I linked my arm with his and we headed for the café.

Life might have been a bit shit, but I would survive. I would survive and I would make sure I would thrive. And I had people around me who would help me with that. Starting with my very own guardian Angel.

† † † †

The next Thursday, my phone buzzed.

Apollo

Can we talk? Before the holidays. Please?

I looked at the message and sighed.

"What's up?" Florence asked.

"Apollo wants to talk."

"About what?" she asked very quickly.

I shrugged, ignoring the squeak in her voice. "I don't know. He didn't say."

She cleared her throat. "Do you…*want* to talk to him?"

After talking to Marco the weekend before, I did.

I didn't think that Marco would embellish Apollo's behaviour. He wasn't that kind of guy, and he *was* professing to be fighting my battles. So, I believed him when he said Apollo wasn't instantly back to fucking any idiot who'd spread her legs for him. I chose to see that as Apollo growing as a person. Maybe he didn't even realise it yet, but it was a step forward. Or back, in his case. Back to the decent guy I knew was in there somewhere.

When I'd told Marco that Apollo was like a really annoying brother, I think I'd finally hit on exactly how I felt about him and had felt about him all this time. He was ingrained in my soul as someone I could never choose to live without, but that didn't mean he wasn't going to fuck up or piss me off. It did mean that I knew, eventually, I was going to forgive him, and we'd get past it. Because family was, annoyingly, like that.

The only problem was that I was currently still mad at him. I was mad at him *and* I missed him, and I didn't like feeling either of those things, even if he totally deserved both and more.

"I'm going to have to at some point," I told Florence. "I might not want to marry him and have his babies, but I do love him, and I do

191

miss him."

"Even after everything?" she asked.

I nodded, feeling conflicted. "He's like family, Floss. I don't want to forgive him yet, but I don't want to be mad at him forever either. He's like a part of me I can't let go of no matter how much he fucked up. It may as well be now."

She nodded slowly. "Okay…"

"You disagree?"

She shook her head quickly, her curls bouncing. "No! No, I don't disagree. I just don't want you to feel obligated one way or the other. I want you to stick to the whole doing things at your pace, no more people pleasing unless it pleases you."

I smiled at her. "Thanks, but this isn't for him. It's for me."

"Okay. Good. Let me know how it goes?"

My smirk grew as I finally took in her demeanour, and she was unusually agitated. "Why does it feel like you expect him to say something scandalous?"

She blinked. "Uh. Don't know. I guess I just know him?"

"Sure," I said. "Why not."

I decided not to press her. She was probably just nervous about her next Art retreat. If she wanted to talk about it, there was nothing I could do to stop her. If she didn't want to talk to me about it, there was also nothing I could do about it.

Harlow

I'll meet you at the café in ten minutes.

"In the meantime, can I bring you back a croissant?" I asked her.

"Yes, please. That would be awesome."

Apollo

I'll be there.

Thank you, Harlow.

I collected up my phone, grabbed a jacket, and headed down to the café.

On the way, I saw Wyatt and Smith. They both inclined their heads to me in deference.

"Harlow," Smith said evenly.

I nodded back to them. "Boys."

"Have a nice day," Wyatt said.

It was pathetic really, the inane small talk they directed at me now. But instead of feeling outside it all like I used to, I felt above it all. Above *them* all. They'd raised me up onto that pedestal that Apollo had once had me on, and they worshipped me accordingly. To them, I was the Goddess of Saint Benedicts and, while I still showed the world the pastel-wearing proper lady, they all knew I had claws when I needed them. They also knew *no one* was safe from those claws.

It wasn't what I'd wanted at the start of the year, it wasn't what I'd envisioned when Apollo and my relationship inevitably changed, but I found I was fine with it. It was preferable, actually. Had they tried to buddy up to me, it might have been harder to maintain the lie that Apollo and I were still the happy couple. As it was, I had to be aloof and cold, pretending I was so full of myself as the properly crowned Goddess of Saint Benedicts, because no other explanation would hold.

When I walked into the café, Apollo was already there, tucked away in a back corner where we'd have some privacy. I saw he had two cups between him and assumed that he'd ordered for me, so I made my way straight there.

"Harlow," he said, with his warm fake smile.

"Apollo." My smile was just as warm and just as fake. I leant down to kiss his cheek before taking the seat across from him. Always the charade. "What did you want to talk about?"

He nodded. "Okay. Straight into it. Fair."

We leaned closer together to aid in both the pretence of being madly in love and to avoid being overheard.

"I won't try apologising again. I know it won't help. Instead, I want to talk to you about how we break the news to our fathers."

"About what?" I asked.

"About us. About the fact there won't be a wedding."

"We can't just break the contract, Apollo. Do you even know what's at stake?"

He levelled a look on me. "I know better than you, Harlow, but it's the least I can do after I fucked up so badly."

I shifted uncomfortably in my seat. "You're damn right it's the least you can fucking do, but I won't have people die because you couldn't keep it in your pants!" I hissed.

His hand reached for mine and I had to force it to stay there so people didn't see me snatch it from him. He gave it a light squeeze before slowly sliding it away – keeping up the ruse while also realising I didn't want him touching me. He got a point for that. Maybe half a point.

"Harlow–"

"Look," I interrupted. "I know this wasn't just about you being unable to keep it in your pants. This is about the fact that we didn't love each other right."

"Harlow, I do love you…" he disagreed.

I sighed resignedly. "And I love you…"

"But just not like that," he finished for both of us.

I nodded. "No."

He looked down and took a breath. "I confused the love I feel for you with teenage lust and the knowledge we're expected to marry. I love you, so much, but it's platonic. No. More like familial. What I felt for your body and for you as a person…they weren't…"

"Connected," I finished for him this time, and he nodded.

"Exactly."

"Like they were separate things. We were friends with benefits – amazing benefits, true – but then also just really good friends."

He nodded. "I confused the two and that meant I wasn't… I didn't treat you the way you deserved."

I sighed. "I didn't either."

im   his head. "I made promises and *I* broke them, Harlow."
           reach for his hand, and he wrapped it up tightly. "And
           you needed."
           on you."
we   head. "No, it's not on either of us. But I'm still sorry
ntic
l for   Me, too."
ell, I   t forgiven you," I warned him.
you.   t." He paused. "What about Valk?"
so I'd   nd from his, heedless of any watching eyes. "No.
t like   ut him."
urvive   towards me. "Harlow," he said softly. "He only
but it   you'd choose me. He was doing his duty. The one
           beaten – for Valk, quite literally – into us since
in his.
           snapped quietly. "I don't want to hear it. Okay?
n. "No.   cks. But once, just once, I'd like to be worth
           You know? It's a silly and futile wish, but
now he   vorth breaking the rules for just once in their
ike that. ear trying to steal down my cheek and cleared
t me on   talk to you about anything but him."
           long, I thought he was going to keep pushing
er of us   e didn't mention Valen again. "Okay. Where

our in it.   I asked.
           he breakup. People will start to guess
           school, our families."
How to be No one can know until we know if our
           ct. We can't risk it, Apollo."
pollo. Our we just keep on going, then?"
words from ice. We're back to the way things were

ole lifetime

I forced myself to take his hand because, as much as I did hate h
just then, I also loved him. "I hate you and I love you."

He nodded. "Can I...?" he started.

I shrugged uncertainly. "I guess so."

His fingers played with mine, but the way they used to when
held hands for the pretence, a platonic fidgeting rather than a rom
playing. "I think I realised it all. About us. The way we really fe
each other. I realised it when I found out about you and... W
didn't feel betrayed by you at all. I actually thought, good on
But...him?" I noticed he was being careful not to say His name,
let him continue. I think we both needed him to. "His betrayal c
a knife, Harlow. We rely upon each other to literally fucking s
and he..." Apollo sighed. "I'm not advocating on his behalf,
made me realise he must love you."

I cleared my throat and shifted in my seat but left my hand
"Sorry," he said.

I shook my head, as much to clear the tears as assure hi
It's... Go on."

Apollo shook his head as well. "He wouldn't have... I
wouldn't have if he didn't. He's not like that. He and I aren't
He's my brother, Harlow, in all but blood. He'd never hu
purpose."

I took a breath. "No," I agreed. "He wouldn't. Neith
would."

Apollo spared me a small smile, but there was no hum
"I'm breaking, Harlow."

"What do you mean?"

"It's like I've forgotten how to survive in this world.
God."

I squeezed his hand gently. "I'll always protect you, A
world will never hurt you," I promised him, echoing his
so many years ago.

After everything we'd been through, it felt like a wh

ago that we'd been promised to each other, and we'd started losing each other. I knew now that we'd never find each other again, not like that. But we had a new path now. A new potential.

Even if we were still forced to marry, we could do so as friends knowing we'd given a real relationship our best shot. We tried it and failed at it. Both of us. And we still loved each other. That, to me, counted for a lot. I didn't know how we were going to manage the specifics of a life together, but I didn't feel the bars around my cage, the walls weren't closing in. I still felt some shred of hope for the future that, even if it wasn't what we'd hoped for originally, we could still – together – make living someone else's life bearable. And dare I say, somewhat enjoyable.

He lifted our clasped hands and kissed the back of mine. "We'll get through this. Together," he agreed.

CHAPTER TWENTY

On Valentine's Day, Florence and I were both sitting in my rumpus room at the Vanguard Estate, watching cheesy rom-coms and our favourite period drama films in our pyjamas. It was the first proper day of the winter holidays, and we were pretending that we didn't currently hate men.

It was working, for the most part. The amount of wine we'd consumed probably helped.

While we were jumping around on the couches to a loud musical interlude in the new *Persuasion* adaptation, we heard the loud clang of the front doorbell sound.

"Trust Dad to be conducting business on the most romantic day of the year," I huffed to Florence.

"They way our mums are treated, every day may as well be the most romantic day of the year," she replied sardonically.

"Yes," I teased sarcastically. "Simultaneously furiously ignored, and yet lavished with gifts and money and lifestyle and luxury."

"It's a tough life," Florence deadpanned and my smirk broke free.

"Miss Vanguard?" Fletcher's voice came at the door.

Florence and I both stopped jumping and looked at the Vanguard butler expectantly.

"You have a…visitor, miss," Fletcher continued, taking in and studiously ignoring the fact that we were acting without a single shred of decorum and didn't care one whit.

I frowned as I schlumped off the couch. "A visitor?" I asked.

Fletcher nodded. "A visitor."

Florence joined me on the floor and paused the movie.

"Uh, okay…" I said slowly.

"Don't be mad," Florence said as Fletcher left to show them in.

I looked at her in panic. "Excuse me?"

I turned to the door and saw Apollo and Valen both standing there. My heart tried leaping and crashing at the same time, and I honestly just felt like I was about to go into cardiac arrest. They were both sporting bruises they hadn't been last I'd seen them, not that I cared.

I looked back at Florence, all incredulous now. "Excuse you!" I yelled at her. "I thought we were hating men for at least the rest of this week?"

"Hate me all you want," Valen said. "But at least let me speak."

I turned a glare on him. "You think you get to speak now? You, who had your chance and fucked it up? Twice!"

"Love, I—"

"Oh, no. Don't 'love' me, Valen Kincaid," I said, all fiery passion threatening to undo me.

He was here. That had to mean a shit tonne. But I didn't know if I was prepared for this to be a shit tonne. I'd already had my heart broken more times than I cared to count in the last year, and I didn't want to risk it again. Not so soon. And certainly not making potentially the same mistake.

Florence put her hand on my arm. "Please hear him out."

I shook my head. "No. No. I'm either too sober or too drunk for this right now, and I'm not sure which."

"That may have been by design," Florence admitted.

"What?" I asked.

"I told you that was a bad plan," Apollo interjected.

I pointed at him wildly. "Nothing out of you, right now," I warned him. "You've brought…him," my finger span to Valen now, "into my house under…what? Some misguided belief that I'll listen to either of you?"

"You just need to listen to him, Harlow," Apollo said. "Please. The fucker's here to grovel."

"Epic levels of grovelling," Florence added, and I frowned at her for the part she had dared to play in this.

I looked at Valen. "Again, you let other people do all the talking for you. Have you decided it's not going to make a difference?" I huffed.

He shook his head. "You know me, Harlow. I don't waste words. I'm not going to waste the ones I do have."

"That is still not grovelling," I pointed out.

Part of me didn't want him to grovel. I didn't want him to worm his way back into my head when I knew he was still firmly planted in my heart. I was just about ready to get over him for good, and now this? Well, fine. I'd listen to what he had to say and…I'd leave my judgement until he'd said his piece.

Ha. Like I had the strength to turn him down if he was here to win me back.

"You *are* worth breaking all the rules for, princess," is what he started with, his voice low. "I broke so many just wanting you that the idea of breaking them all…fucking terrified me. It wasn't just my life that could be forfeit, but the Black Bloods were coming for yours and I was risking that. Risking you. Cowardice more than obligation made me drive you to Apollo, but I won't make that mistake again. I will break *all* the rules for you, if you'll let me."

Clearly, Apollo and Valen had been talking about me for a second time.

I looked Valen over slowly, feeling the ice around my heart cracking but not willing to risk it thawing entirely. "Except you can't. Apollo and I have to pretend we're together until a better opportunity presents itself, and I don't see a better opportunity presenting itself."

"We'll find a way," he said. "There has to be a way."

"Why?" I asked. "Why does there have to be a way? Why does something that should be so simple have to be so hard? Why does being with the man I *love* have to be so hard?"

"Save me, Harlow, love," he begged. There was a broken gruffness to his voice now. "Save me from myself. From our world. From a life of emptiness without you."

"Take him back, Harlow," Apollo said, and I heard the humour in his voice at Valen's grovelling. "For the love of God," here, a wink, "please. And I'll help you two be together while we still have to pretend. If you want. I will help us find a way out of our contract so you can be with him for real. If you want. I don't know how long it will take, but we'll find a way until we work it out."

I took a breath.

Until we work it out. Apollo truly believed we'd find a way to break our contract. I didn't want to risk anyone dying for me and my selfish choices, but I was being handed a chance at a life I wanted, even just a semblance of one, and it was so tempting to just reach out and take it.

"Me, too," Florence added. "Fuck, I'll pretend I'm fucking Valen if it helps."

I took another breath, this one shaking with a small laugh.

"It's Harlow's choice," Valen said.

We all knew what my choice was. I'd told them all. I just had to admit it to myself and take the risk on owning it was still what I wanted.

"I agree. In theory. But if you think I'm going to forgive him that easily, you've got another thing coming. If you want to be with me, Valen, you have to fucking earn it."

Valen dropped to his knees in front of me. "You have my oath I will."

Apollo fake-gagged but was smiling. "Flo, I think we probably need to go and see something…not in this room."

Florence nodded as she stepped gingerly around Valen and me. "Yes. Definitely. I'm sure there was a…suit of armour I haven't seen yet."

"Yes. It's…new," Apollo added.

I rolled my eyes. "Just get out, the both of you," I told them.

They ushered each other out, whispering and laughing between themselves. No doubt thinking they were terribly clever in getting Valen and me back together. But it left me alone with Valen.

I looked down at him. Seeing him on his knees in front of me was a pleasant sight.

"You want me to save you?" I asked him.

He nodded. "Yes."

"That's a lot to put on me, Valk," I said slowly, taking a step back.

He actually crawled towards me, and my heart lurched expectantly. "Except, you know it's not," he countered, and I knew he was right; wanting to save the person you loved wasn't a hardship, especially when just loving them could do it.

I looked him over shrewdly. "Even on your knees, you're defiant."

A smirk lit his eyes. "How else would you have me?"

To get what I wanted here, I had to walk a very fine line. We weren't the kind for romantic soliloquies, as nice as they were. If he gave me one now, I'd start to doubt he was the man I wanted. And if I expected one from him now, I wasn't the woman he thought I was.

"You don't strike me as the kind to grovel, Valk."

"Maybe it was *you* who tamed the big, bad wolf after all?"

I scoffed and made to step away, but he wrapped his arm around my legs. I leant down, touching my fingertip under his chin. There was a challenge in his eyes, but I met it with one of my own.

"I didn't fall in love with God's tame wolf," I told him pointedly.

"And I didn't fall in love with God's timid princess," he replied, just as pointedly.

"If you want me, Valen, then take what's yours," I demanded.

As he stood up, his hand went to my throat. "You think I answer to you, princess?"

"There are worse powers to obey," I sassed.

A smirk lit his eyes. "The only place I ever want to be is on my knees at your feet."

I grabbed the front of his shirt and pulled him to me. A flash of silver caught my eye under his collar. Jealousy flared as I ripped his collar aside. When I saw what hung on that chain, my heart didn't beat any slower, but it beat for a very different reason. Valen's hand gently wrapped around the wrist of the hand gripping his shirt and I finally looked up into his eyes.

"I don't have to hide it anymore, love," he said slowly. "Not from Apollo, and I doubt anyone else would look at it and realise it's yours. Much like no one's looked at the one around your neck and realised it's mine."

"You're wearing my cross, Valen."

He nodded, a soft smile in his eyes. "I'm wearing your cross, Harlow."

"Why are you wearing my cross?"

"Because it means everything to me. The only thing that means more is you."

"What about your contract with Archer?"

He dropped his forehead to mine. "No one in our world just walks away from a contract, love. You know that. But you will always be first. You can't not. You're mine. But more importantly, I'm yours. I am bound to you whether you'll have me or not, and I will forever be yours. To serve you. To protect you. To love you. If you'll let me."

I nodded. "And what's going to stop you from deciding to do the right thing again and push me to Apollo?"

"I know now that you don't love each other. That neither of you want to be together. I owe Apollo my life and my service, princess. I don't owe him the woman I love for no reason."

"Those are very pretty words, Valen. But I don't know if I can trust your words anymore."

"What can I do?" he begged.

"Are you serious about this? About me?"

"You walking out my door that night didn't stop you being mine, and it won't now. What can I do?"

"You can spend every day of the rest of our lives showing me I can trust you."

He nodded. "Easy."

"Easy? Even when I have to pretend to be with Apollo?"

"Less easy, but I'm not scared off by things being a little difficult."

"Are you really going to break all the rules for me, Valen?"

He shrugged nonchalantly. "It's a free country."

"Only until you get caught."

"A Kincaid is never caught," he reminded me.

"A Kincaid also never marries," I reminded him.

He nodded. "Aye. They beat that into us young."

"And you?"

"And me?"

"What exactly are you offering me, Valen?" I asked slowly. "You say you want to love me forever, but what does that look like to you?"

He shook his head. "I don't care. As long as we're together, I don't care. Your contract with Apollo will either break, or it won't. We can't know that now. But I want a life with you, love. I want us."

I chewed on my lip, and I thought about what he was saying. He was here, promising me a future. A future I'd firmly told myself he couldn't – wouldn't – ever offer me. Did that make him more or less the man I loved?

"What?" he asked. "What are you thinking, love?"

"I'm trying to work out if you're the sort of man to offer a future, Valen," I said, and he frowned in confusion. "I fell in love with a man who couldn't–"

"The man you fell in love with *couldn't*, but he wanted to. I always wanted it, Harlow. Before you, the idea of marriage, kids… It was nothing I thought twice about. I was told I couldn't have it, but I didn't want it or need it. Then there was you and I couldn't stop thinking about it. You in a white dress. Just for me." He ran his hand over my stomach. "Pregnant with my baby. I tried to stop, but I'd never wanted anything more than I wanted us."

I'd thought we weren't the type for romantic soliloquies, but maybe we could be. They definitely were nice.

I thought of something. "That day you thought I was going to tell you I was pregnant…?"

A rueful smile lit his eyes. "They would have lined up to kill me, but I'd have died happy."

I couldn't help smiling. "Really? Why?"

His eyes were soft as he looked me over. "Because I'd have had a claim to you, love. It was foolish to think it, but I was ready to face any consequence of our actions. Had there been any."

"I'm not ready for kids, Valen…"

He gave me a soft smile. "Neither am I, but that doesn't mean I wouldn't accept them if they happened."

"And these kids…" I started.

"Mm…?" he asked as he put his arm around my waist.

I leant my hand on his chest. "Whether I'm with you or forced to marry Apollo, I'll be expected to have kids."

His nose dipped to my hair. "You will," he murmured.

"You'd really be their father? They wouldn't be considered…unworthy?"

"My da can think what he likes about it," Valen said vehemently, holding me closer. "Any child I have will be half Kincaid and half Vanguard. I can't think of a stronger pairing."

"Are you just saying that because you love me?"

"I love you because you're strong, Harlow. You're fearless."

I shook my head. "I'm not fearless, Valen."

"Why would you say that?"

I looked up at him. "Because I'm afraid of what my life looks like – feels like – without you, but I'm also afraid of how my life looks if I'm forced to marry Apollo. A man like you playing mistress?"

He scoffed, a smile playing at his lips. "Love, I will be anything for you."

I raised my eyebrow. "Anything?"

He nodded. "Anything. I came to you, princess, you're in charge."

I gave him a wry smirk and pushed him onto the couch behind him before crawling into his lap. His hands slipped under my pyjama top and gripped my waist firmly.

I leant forward to whisper in his ear, "You will have me screaming your name. You will make me cum, but even then you will thrust deep into me. Relentlessly. You will be so deep inside me that I'll never forget the feel of you. And you won't stop until you've given me every ounce of pleasure my body can handle." I lay my hand over his throat. "Understood?"

He nodded eagerly. "Understood."

I rubbed myself over him as I nipped his earlobe. "And you will not touch any woman other than me," I commanded.

"Never," he breathed as we rocked together.

I put my finger under his chin and stared into his eyes. "And you will tell me at least three times a day that you love me."

Humour lit his eyes, but he nodded. "At least."

I gripped his jaw tightly and steeled myself. If I let him in now, then this was it. If this went sideways now, I might not survive. But then, I wasn't sure he would either. He searched my eyes, and I could see the message in his. The earnest sincerity that had my heart melting for him.

But it didn't hurt that he voiced out loud, "I love you, Harlow. With everything I am. All of me is yours."

I couldn't resist him any longer. I'd been his since the day I first saw him. When I was that clueless twelve-year-old standing on the staircase at the Callahans and he'd pinned me with that piercing grey stare.

My hand still gripping his jaw, I kissed him hard.

He wrapped his arms around me, and I wrapped mine around his shoulders, my hands finding their way to his hair. We just kissed for the longest time. Like we were making up for lost time.

Finally, I gripped his tee in my hands and breathed, "Valen, I need you."

He stood up, picking me up easily so we didn't have to stop kissing. He took a couple of purposeful steps towards the doors, then stopped.

"What?" I asked.

He leant his forehead to mine. "I've just realised, I don't know where your room is here."

I smiled as he lowered me gently to my feet. I held my hand out for his. "Well, we're going to have to change that."

He gave me a rough laugh, looking up at me through his hair with a sinful smile. He took my hand, and I pulled him to my room.

Chapter Twenty-One

We fell through my bedroom door, hands and lips refusing to leave each other.

"Jesus, Harlow," he breathed my name like a prayer against my lips as my hands went for his jeans button.

He kicked my door closed behind us and we set to getting each other's clothes off. I felt his smile against my lips as he tried – and failed – to get his boots off without his hands. I ran mine up his chest and grasped his hair.

"Need a hand with that?" I teased him.

"You're at a distinct advantage here, princess," he pointed out.

"It's not my fault you decided to *beg* for my heart while I was in my pyjamas."

"You can say that like it's shameful, love," he whispered huskily. "But begging for your love is one of the least shameful things I've ever done."

In his words was all the implications of that. The fact he'd killed. Kidnapped. Fought men twice his size and beaten them into the dust. No doubt done far worse things I would never know the half of. Valen knew about shameful things.

"Loving you," he said, "is the least shameful thing I will ever do, and I will get on my knees at your feet and beg you to keep me every day if I have to."

"Just don't break my heart, Valen…" I was the one begging now, even if my hand was running over his cock like I was desperate for it.

"Not again."

His nose ran over mine. "Just let me have forever, love," he whispered before kissing me again.

Somehow, we got the rest of our clothes off, then we were in my bed, and he was sliding inside me. He filled me and a blissfully aching clarity descended on me. This was where he was supposed to me. Him and me. Together. Whatever life threw at us, all I had to do was hold on to that fact and I was sure we'd find a way through.

Valen had fucked me plenty over the last four months but what we did that night couldn't rightly be called fucking. There was too much in it. It was slow, both agonising and incredible. We spent more time exploring each other's bodies, murmuring incomprehensible nothings to each other, and just being together without any hate or the knowledge that we only had a short time together than we did trying to wring untold pleasures from each other's bodies in the time we did have. There was no fight for supremacy, serious or in jest. We were just two people who needed to show each other how we felt.

The first time, at least.

Which is not to say that Valen didn't make me cum as many times as he could.

By the time his cock was pressing against me, hard and ready, for the fourth time, we were done with the purely emotional, as nice as that was.

"Come, there's something I've been wanting to do for years," he said. He planted a kiss on my shoulder, then got out of bed.

I looked at him questioningly but let him pull me with him over to my window seat.

"Is this one even bigger than at the Callahans'?" he asked.

I nodded. "Yeah. I used to pull the curtains closed and hide in here for hours."

His smirk was a promise of delicious sinfulness. He lifted and turned me, so I was on the window seat on my knees, my back to him. He peppered kisses along my shoulder and neck as his fingers trailed between my legs.

I breathed in deeply as I leant back against him and he wrapped his other arm around me, his forearm sitting between my breasts so he could drape his hand lazily around my throat. Pleasure zinged around my body, accompanied by the opposing chill on my skin from cold coming through the window. Everything was heightened and my nipples pulled tight from more than just the chill.

Valen rubbed me, his hand tightening around my neck slightly along with the coil in me. My breath came heavier. I rocked against him, but he held me firm. My body started shaking as he unleashed wave after wave of pleasure through me. And still he held me firm.

"Tell me you're mine," Valen said in my ear.

"I'm yours," I told him, unhesitatingly. "Only yours." My hand snaked behind me and gripped the back of his head. "Tell me you're mine."

"Forever, love," he growled, then bent me over and plunged deep into me.

I braced myself on the window with one hand, my other holding his leg and he pounded into me.

"Shit, Valen…" I breathed.

He pulled my back to lie flush against his chest again and squeezed my breast hard. Pain and pleasure shot through me in a delicious mix that sent my senses into overdrive. And still he drove into me.

"Harlow," he groaned as his arms wrapped around me. "Fucking…"

He pulled out of me and flipped me over. He claimed my lips with his as he slid into me again. We were well past slow and gentle with a hint of sweet. This was all fucking for the sake of fucking, for the singular purpose of satiating the ache inside us that the other caused. It was hard, fast, relentless. Everything Valen had promised me when I'd refused him on Halloween.

I came hard, my back arching, and I was pretty sure I was close to seeing stars. Still, Valen drilled me. Swift, long, steady thrusts. Each one eliciting a shiver of ecstasy through me. He was so deep. Everything tingled and warmed. Another orgasm was building.

And I actually did scream, "Valen!" as I dug my nails into his back and my whole body wrapped around his.

I felt his smile as he trailed his lips over my neck. "Scream for me, love," he begged as he dragged his teeth across my skin.

So, I did. My moans wouldn't be muffled. I encouraged him very vocally.

"Fuck, yes. Harlow," he groaned in satisfaction at my gratification as he fucked me hard.

Valen came and it sent me over that precipice one more time. My body convulsed under him, and he chuckled a rough laugh as he grazed my nipple with his teeth. Then he sucked on it and much more purposefully dragged his teeth over it. My back arched into him again as I inhaled sharply.

He dropped beside me with a contended sigh and pulled me to him.

I ran my fingers gently over the bruise on Valen's cheekbone as we lay there in the window seat. The chill through the now very fogged up window helping to cool me down after our exertions.

"Did you two come to fisticuffs again?" I asked him, thinking they both deserved it.

Valen shook his head. "Marco saw fit to fuck the both of us up for how we treated you. And rightly so."

I smiled. "He is my guardian Angel," I teased.

Valen nodded solemnly as he ran his nose over my cheek, his lips trailing softly behind. "He's done a better job than me."

"That's because you're Apollo's Angel first."

I felt Valen smile against my temple. "And Marco's yours first? Is that it?"

"I'm still the goddess of Saint Benedicts," I reminded him. "Maybe I should have my own Angels?"

"God's Angels are your Angels, princess. But you're not *Saint Bens'* Goddess…"

"Oh, is that so?"

He nodded. "It is. You're mine."

"Are you sure about that this time?" I asked softly, only really half-teasing.

"You wanted to know what would happen if you pushed me, princess?" he asked, and I nodded. "I fell in love with you, Harlow Vanguard. You pushed and pushed and your carved your fucking name in my heart, and I want to spend every second until my dying breath loving you, not hating you."

"You won't get bored?"

"Why do you think I'll get bored?"

"I might like it hard and fast, but I don't think I'll ever really like it proper rough and dirty," I admitted to him.

He nodded. "I know."

I frowned. "You know?"

"I've known since that time I slapped your arse, and you didn't care for it."

I'd guessed since then, too. "And you don't mind?"

"Mind? No, love. You get my dick hard. You with your tiny fury and dirty mouth and no time for my shite. Not how hard I can choke you to make you cum."

When he put it like that, it wasn't something I was going to say a hard no to...

But I just asked him, "I thought you liked it rough and dirty?"

He shrugged. "I have done, but I don't need it. I want to fuck you how you want to be fucked. I want to please you. If rough and dirty's not your thing, I don't want it either."

"I'm not saying never..." I told him.

A wicked gleam lit his eyes as he looked me over. "I'd be happy to give you proper rough, love. But only if it's what you want. You're in charge."

I smiled at him, and he actually grinned as well. It looked completely unbidden, but it transformed him. I loved him at his darkest, but a thrill ran through me at the idea there were different layers to him that I was going to get to explore, more depth to him that I could fall in love with. And that we had forever for me to do that.

"I never gave you your Christmas present," Valen changed the subject as his nose trailed over my shoulder.

I remembered now. "You got me a Christmas present."

He nodded. "I was going to give it to you on Christmas Eve. Then Archer interrupted us, and we didn't have time."

I rolled over and looked at him. "What was it?"

He smirked at me. "You mean, what is it?"

"You still have it?"

"Of course. Do you want it?"

"Do you still want to give it to me?"

His eye flashed mischief at my word choice, but he stuck to the current conversation. "Now more so than ever."

I nodded, intrigued. "Then of course I want it."

He reached over to find his jeans and pulled a small box out of his pocket.

"Have you been carrying that around since Christmas?" I asked, trying and failing to hide my amusement at him being so sentimental.

He looked at me like I should keep all further thoughts of that to myself.

"It's not diamonds," he said slowly. "In contrast, it's pretty shit. But it does mean something. To me."

I took the box gingerly and opened it. Nestled inside was a little ring. It wasn't garish. It wasn't ostentatious. It wasn't making up for indiscretions with a ridiculous price tag.

A simple black band with a small black cross in the middle.

I smiled up at him. "I love it."

"May I?" Valen asked.

I nodded and he took the box back. He took the ring out, dropped the box, and picked up my right hand.

"Did you know," he started as he slid the ring onto my third finger.

"Traditionally, we wore the engagement ring on the right hand?"

"We?" I asked.

He nodded. "Catholics."

I wasn't quite sure what to say to his words. There was this little flurry of excited happiness in my chest, but Valen wasn't the excited flurry of happiness kind of guy. It was one reason I loved him. "Oh," seemed hardly fitting, but his eyes lifted to mine, and I saw the smile in them.

"It's not, mind," he said.

"Not what?" I asked.

"An engagement ring."

I nodded. "No. Of course not."

"Ye can hardly be engaged to two men at once." There was a note of teasing in his voice. "But consider it a promise."

"A promise of what?"

"My intentions."

He turned his right hand over, the one on which he'd always worn his big black ring on the third finger, and I saw there was a cross cut into it. A cross that matched the one on the third finger of my right hand.

The full implication of Valen's actions hit me. He'd done this, organised this, at Christmas. Three months earlier. He'd been willing to make me this promise even back then, though maybe it hadn't meant quite so much before. And maybe that was good. Maybe it was good that we were here, making this promise now when it could mean as much as we both wanted it to.

"I don't have anything to give you in return."

Thankfully, he knew what I meant. "If you deign to wear it, that will be promise enough for me, love. You have nothing to prove to me," he said, like he was the one with something to prove.

I almost told him he didn't either, but then I thought it wouldn't hurt for him to prove it. I wanted to trust his love, and I was going to give him the chance, but I wasn't that naïve princess with the rose-coloured glasses anymore.

Valen had my heart, and I wasn't going to hold any part of it back from him, but I also knew that I was still contracted to marry Apollo and we didn't know what the future held. But as they said, you had to love like there was no such thing as a broken heart. Anything else would guarantee failure.

I trailed my fingers over the cross cut into his ring and looked up into his eyes.

"And I'll consider your promise enough so long as you still wear this ring," I told him, and he smirked like he knew – and liked – what was coming next. "You will not like what I do to you if you take it off."

Valen rolled onto his back, pulling me onto his body. "Deterrent works best for me, love," he said. "Maybe you'd best show me exactly what you'll do to me?"

I nipped his earlobe. "Sounds to me like you're after encouragement, Valen."

His strong arms went around me, and I felt him tilt his tip to my centre. He was rock hard for me again. "Encouragement isn't what's lacking, princess. All I need to do is think about you. Catch a hint of your scent. I couldn't sleep in my own bed for a fucking week after that night you came to my room in that fucking sexy lingerie."

"Why not?" I asked, my heart pounding so hard in my chest I was sure he could feel it in his.

"Because every time I lay down, all I could smell – all I could remember – was you."

"I'm more than a memory now, love," I whispered, and I saw something thaw in his eyes.

He brushed his fingers down my face. "Aye. But I hope we'll be making memories for the rest of our lives."

What started out as soft and sweet quickly devolved and somehow, at some point in the shenanigans, we made our way back to the bed.

By the time Valen and I finally fell asleep in a tangle of bedsheets, the sun was peeking over the horizon, and I felt utterly spent. Fantastically used and tucked safe and warm in Valen's arms.

And when I woke later that morning, he was still there beside me, looking the most at peace I had ever seen him.

CHAPTER TWENTY-TWO

"Well, this is all very nice," Florence said as the four of us sat around the next afternoon. "But what are you going to do about it?"

"What do you mean?" Apollo asked.

She rolled her eyes. "I mean, how do you plan to sneak around behind our world's eyes and ears. Apollo and I will go to the ends of the earth to help you–"

"Team Apollo and Florence," I snorted, and she glared at me to shut it.

"–BUT," she continued as though I hadn't spoken. "But we'll only get so far."

I shrugged. "I guess we cross that bridge when we come to it."

"Do the two of you plan to get married in secret and then be all 'surprise Archer, fuck you'?" Florence asked.

We could, but it wouldn't solve anything. Being married wouldn't suddenly make Valen immortal or invulnerable. It wasn't something I enjoyed thinking about.

"I don't know," I said more vehemently. "Can I not just enjoy the now?"

"What if we offer Valk up instead of me?" Apollo asked slowly, like he was still working out the details in his head.

Valen looked at him quizzically. "What do you mean?"

"I mean you in my place. With Rex."

He wasn't the first person to suggest that an official alternate marriage contract might be enough to at least convince my dad to break the contract with Archer. When Marco had suggested it, I took it with a grain of salt and didn't think much of it. Now, I started considering it more seriously. But I wasn't the only one who'd have to agree to this marriage before they'd finished school and, for all Valen's words and promises, he hadn't said anything about the practicalities of long-term.

"I can't just risk throwing everything away on a whim, Apollo," I said gently.

But it was Valen who interjected. "It's not a whim, love. You are not a whim. Any other couple at our age wouldn't have to go this far yet, but–"

I knew what he was saying. "We're not any other couple."

He shook his head. "No. You're contracted to marry. I have to offer you at least the same."

"You don't have to–"

"Yes, I do. I want you – us – and the only chance our world's going to let that happen is if I offer to marry you instead."

"Valen…" I started, looking him over.

"I'd have done it anyway, love. It's just a little earlier than I planned."

Florence cheered, but Apollo nudged her quiet, even if he did wear a ridiculously large grin.

I smirked. "Earlier?"

Valen shrugged coyly. "I was all in from the moment you told me you'd have me on my knees worshipping you. My heart bowed to you that day, even when my body couldn't, and it's never fucking got back up again."

"What are you saying, Valen?"

"I'm saying, Harlow, that I'd want to marry you even if we lived normal lives."

"Naw," Florence cooed as Apollo fake-gagged, then laughed as Florence nudged him.

I threw them both a look that told them to shut up before turning back to Valen. I took a deep breath, realising I was about to exchange one contract for another, if all went to plan. But this time, I'd make sure I had some say in the matter.

I nodded. "Okay. We can only try. Give my dad the option and see what he says."

"I'll go and talk to him, then," Valen said.

Apollo nodded. "Okay. Good."

I put a hand on Valen's chest. "No," I said, my voice firm despite the trepidation making my stomach flutter.

"I thought you wanted–" Apollo started, but Florence smacked him, knowing exactly what was going through my head.

I swallowed hard and nodded. "No. I do." I looked into Valen's eyes to reassure him. "I want to be with you, but I've had men dictate everything for me my whole life. I need to be the one to talk to him."

Valen dropped his forehead to mine as his hand lighted on my elbow. "Are you sure?"

I nodded, feeling stronger and more determined. "Yes. I'm not going to be the princess locked in the tower anymore. I'm a fucking goddess in my own right."

"Fuck yeah, you are!" Florence cheered and I threw her a smile.

"We'll be here if you need us," Valen said, and I reached up to give him a kiss.

"I'll fight for you both, Harlow," Apollo added.

"You're no use to anyone dead," Florence muttered sardonically.

"I can hold my own," Apollo argued.

"Almost," Valen conceded. "We've still got work to do."

Florence looked to Apollo in surprise. "You're actually training to fight? Properly? As in, not just for show?"

Apollo shrugged like it was nothing. "The two people who matter most to me are about to start a war, just for loving each other. Of course, I'm fucking training to fight."

I'd have recognised then that Florence seemed to look at him with new eyes, but I was gearing up to start that war. It was not a decision to be taken lightly, but it was the right one. There was no way Apollo and I could ever be more than friends, and sneaking around with Valen for the rest of my life wasn't an attractive prospect. And it would have to be some next level sneaking because there was no doubt that Archer would kill Valen to force me to be 'faithful' to Apollo and secure his son's inheritance.

The next step was convincing my father I knew my own mind – and heart – well enough to risk breaking what was no-doubt an iron-clad contract with Archer Callahan.

I left the others, went and knocked on Dad's door, and waited for the, "Enter," before pushing it open.

Dad looked at me in surprise. "Harlow. What can I do for you?"

I cleared my throat. "There's no easy way to say this, but I'm not marrying Apollo."

Dad put his pen down carefully and steepled his fingers under his chin. "Really?"

I nodded as I took a hesitant step forward. "Really."

He indicated I sit in the seat on the other side of his desk, so I did. "How much did your mother tell you about the contract with Archer Callahan?" he asked.

I forced myself to keep my eyes out of my lap. "Enough."

His eyebrow rose for merely a split second. "Then you know what happens if we renege on our part of the deal?"

I swallowed hard. "Mostly…?" I was ashamed of how uncertain I sounded.

He inclined his head. "I think you're old enough now to tell you. Especially if you're entertaining ideas of breaking the contract. You may as well know exactly what we're risking."

"You haven't said no…" I pointed out.

He looked at me seriously. "Harlow, everything in life is business. Agreements. Understandings. Negotiations. You can't make an informed decision to break off the contract with the Callahans without me giving you all the information. If you're still adamant after I do so, then we will discuss."

"Okay," I said, thinking it sounded more fair than I was expecting.

"It is understood that you marrying Apollo gives him better legal claim to your inheritance, yes?" he asked, and I nodded. "Good. What you may not realise is that Archer is not above taking that inheritance by force."

"Force?" I clarified and now he nodded.

"If you don't marry Apollo, then Archer will not hesitate to have me killed and take over my holdings with whatever force is necessary."

"What's stopping him doing it now?" I breathed.

"There is a tentative truce between the families of our world, Harlow. Have you heard of the Nameless?"

I nodded slowly. "I've heard them mentioned once or twice."

"The Council of the Nameless governs our world, as much as we can be governed. We have unspoken understandings about what is and is not above board. We have…for lack of a better word, laws we are expected to follow as members of the Nameless. A code. Archer Callahan has been plotting to get his hands on the Vanguard fortune since before you were born. If he has to take it by force, he'll be starting a war."

So, Apollo had chosen his words well, and clearly did know more about the situation than me. Valen and I being together *was* risking actual war.

"I won't be the only casualty," Dad continued. "It won't just be our personnel who die, our suppliers, but O'Malleys and Kincaids–"

"Kincaids?" burst out of me as my heart strangled uncomfortably.

Dad looked at me like I'd just confirmed something. "Mmhm," he said.

"What?" I asked, failing at any kind of nonchalance.

"This is why you want to break the contract." It wasn't a question.

I tried to steer him away from that train of thought. "Apollo and I are poorly suited to anything more than friends. It will never work.

We'll keep trying to make it, and keep failing, resenting each other more and more as the years go by. It won't work and it won't last. We cannot marry."

Dad raised a single eyebrow. "Mmhm," he said, and I knew he didn't believe that was the only reason.

I took a deep breath. "It... It doesn't help that I fell in love with Valen..."

Dad was surprised now. "Love?"

I nodded and felt my cheeks blush. Somehow, talking about love felt taboo. "Yeah. I didn't mean to. It just..."

"Took you by surprise," Dad finished for me, like he had some understanding of the concept.

"Yeah," I answered.

"Does Apollo know?"

"He does. He... He actually brought Valen here this week to..."

Dad held up a hand. "I don't need the details."

I smirked. "Not what I meant. There was a...misunderstanding of sorts. Apollo brought Valen here to make amends."

Cue even more surprise. "Valen returns your feelings?"

I stilled my wringing hands in my lap. "I think–"

"Yes," Valen interrupted. "I do."

I didn't know how Valen had got in the room without either of us noticing, but then that was kind of his job. The interruption wasn't unwelcome. If Dad needed to know the truth, then Valen would need to say his piece as well. As independent as I wanted to be, his feelings weren't something I could prove alone.

Dad sat back in his chair and watched Valen walk out of the shadows. "Valen Kincaid. I thought you were supposed to be keeping my daughter pure for her future husband, not seducing her."

I looked between them. "What?"

Dad smirked as Valen came to a stop next to me. "Archer gave Valk very specific instructions regarding his son's intended. Do not let another man touch her."

Valen growled. "He was just lucky I had a personal interest in doing so."

So many more things made sense now. Why Valen had been roughing kids up even before the contract. Why Apollo hadn't cared, but Valen had. All of that purity bullshit came from outdated ideals on Archer's part, and jealousy on Valen's. He'd better believe I'd hang that over him for years.

Dad's eyebrow quirked and there was a hint of amusement at his lips. "I've no doubt. And you profess to love my daughter, Valk? You, a Kincaid?"

"I want to offer myself in place of Apollo," he said.

Dad looked impressed. For a moment. "That's not a yes," he pointed out.

Valen growled again. "Yes. I love Harlow."

"And you intend to marry her?"

"One day."

"Help her run the Vanguard family business? Give her heirs?"

"Yes." It sounded like it cost some effort for Valen to agree.

"Kincaids don't marry," Dad seemed to be reminding him.

"This one will."

"And when your father forbids it?"

"I will kill him if I have to," Valen snarled, and Dad looked like he believed him.

Dad tapped his desk. "And what would the Kincaids get out of it?"

"Same as the Vanguards. Power."

"The Vanguards have power in spades, son," Dad said lazily. "What power could an alliance with the Kincaids bring me?"

"How about a private contract?" Valen asked.

Dad sat forward. "A private contract?"

Valen nodded. "If you let your daughter have me, then I'll convince my old man to enter into an exclusive contract with the Vanguards."

Dad looked at me. "That could do it, although the Council won't like it.”

“You’ll need it,” Valen seemed to agree. “It could be justified.”

So, even Valen knew the consequences of me breaking the contract with the Callahans. Great. I promised myself that was the last time I was the last to know anything.

“Is this really what you want, Harlow?” Dad asked me and, for once, I felt like he was really asking. Like it actually mattered what I wanted.

I looked at Valen and I felt the smile on my lips. “Yeah,” I told Dad, my eyes still on Valen. “Yes. I want to be with Valen.”

“A Kincaid and a Vanguard,” Dad chuckled. “All right. Who am I to deny my little princess what she wants?”

My eyes swung back to Dad. “Really?”

He nodded. “Really. I don’t know how long it will take, but I’ll open negotiations with Cillian. Until then…”

I sighed and nodded, playing with Apollo’s heavy diamond on my finger. “I know. Keep up the ruse.”

“We cannot afford to let Archer get wind of our plans before everything is set,” he said, like he was trying to reassure me, like it was an apology. “We need a solid contract with the Kincaids before risking the wrath of Archer Callahan.”

“He’d be stupid to start anything with my family and his son already guaranteed on your side,” Valen said.

“We have Apollo?” Dad clarified.

I nodded. “He just wants me to be happy. He’s willing to do whatever it takes.”

“I think it says a lot about you, darling,” Dad said fondly, “that you have three very powerful men who feel that way.”

“You don’t think much of yourself, do you?” I teased.

Dad cracked a full-on, warm smile. “Not at all,” he laughed, then looked at me with adoration in his eyes. “I suppose I’m going to need to show you the ropes then.”

I blinked, confused. “What do you mean?”

Dad shrugged. "Well, if you're going to be head of the Vanguard empire, then you'll need to know how things work."

Me? Head of the Vanguard empire?

I'd seen more of the men's business lately, but I knew there was a lot I still had to learn. One thing I didn't need to learn was that women never inherited. Never. If Dad was actually suggesting I would inherit...?

"Seriously?" I asked.

He nodded. "Seriously. Valk, I presume I don't need to ask that my daughter has your backing?"

"She has God and all his Angels behind her, Mr Vanguard."

Dad looked Valen up and down. "If you're really planning to go through with this, you'd better call me Rex, son."

"That's not my place," Valen answered, like it was rote.

"Valk, you're about to risk the wrath of the whole of Family Kincaid, don't risk mine as well."

The corner of Valen's lip tipped up. "Of course, Rex."

"How much does Marco know?" Dad asked suddenly and I was surprised by the turn the conversation took.

Valen shrugged and helped himself to the seat beside me like some unspoken permission had been given. "Everything."

"Are you not as good as your reputation, Valk?" Dad actually cracked a joke.

Ah, this time I wasn't the last to know something.

Valen almost smirked in reply, but I answered before he could, "Or Marco's a lot better at his job than you give him credit for."

Dad smiled at me. "You worked it out." Another not question.

"Not that long ago, but yes. I accused him, he came clean."

"The beating he gave us for the way we treated you," Valen said, sounding proud of Marco.

"You want to rethink that admission, Valk?" Dad asked sternly.

I put a hand on Valen's arm. "Apollo acted... Let's just say he has a long way to come before his redemption. Valen did nothing more than what he thought was best. He was wrong – very wrong – but he meant well. By me and Apollo.”

Dad looked at Valen like he saw him with new eyes. “I see. Archer has always extolled your loyalty, Valk.”

“Unlike many in my family, my loyalty can’t be bought, Rex,” Valen answered, almost like a warning. “But your daughter has held it since the first time I saw her.”

Dad’s gaze swung to me again. “Well, then. Consider our estate a safe haven for this week, then,” he said to both of us. “My staff know better than to spread anything that could harm our household. Take this week to be very sure that this is what you want. Once you’re back at school, you will not have the luxury or the freedom. And Valk, I will be in contact with your father. You may like to give him a head’s up.”

Valen nodded. “Apollo and I will make sure he’s ready for you.”

Dad nodded once. “Good. Now, go. Do whatever it is you young people do when our world isn’t threatening to crush you alive.” So, even dad was under no pretences about the realities of our world, on any of us.

I jumped up and ran around his desk to kiss his cheek. “Thank you, Dad.”

He smiled. “I would do anything for you, Harlow. I’m just sorry I didn’t realise how unhappy you were sooner.”

I shook my head. “I played my part too well, maybe.”

“You did. Which makes me believe that, while this next part will be hard for you all, you’ll survive it.” He squeezed my hand gently. “Just promise me that next time you want something, you just come and talk to me about it.”

I bit my lip against a smile and nodded. “Promise.”

“Good girl. I love you, Harlow.”

“I love you, too, Dad.”

“Go. I have work to do. Valk, if you can get Marco here sometime tomorrow?”

"Will do, Rex."

I went to Valen, took his hand, and led him out of Dad's office. Valen and I didn't bother looking for Florence and Apollo, we just went straight to my room and got lost in each other in celebration. Florence had some choice words about having to wait until dinner to find out that we were one step closer to a happy ever after, but she got over it.

Chapter Twenty-Three

It was back to school the next Sunday night and out of the bubble we'd created for ourselves once more. But this time, after the bubble burst, I didn't have to leave Valen behind.

I didn't have to walk into the sunlight the next morning with regrets, I walked into it with nothing but hope for the future. That future wasn't perfect yet, but it's potential was so much more than the potential I'd almost settled for.

At school, it was back to pretending that Apollo and I were the loved-up couple. It was easier for me this time around. It felt like playing again, not walking to the gallows. I knew it wasn't as easy on Valen, but we both more than made up for it nearly every night in his bed.

At school, only five of us knew the truth.

Me.

Valen.

Apollo.

Florence.

Marco.

We all had the secret to keep, and we all knew now who Marco really was to me.

I understood that knowledge had put a bit of a dampener on whatever kind of relationship Florence and Marco had been entertaining, but they both – independently – assured me that it was mutual and amicable.

"Mrs Kincaid for the endgame?" Florence teased as she nudged me playfully.

We were sitting on her bed that Monday night, scoffing biscuits and sharing a bottle of 'Elle and Lui' in our own celebration.

I laughed. "You are *very* obsessed with me giving away my last name."

"Mr Vanguard for the endgame, then?" she posited.

I nodded. "That's better."

There was a knock at our dorm door and we both looked up to see the future Mr Vanguard himself coming through it.

"Help yourself, why not?" Florence said to him.

He looked at her with the vaguest hint of a smile. "You do not want to test me, Miss Walton."

She was trying very hard not to be impressed with him. I could see it. Much like her and Apollo, she and Valen had the whole 'my horse is bigger than your horse' fight going on, but this felt more borne out of shared humour than actual hate.

"You're fucking my best friend. I get to test you all I want, Valk," was her reply.

"I love your best friend, Miss Walton. Do your worst."

"Her best friend *does* have a name," I reminded them pointedly.

Florence nodded like it was a good point, but she'd just thought of a better one. "And enough of this 'Miss Walton' bullshit. You call me Florence, Valk."

"That's not my place." He looked to me meaningfully and I warmed. "Yet."

Florence did show how impressed she was with him now. "All right, then. But the minute it is your place…"

He inclined his head. "You have my oath."

"And you have my best friend." She waved her arm from me to Valen as though giving him her permission to do with me what he would.

"And my axe," I muttered as I looked between them.

Suddenly, having my best friend and my future husband – all going well – in the same room seemed dangerous for a very different reason than it had the last four years. I wasn't so much worried that they'd come to blows, but rather that they'd get along far too well, without me needing to mediate.

Valen held a hand out to me. "Come, princess."

I folded my hands over my chest. "Why?"

"Come." This time it was far less a request and much more an order.

I tried to repress my smile. "Why?"

His eyebrow quirked. "What have I told you about pushing me, love?" he asked sternly.

I grinned. "That it makes you love me more," I said playfully.

He rolled his eyes and looked very much like he wished he hadn't told me that. But I saw the humour on his face. "Just trust me, will ye? Please."

"One of these days, you're going to say please and I'm not going to give in," I told him, pretending that was at all true.

"And on that day, I'll bow before you in front of the whole school if you want it, love. But, for tonight, you'll do as ye're told."

When he put it like that, yes, I would. Call me weak. Call me a pushover. Call me the woman who knew what she liked. It made no difference to me.

I stood up. "Now what?"

Valen narrowed his eyes at me. "Come," he commanded, and my feet went to him willing. "Do not wait up, Miss Walton," he told her with a wink before pulling me out of the room.

We slipped out of the girl's dorm and Valen took me to the main building. The Callahan building where we had most of our lessons. He wrapped me in his arms and kissed me as he pulled something out of his pocket. It was a keycard and he used it to unlock the doors.

"Who did you beat up to get that?" I asked him.

He grinned at me, all cheeky cockiness. "We've got our whole lives, princess. I'm not giving up all my secrets just yet."

I smirked as he pressed another quick kiss to my lips before pulling me inside and pushing the door locked behind us. I said nothing as he took my hand and dragged me up two flights of stairs and then halfway along the corridor.

"Valen, what are you doing?" I asked as he pulled me into a classroom.

"Doing what I should have done nearly four years ago," he said, his voice low and husky.

He propped me on the teacher's desk and kissed me hard as his fingers slid in my panties. It was only then that I registered whose classroom we were in.

"You going to bend me over Mr Galikani's desk and make me yours?" I teased.

"You fucking know I am."

The prince had forfeited his princess, but the big, bad wolf had his goddess. I knew, now he had me, he would never let me go. Valen Kincaid would do whatever it took to stay mine. I just had to hope that I'd be worth the shitstorm that was coming next.

THE END...for now.

Read on for the epilogues.

Epilogue 1: Valen

I was the first Angel to rebel against his God in the whole sordid history of Saint Benedicts. Morningstar, they called me now. Those who knew. And that list was disconcertingly growing.

No longer God's tame wolf, but a leader in my own right. Only my future was a tad less grim than my namesake. Instead of being banished to rule the underworld, I was instead going to serve as consort to the new queen, to a Goddess. Not even consort. Yet.

Mistress.

Whore.

All words more commonly reserved for a woman in my position. Funny how men were always free to fuck about, and women were not.

The Goddess was mine, but we still had a long way to go before the world – our world – could know she owned my heart.

For now, negotiations had stalled due to the Kincaids gearing up for another war. This one for Archer Callahan against Vinnie Rossano. At least this one paid in money and power if – when – we won. And both would help when we openly turned that war on Archer Callahan.

My father looked at me over the table where we were nutting out our most recent battle plans. He was the only Kincaid to know negotiations had opened between the Kincaids and Vanguards for a marriage alliance. And all he'd done is agree to negotiate. Then Archer Callahan had opened his coffers and called for the Kincaids to fight his battles for him.

"The train is due in at ten," Neo was saying. "Our man inside says it'll be under heavy guard."

"How heavy is heavy?" Da asked.

Neo shrugged. "Twenty-odd."

Da scoffed. "Pfft. Twenty Rossanos? Five Kincaids can get the job done."

Neo shared a look with me that suggested he was less optimistic. He didn't dare mention that to Chief Kincaid. "They've got armoured–"

The door crashed open, and we all turned, weapons drawn. Suddenly, I was staring face to face with a female version of...me. Right down to the grey eyes and nearly black hair. Her bone structure was the same. She could only have been a couple of years older than me.

"What the fuck?" I muttered.

She looked around the room, clearly unimpressed with the men she saw in there. I had never seen a woman look so brazenly unafraid of any Kincaid man, let alone a room full of them. Not since my da's mother, and she still threatened to make me piss myself.

"Where is Valen?" she asked. Her accent was thick but, where ours was Scottish, hers was all Russian.

I stepped forward. "Who are you?" I asked, not believing for a second she could be who I thought she was.

She gave me a cocky smirk the likes of which rivalled mine. "Can a woman not check up on her little brother now?"

"Valentina," Da said carefully.

"*Otets*," she replied just as carefully. "Is this how you welcome your daughter home?"

"This is how we welcome intruders to our home," Da told her, his weapon not lowered.

Valentina didn't seem to care she had three Kincaids training a gun on her, and mine was still in my hand.

"*Net*," she said with a nod. "This is how you welcome women into your home."

"State your business," Kane said, closing the distance between them and holding his gun right in her face.

She seemed to find him amusing. "I should have brought my white flag, *da*?" She knocked Kane's gun aside, then her eyes narrowed on his arm.

She grabbed Kane by that arm and looked down at the tattoo on it. "I'd heard stories about you, Kincaid," she said to our father, her voice implying she didn't think much about the reality behind those stories. "They say loyalty to the Family is first. Even over blood." She left the 'I'm clear evidence of this' hanging. "Why then have you allowed your son to pledge to the Black Bloods?" she demanded, throwing – actually fucking throwing – Kane to the ground at our father's feet.

Da frowned down at Kane. "The Black Bloods, Kane?"

Trust the older generation not to notice the meaning of the tatts of the younger, but even I hadn't pieced together that Kane's new tatt had ties to the Black Bloods. The Black Bloods were usually most recognisable by their jackets. A small faction of Nameless try-hards from all Families who liked to get together to drink and fuck and complain about their bosses; they were too hard on them, they weren't hard enough on them, didn't matter. We'd had a few run-ins with them over the year and they were a nuisance more than they were an actual threat.

"It's just a bit of fun," Kane laughed.

Da rolled his eyes at him. "A bit of fun, Kane? Fucking hell. You're off running around with those idiots when we need you here? I will deal with you later. Valen, find your sister a room."

"Am I a guest or prisoner, *otets*?"

"Until your motives can be cleared with the Motherland, that remains to be seen." Da kicked his head at me to tell me to go and I ushered Valentina out.

"The men call themselves stronger and yet all I see here is a little boy obeying the demands of his father," she said to me as we walked up the stairs.

"Don't pretend you know anything about my life, and I won't pretend I know anything about yours," I told her harshly. "We may share blood, but that won't stop you from shedding mine."

She grabbed my arm and pulled me to face her. She was almost as tall as me and, dare I even think it, probably twice as fierce. "Unlike the Kincaids, the Volkovs put loyalty in blood."

I leant into her. "Tell that to Peskov."

She grinned. "I hear you made him bleed first."

She sounded proud of me. I don't think anyone had ever actually been proud of me before. I wasn't sure I liked what it did to me.

"Why are you really here?" I asked her.

"I hear you are to be married."

My eyes narrowed. "How?"

"*Babushka* Kincaid thought I should know."

Of course, she knew. Da's worst kept secret was that he still told his mother everything. For a hardened criminal who threw women away as easily as a used cigar butt, he was a proper mama's boy. What did surprise me was that Nana Kincaid had reached out so far East with that information.

"You keep in touch?"

"Women know better than men the worth we can be."

"I'm not going to argue with that. It still doesn't explain why you're here."

She clapped me on the arm. "Did you think my little brother, a fucking Volkov, would be allowed to get married without me first approving of his woman?"

I would pay good money to see Harlow square off against my sister, but, "I'm a Kincaid," is what I told her firmly.

"*Fignya*," she spat, and I didn't need to understand Russian to get the gist. "You are a Volkov."

"The point is fucking moot. We have a long road ahead of us before anyone's getting married." I didn't bother mentioning at that point that there was still a very real chance that Harlow would be forced to marry Apollo.

"So I hear. How can I help?"

Is that why she was here? To help? I may as well send her straight home now.

"Help?" I scoffed. "Unless you can fuck up centuries of misogynistic arseholes' laws, you can't."

She winked at me. "*Da zdravstvuyet revolyutsiya,*" she said, and I blinked slowly in reminder that I didn't speak Russian. "Long live the revolution, little brother."

MEN & MONSTERS: Harlow Trilogy Book 3 coming soon
MORNINGSTAR: Book 4: Valen's POV coming soon

Epilogue 2: Apollo

I was a broken, fractured version of the man, the God, I used to be. One fiery woman had brought me to my knees and turned my world upside down and inside out.

She'd left me a hollow carcass of a man, disconnected from his kingdom and all those who still worshipped in it. I was left not knowing who I was, who I wanted to be, who I could be. It felt like everything I'd ever been told was a lie, and the only person I could trust was the woman who'd secured my downfall.

Because Harlow Vanguard had ruined me.

I'd failed her.

I'd failed her. I'd failed me. I'd failed our parents.

My father was yet to know about the monumental failure, but hers knew all about it and I knew my esteem had somehow both tanked and soared in his eyes. I lost all respect in every way that counted for a member of the Nameless. But in the eyes of a father, he could see the amends I was willing to make, and he appreciated that. It was too bad that our world were Nameless members first and fathers second.

I didn't know how long it would take to get Harlow the happy ending she deserved, but I would do everything in my power to make sure she got it. Even if that meant I had to spend the foreseeable future pretending I wasn't in love with the woman pretending to be my fiancée.

They say you don't know what you have until it's gone, and it was true in my case. Or at least it took losing what I had to realise what it meant to me. What I'd dismissed as something far more platonic very quickly became anything but. While Harlow was busy comparing me to a brother, everything in me ached for her, for some reparations to the mess I made.

But the only reparations I could make now was to make sure that she and my closest friend lived their happily ever after. Or at least their happy for now. Even if it killed me inside. But it was a small price to pay and I knew, without a shred of doubt, that it was exactly how Valk had felt for the past few months. Maybe even longer.

So, I wore my mask, and I played my part to perfection. We'd only been practising for the previous four years. It was second nature by now. Even as I was crumbling to dust on the inside. Even as everything that had made up Apollo Callahan seemed to have been carved out of me and I wasn't sure how to start replacing it, or what to replace it with.

The one thing that made it bearable was something I'd never have seen coming in a million years.

No strings.

No contract.

Just pleasure.

Desire.

Fun.

An unlikely friendship with spectacular benefits I'd never even imagined possible.

It was new territory.

New Apollo. New territory.

Between her and Harlow, I was sure that I'd be able to rebuild myself as a man not just they but I could be proud of. It wouldn't be easy, not while I'm fighting for my throne, the people I love, and preparing to unleash full-scale war on my own father. But who said the high road was the easy road?

"Come back to bed, Apollo," came the grumbled murmur from behind me.

I looked back to her and felt my heart soften. I wouldn't fall into the trap of mistaking friendship and love again, but she had the power to make me forget where the line between lust and hate ran. Or at the very least, friendship and lust.

BROKEN GOD: Book 5: Apollo's POV coming soon

SINS & SAINTS: Sinners of Saint Benedicts Book 6 coming soon

Men & Monsters

Harlow, Valen and Apollo's story will continue in *Men & Monsters*.
Available in eBook and print.

A broken man. A dangerous monster. And the woman that binds them.
In the epic finale to the Harlow Trilogy, will Harlow find her happily ever after?

tHE SINNERS OF St BENEDICtS

If you liked *Princes & Wolves*, share the love and let me know!
While the duet currently sits as a standalone, I've got ideas for a
whole series of follow-ups, including a sequel to turn Harlow's story
into a trilogy, Valen's and Apollo's POVs, a HEA for Florence,
'next gen' plotlines, as well as a sequel to the alternate endings.

Print Books

Print versions of the Sinners of Saint Benedicts duet will be available from Elizabeth Stevens' webstore. They come in three versions:

1) the original duet version with all endings
2) the Harlow trilogy version, which will be what the Main Timeline follows on from.
3) the Why Choose trilogy version, which will tie-in with a sequel for the three of them.

Little Nymph

A New Adult darker, enemies-to-lovers, mafia romance, perfet for fans of *365 Days*. Get it here: https://books2read.com/u/bW0GdW

From Elizabeth Stevens, writing as E.J. Knox, comes…
Forbidden lust, a marriage pact, and the dangerous secret that could ruin it all.

My job is simple; protect Olive. Whatever she needs. Including spending the summer with the family of her intended fiancé.

Mav Vitali is anything but simple. Olive's future husband. Heir to his father's crime empire, he's as deadly as he is gorgeous.

I have one job. One. Goddamned. Job. My life is hers. So, of course I fall head over heels into lust at first sight with Mav.

I could have resisted – he's an arsehole, after all – if the feeling hadn't been mutual. And it takes just one inadvisable kiss for him to decide I will be his at any cost. Luckily, Olive's had more spark with a wet towel but, when a stalker comes after her, we've all got other things on our minds.

To save her, I'll have to team up with the man I love to hate. As the stalker grows closer, so do we. But what price will we pay to be together?

Princes & Wolves

Thank you so much for reading this story! Word of mouth is super valuable to authors. So, if you have a few moments to rate/review Harlow's story – or, even just pass it on to a friend – I would be really appreciative.

Have you looked for my books in store, or at your local or school library and can't find them? Just let your friendly staff member or librarian know that they can order copies directly from LightningSource/Ingram.

If you want to keep up to date with my new releases, rambles and writing progress, sign up to my newsletter at https://landing.mailerlite.com/webforms/landing/y1n6q2.

You can find the playlist for *the Sinners of Saint Benedicts* on Spotify:
I also have a generic writing playlist you can check out 😊

Follow me:

Thanks

I can't believe that's it for book two already! It felt like this book simultaneously took me forever to write, but also just flowed so easily.

A huge thanks to Kaity for all our chats. Whether we were creating new backstories or you were just reassuring me that I'd made the right choice, you're help, as always, was invaluable.

One great big, unending thanks goes to my husband and our parents. Packing up our whole house AND looking after the Sprog can't be an easy task. Thanks for getting started without me while I got this finished.

Thank you, also, to the Sprog who rightly believes that it's very important to interrupt Mummy's "hard work" to show off one's potty training efforts.

And lastly, to the characters. Every chapter I write seems to grow the world of the Sinners of Saint Benedicts and I can't wait to see what adventures we all go on next.

My Books

E.J.'s list is firing up. While you wait for the next release, you can find where to buy all my books in print and eBook at the website; www.elizabethstevens.com.au/ej-knox.

About the Author

E.J. Knox is the Darker/Bully Romance penname of Elizabeth Stevens. E.J. is the name to read if you want darker/bully romance in the Mature YA/NA crossover space. Think high school, college, and academy. E.J. brings my usual wit, banter, and repartee in good old enemies-to-lovers showdowns between alpha males and the sassy heroines strong enough to knock them down a peg or two. There'll be fake-dating, love triangles, kidnapping and danger, second chances, and more.

Writer. Reader. Perpetual student. Nerd.

Born in New Zealand to a Brit and an Australian, I am a writer with a passion for all things storytelling. I love reading, writing, TV and movies, gaming, and spending time with family and friends. I am an avid fan of British comedy, superheroes, and SuperWhoLock. I have too many favourite books, but I fell in love with reading after Isobelle Carmody's *Obernewtyn*. I am obsessed with all things mythological – my current focus being old-style Irish faeries. I live in Adelaide (South Australia) with my long-suffering husband, delirious dog, mad cat, two chickens, and a lazy turtle.

<u>Contact me:</u>
Email: ejknox@elizabethstevens.com.au
Website: www.elizabethstevens.com.au/ej-knox
Twitter: www.twitter.com/writer_iz
Instagram: www.instagram.com/writeriz
Facebook: https://www.facebook.com/elizabethstevens88/